frozen, like an
insect in amber
knowing that a
free meal was
one that he wouldn't
have to pay for

TICKLED
TO
DEATH

and
other stories of
Crime and Suspense

SIMON BRETT

A DELL BOOK

Published by
Dell Publishing Co., Inc.
1 Dag Hammarskjold Plaza
New York, New York 10017

This work was first published in Great Britain as *A Box of Tricks*.

Dell ® TM 681510, Dell Publishing Co., Inc.

ISBN: 0-440-18541-6

Reprinted by arrangement with Charles Scribner's Sons

Printed in the United States of America

March 1987

10 9 8 7 6 5 4 3 2 1

WFH

CONTENTS

BIG BOY, LITTLE BOY

UNDER NORMAL CIRCUMSTANCES he would have thrown away the letter as soon as he recognized the cramped handwriting, but Larry Renshaw was in the process of murdering his wife, and needed to focus his mind on something else. So he read it.

Mario, the barman, had handed it over. Having a variety of postal addresses in pubs and bars all over London was a habit Larry had developed in less opulent days, and one that he had not attempted to break after his marriage to Lydia. The sort of letters he received had changed, though; there were less instructions from "business associates", less guilty wads of notes buying other people's extramarital secrets; their place had been taken by confirmations of his own sexual assignations, correspondence that could, by the widest distension of the category, be classed as love letters. Marriage had not meant an end of secrets.

But it had meant an upgrading of some of the "postes restantes". Gaston's Bar in Albemarle Street was a definite advance on the Stag's Head in Kilburn. And the Savile Row suit, from which he flicked the salt shed by Mario's peanuts, was more elegant than a hotel porter's uniform. The gold identity bracelet that clinked reassuringly on his wrist, was more comfortable than a handcuff. And, Larry Renshaw sincerely believed, much more his natural style.

Which was why he had to ensure that he continued to live in that style. He was nearly fifty; he resented the injustices of a world which had kept him so long from his natural milieu; and now that he had finally arrived there, he had no intentions of leaving.

Nor was he going to limit his lifestyle by removing those elements (other women) of which Lydia disapproved.

Which was why, while he sipped Campari and vodka in Gaston's Bar, he was murdering his wife.

And why he read Peter Mostyn's letter to take his mind off what he was doing.

. . . and those feelings for you haven't changed. I know over thirty years have passed, but those nights we spent together are still the memories I most treasure. I have never had any other friends. Nothing that has happened and no one I have met since has meant as much to me as the pleasure I got, not only from being with you, but also from being known as yours, from being made fun of at school as your Little Boy.

I know it didn't mean as much to you, but I flatter myself that you felt something for me at the time. I remember how once we changed pyjamas, you let me sleep in yours in your bed all night. I've never felt closer to you than I did that night, as if I didn't just take on your clothes, but also a bit of you, as if I became you for a little while. I had never felt so happy. Because, though we always looked a little alike, though we were the same height, had the same colouring, I never had your strength of character. Just then, for a moment, I knew what it was like to be Larry Renshaw.

It was wonderful for me to see you last week. I'm only sorry it was for such a short time. Remember, if there's ever anything I can do for you, you have only to ask. If you want to meet up again, do ring. I'm only over here sorting out some problem on my uncle's will and, as I'm pretty hard up, I spend most of my time in my room at the hotel. But, if I am out when you ring, they'll take a message. I'll be going back to France at the end of the week, but I'd really like to see you before then. I sometimes think I'll take my courage in both hands and come round to your flat, but I know you wouldn't really like it, particularly now you are married to that woman. *It was quite a shock when you told me about your marriage. I had always had a secret hope that the reason you never* had *married was . . .*

Larry stopped reading. Not only had the mention of his marriage brought his mind back to the murder of Lydia, he also found the letter distasteful.

It wasn't being the object of a homosexual passion that worried or challenged him. He had no doubt where his own tastes lay. He didn't even think he had gone through a homosexual phase in adolescence, but he had always had a strong libido, and what other outlet was there in a boys' boarding school? All the other Big

Boys had had Little Boys, so he had played the games tradition demanded. But, as soon as he had been released from that particular prison, he had quickly discovered, and concentrated on, the instinctive pleasures of heterosexuality.

But Peter Mostyn hadn't changed. He'd make contact every few years, suggesting a lunch, and Larry, aware that a free meal was one he didn't have to pay for, would agree to meet. Their conversation would be stilted, spiralling round topics long dead, and Larry would finish up his brandy and leave as soon as the bill arrived. Then, within a week, one of the "poste restante" barmen would hand over a letter full of closely written obsequious gratitude and assurances of continuing devotion.

Obviously, for Mostyn the dormitory grappling had meant more, and he had frozen like an insect in the amber of adolescence. That was what depressed Larry. He hated the past, he didn't like to think about it. For him there was always the hope of the big win just around the next corner, and he would rather concentrate on that than on the disaster behind him.

He could forget the past so easily, instinctively sloughing off the skin of one shady failure to slither out with a shining new identity ready for the next infallible scheme. This protean ability had enabled him to melt from stockbroker's clerk to army recruit (after a few bounced cheques); from army resignee to mail order manager (after a few missing boxes of ammunition); from mail order manager to pimp (after a few prepaid but undelivered orders); and from pimp to hotel porter (after a police raid). And it had facilitated the latest metamorphosis, from hotel porter to Savile-Row-suited husband of rich neurotic dipsomaniac (just before the inevitable theft inquiry). For Larry change and hope went hand in hand.

So Peter Mostyn's devotion was an unpleasant intrusion. It suggested that, whatever his current identity, there remained in Larry an unchanging core that could still be loved. It threatened his independence in a way the love of women never had. His heterosexual affairs were all brisk and physical, soon ended, leaving in him no adverse emotion that couldn't be erased by another conquest and, in the women, undiluted resentment.

But Peter Mostyn's avowed love was something else, an unpleasant reminder of his continuing identity, almost a *memento mori*. And Peter Mostyn himself was even more of a *memento mori*.

They had met the previous week, for the first time in six years. Once again old habits had died hard, and Larry had instinctively taken the bait of a free meal, in spite of his new opulence.

As soon as he saw Peter Mostyn, he knew it was a bad idea. He felt like Dorian Gray meeting his picture face to face. The Little Boy had aged so unattractively that his appearance was a challenge to Larry's vigour and smartness. After all, they were about the same age—no, hell, Mostyn was younger. At school he had been the Little Boy to Larry's Big Boy. A couple of forms behind, so a couple of years younger.

And yet to see him, you'd think he was on the verge of death. He had been ill, apparently; Larry seemed to remember his saying something over the lunch about having been ill. Perhaps that explained the long tubular crutches and the general air of debility. But it was no excuse for the teeth and the hair; the improvement of those was quite within his power. Okay, most of us lose some teeth, but that doesn't mean we have to go around with a mouth like a drawstring purse. Larry prided himself on his own false teeth. One of the first things he'd done after marrying Lydia had been to set up a series of private dental appointments and have his mouth filled with the best replacements money could buy.

And the hair . . . Larry was thinning a bit and would have been greying but for the discreet preparation he bought from his Jermyn Street hairdresser. But he liked to think that, even if he had been so unfortunate as to lose all his hair, he wouldn't have resorted to a toupee like a small brown mammal that had been run over by a day's traffic on the M1.

And yet that was how Peter Mostyn had appeared, a hobbling creature with concave lips and hair that lacked any credibility. And, to match his physical state, he had demonstrated his emotional crippledom with the same adolescent infatuation and unwholesome self-pity, the same constant assertions that he would do anything for his friend, that he felt his own life to be without value and only likely to take on meaning if it could be used in the service of Larry Renshaw.

Larry didn't like any of it. Particularly he didn't like the constant use of the past tense, as if life from now on would be an increasingly crepuscular experience. He thought in the future tense, and of a future that was infinite, now that he had Lydia's money.

Now that he had Lydia's money . . . He looked at his watch. A quarter to eight. She should be a good five hours dead. Time to put thoughts of that tired old queen Mostyn behind him, and get on with the main business of the day. Time for the dutiful husband to go home and discover his wife's body. Or, if he was really lucky, discover that his sister-in-law had just discovered his wife's body.

He said goodbye loudly to Mario, and made some quip about the barman's new apron. He also asked if the bar-room clock was right and checked his watch against it.

After a lifetime of obscuring details of timing and squeezing alibis from forgotten minutes, it was an amusing novelty to draw attention to time. And to himself.

For the same reason he exchanged memorable banter with the driver of the taxi he picked up in a still light Piccadilly, before settling back for the journey to Abbey Road.

Now he felt supremely confident. He was following his infallible instinct. The plan was the work of a mastermind. He even had a twinge of regret to think that, when he had all Lydia's money, that mind would be lost to crime. But no, he did not intend to hazard his new-found fortune by doing anything mildly risky. He needed freedom to cram into his remaining rich life what he had missed out on in poorer days.

Which was why the murder plan was so good; it contained no risk at all.

In fact, although he did not consciously realize it at the time, he had got the murder plan at the same time that he had got Lydia. She had come ready-packed with her own self-destruct mechanism. The complete kit.

Lydia had fallen in love with Larry when he saved her life, and had married him out of gratitude.

It had happened two years previously. Larry Renshaw had been at the lowest ebb of a career that had known many freak tides. He had been working as a porter at a Park Lane hotel, whose management was beginning to suspect him of helping himself from the wallets, handbags and jewel-cases of the guests. One afternoon he had received a tip-off that they were on to him, and determined to make one last, reasonable-sized haul before another sudden exit and change of identity.

Observation and staff gossip led him to use his pass-key on the door of a Mrs Lydia Phythian, a lady whose Christmas tree appearances in the bar left no doubts about her possession of a considerable stock of jewellery, and whose consumption of gin in the same bar suggested that she might be a little careless in locking away her decorations.

So it proved. Necklaces, brooches, bracelets and rings lay among the pill bottles of the dressing table as casually as stranded seaweed. But there was also in the room something that promised a far richer and less risky haul than a fence's grudging prices for the gems.

There was Mrs Lydia Phythian, in the process of committing suicide.

The scene was classic to the point of being corny. An empty gin bottle clutched in the hand of the snoring figure on the bed. On the bedside table, an empty pill bottle, dramatically on its side, and, propped against the lamp, a folded sheet of crisp blue monogrammed notepaper.

The first thing Larry did was to read the note.

THIS WAS THE ONLY WAY OUT. NOBODY CARES WHETHER I LIVE OR DIE AND I DON'T WANT TO GO ON JUST BEING A BURDEN. I'VE TRIED, BUT LIFE'S TOO MUCH.

It was undated. Instinctively, Larry put it in his pocket before turning his attention to the figure on the bed. She was deeply asleep, but her pulses were still strong. Remembering some movie with this scene in it, he slapped her face.

Her eyes came woozily open. "I want to die. Why shouldn't I die?"

"Because there's so much to live for," he replied, possibly remembering dialogue from the same movie.

Her eyes rolled shut again. He rang for an ambulance. Instinct told him to get an outside line and ring the Emergency Services direct; he didn't want the manager muscling in on his act.

Then, again following the pattern of the movie, he walked her sagging body up and down, keeping her semi-conscious until help arrived.

Thereafter he just followed instinct. Instinct told him to accompany her in the ambulance to the hospital; instinct told him to return (out of his hotel uniform) to be there when she came round after the ministrations of the stomach pump; instinct told him to continue his visits when she was moved to the recuperative luxury of the Avenue Clinic. And instinct provided the words which assured her that there really was a lot to live for, and that it was insane for a woman as attractive as her to feel unloved, and that he at least appreciated her true worth.

So their marriage three months after she came out of the clinic was really a triumph of instinct.

A couple of days before the registry office ceremony, Larry Renshaw had fixed to see her doctor. "I felt, you know, that I should know her medical history, now that we're going to be together for life," he said in a responsible voice. "I mean, I'm not asking you to give away any professional secrets, but obviously I want to ensure that there isn't a recurrence of the appalling incident which brought us together."

"Of course." The doctor was bald, thin and frankly sceptical. He did not seem to be taken in by Larry's performance as the concerned husband-to-be. "Well, she's a very neurotic woman, she likes to draw attention to herself . . . nothing's going to change her basic character."

"I thought, being married . . ."

"She's been married a few times before, you must know that."

"Yes, of course, but she seems to have had pretty bad luck and been landed with a lot of bastards. I thought, given someone who really loves her for herself . . ."

"Oh yes, I'm sure she'd be a lot more stable, given *that*." The scepticism was now so overt as to be insulting, but Larry didn't risk righteous anger, as the doctor went on, "The trouble is, Mr

Renshaw, women as rich as Mrs Phythian tend to meet up with rather a lot of bastards."

Larry ignored the second insult. "What I really wanted to know was—"

"What you really wanted to know," the doctor interrupted, "was whether she was likely to attempt suicide again."

Larry nodded gravely.

"Well, I can't tell you. Someone who takes as many pills and drinks as much as she does is rarely fully rational. This wasn't her first attempt, though it was different from the others."

"How?"

"The previous ones were more obviously just demands for attention, she made pretty sure that she would be found before anything too serious happened. In this case . . . well, if you hadn't walked into the room, I think she'd have gone the distance. Incidentally . . ."

But Larry spoke before the inevitable question about why he came to be in her room. "Were there any other differences this time?"

"Small ones. The way she crushed up all the pills into the gin before she started suggested a more positive approach. And the fact that there was no note . . ."

Larry didn't respond to the quizzical look. When he left, the doctor shook him by the hand and said, with undisguised irony, "I wouldn't worry. I'm sure everything will work out *for you*."

The insolent distrust was back in that final emphasis, but mixed in the doctor's voice with another feeling, one of relief. At least a new husband would keep Mrs Phythian out of his surgery for a little while. Just a series of repeat prescriptions for tranquillizers and sleeping pills. And he could still charge her for those.

Subconsciously, Larry knew that the doctor had confirmed how easy it would be for him to murder his wife, but he did not let himself think about it. After all, why should it be necessary?

At first it wasn't. Mrs Lydia Phythian changed her name again (she was almost rivalling her husband in the number of identities she had taken on), and became Mrs Lydia Renshaw. At first the marriage worked pretty well. She enjoyed kitting out her new husband, and he enjoyed being taken round to expensive shops and being treated by her. He found her a surprisingly avid sexual partner and, although he couldn't have subsisted on that diet alone, secret snacks with other women kept him agreeably nourished, and he began to think marriage suited him.

Certainly it brought him a lifestyle that he had never before experienced. Having been brought up by parents whose middle-class insistence on putting him through minor public school had dragged their living standards down to working-class and below, and then having never been securely wealthy for more than a fortnight, he was well placed to appreciate the large flat in Abbey Road, the country house in Uckfield and the choice of driving a Bentley or a little Mercedes.

In fact, there were only two things about his wife that annoyed him—first, her unwillingness to let him see other women and, second, the restricted amount of pocket money she allowed him.

He had found ways around the second problem; in fact he had reverted to his old ways to get around the second problem. He had started, very early in their marriage, stealing from his wife.

At first he had done it indirectly. She had trustingly put him in charge of her portfolio of investments, which made it very easy for him to cream off what he required for his day-to-day needs. However, a stormy meeting with Lydia's broker and accountant, who threatened to disclose all to their employer, persuaded him to relinquish these responsibilities.

So he started robbing his wife directly. The alcoholic haze in which she habitually moved made this fairly easy. Mislaying a ring or a small necklace, or even finding her notecase empty within a few hours of going to the bank, were common occurrences, and not ones to which she liked to draw attention, since they raised the question of how much her drinking affected her memory.

Larry spent a certain amount of this loot on other women, but the bulk of it he consigned to a suitcase, which every three or four weeks was moved discreetly to another Left Luggage office (premarital habits again dying hard). Over some twenty months of marriage, he had accumulated between twelve and thirteen thousand pounds, which was a comforting hedge against adversity.

But he did not expect adversity. Or at least he did not expect adversity until he discovered that his wife had put a private detective on to him and had compiled a dossier of a fortnight's infidelities.

It was then that he knew he had to murder her, and had to do it quickly, before the meeting with her solicitor which she had mentioned when confronting him with the detective's report. Larry Renshaw had no intention of being divorced from his wife's money.

As soon as he had made the decision, the murder plan that he had shut up in the Left Luggage locker of his subconscious was revealed by a simple turn of a key. It was so simple, he glowed from the beauty of it.

He went through it again as he sat in the cab on the way to Abbey Road. The timing was perfect; there was no way it could fail.

Every three months Lydia spent four days at a health farm. The aim was not primarily to dry her out, but to put a temporary brake on the runaway deterioration of her physical charms. However, the strictness of the fashionable institution chosen to take on this hopeless task meant that the visit did have the side-effect of keeping her off alcohol for its duration. The natural consequence of this was that on the afternoon of her return she would, regular as clockwork, irrigate her parched system with at least half a bottle of gin.

And that was all the plan needed. His instinct told him it could not fail.

He had made the preparations that morning, almost joyously. He had whistled softly as he worked. There was so little to do. Crush up the pills into the gin bottle, place the suicide note in the desk drawer and set out to spend his day in company. No part of that day was to be unaccounted for. Gaston's Bar was only the last link in a long chain of alibis.

During the day, he had probed at the plan, testing it for weaknesses, and found none.

Suppose Lydia thought the gin tasted funny . . . ? She wouldn't, in her haste. Anyway, in her descriptions of the previous attempt, she had said there was no taste. It had been, she said, just like drinking it neat, and getting gently drowsier and drowsier. A quiet end. Not an unattractive one.

Suppose the police found out about the private detective and the appointment with the solicitor . . . ? Wouldn't they begin to suspect the dead woman's husband . . . ? No, if anything that strengthened his case. Disillusioned by yet another man, depressed by the prospect of yet another divorce, she had taken the quickest way out. True, it didn't put her husband in a very good light, but Larry was not worried about that. So long as he inherited, he didn't care what people thought.

Suppose she had already made a will which disinherited him . . . ? But no, he knew she hadn't. That was what she had set up with the solicitor for the next day. And Larry had been present when she made her previous will that named him, her husband, as sole legatee.

No, his instinct told him nothing could go wrong.

He paid off the taxi-driver, and told him an Irish joke he had heard in the course of the day. He then went into their block of flats, told the porter the same Irish joke, and asked if he could check the right time. Eight-seventeen. Never had there been a better-documented day.

As he went up in the lift, he wondered if the final refinement to the plan had happened. It wasn't essential, but it would have been nice. Lydia's sister had said she would drop round for the evening. If she could actually have discovered the body . . . Still, she was notoriously bad about time and you can't have everything. But it would be nice. . . .

Everything played into his hands. On the landing he met a neighbour just about to walk his chihuahua. Larry greeted them cheerfully and checked the time. His confidence was huge. He enjoyed being a criminal mastermind.

For the benefit of the departing neighbour and because he was going to play the part to the hilt, he called out cheerily, "Good evening, darling!" as he unlocked the front door.

"Good evening, *darling*," said Lydia.

As soon as he saw her, he knew that she knew everything. She sat poised on the sofa and on the glass coffee table in front of her were the bottle of gin and the suicide note. If they had been labelled in a courtroom, they couldn't have been more clearly marked as evidence. On a table to the side of the sofa stood a second, half-empty bottle of gin. The bloody, boozy bitch—she couldn't even wait until she got home, she'd taken on new supplies on the way back from the health farm.

"Well, Larry, I dare say you're surprised to see me."

"A little," he said lightly, and smiled what he had always believed to be a charming smile.

"I think I'll have quite a lot to say to my solicitor tomorrow."

He laughed lightly.

"After I've been to the police," she continued.

His next laugh was more brittle.

"Yes, Larry, there are quite a few things to talk about. For a start, I've just done an inventory of my jewellery. And do you know, I think I've suddenly realized why you appeared in my hotel room that fateful afternoon. Once a thief, always a thief. But murder . . . that's going up a league for you, isn't it?"

The gin hadn't got to her: she was speaking with cold coherence. Larry slowed down his mind to match her logical deliberation. He walked over to his desk in the corner by the door. When he turned round, he was holding the gun he kept in its drawer.

Lydia laughed, loudly and unattractively, as if in derision of his manhood. "Oh, come on, Larry, that's not very subtle. No, your other little scheme was quite clever, I'll give you that. But to shoot me . . . They'd never let you inherit. You aren't allowed to profit from a crime."

"I'm not going to shoot you." He moved across and pointed the gun at her head. "I'm going to make you drink from that other gin bottle."

Again he got the harsh, challenging laugh. "Oh, come on, sweetie. What kind of threat is that? There's a basic fault in your logic. You can't make people kill themselves by threatening to kill them. If you gotta go, who cares about the method? And if you intend to kill me, I'll ensure that you do it the way that gives you most trouble. Shoot away, sweetie."

Involuntarily, he lowered the arm holding the gun.

She laughed again.

"Anyway, I'm bored with this." She rose from the sofa. "I'm going to ring the police. I've had enough of being married to a criminal mastermind."

The taunt so exactly reflected his self-image that it stung like a blow. His gun-arm stiffened again, and he shot his wife in the temple, as she made her way towards the telephone.

There was a lot of blood. At first he stood there mesmerized by how much blood there was, but then, as the flow stopped, his mind started to work again.

Its deliberations were not comforting. He had blown it. The best he could hope for now was escape.

Unnaturally calm, he went to the telephone. He rang Heathrow. There was a ten o'clock flight. Yes, there was a seat. He booked it.

He took the spare cash from Lydia's handbag. Under ten pounds. She hadn't been to the bank since her return from the health farm. Still, he could use a credit card to pay for the ticket.

He went into the bedroom, where her jewellery lay in its customary disarray. He reached out for a diamond choker.

But no. Suppose the Customs searched him. That was just the sort of trouble he had to avoid. For the same reason he couldn't take the jewellery from his case in the Left Luggage office. Where was it now anyway? Oh no, Liverpool Street. Fumes of panic rose to his brain. There wouldn't be time. Or would there? Maybe if he just got the money from the case and—

The doorbell rang.

Oh my God! Lydia's sister!

He grabbed a suitcase, threw in his pyjamas and a clean shirt, then rushed into the kitchen, opened the back door and ran down the fire escape.

★

Peter Mostyn's cottage was in the Department of Lot. The nearest large town was Cahors, the nearest small town was Montaigu-de-Quercy, but neither was very near. The cottage itself was small and primitive; Mostyn was not a British trendy making a fashionable home in France, he had moved there in search of obscurity and lived very cheaply, constantly calculating how many years he could remain there on the dwindling capital he had been left by a remote uncle, and hoping that it would last out his lifetime. He didn't have more contact with the locals than weekly shopping demanded, and both sides seemed happy with this arrangement.

Larry Renshaw arrived there on the third night after Lydia's death. He had travelled unobtrusively by local trains, thumbed lifts and long stretches of cross-country walking, sleeping in the fields by night. He had sold his Savile Row suit for a tenth of its value in a Paris second-hand clothes shop, where he had bought a set of stained blue overalls, which made him less conspicuous tramping along the sun-baked roads of France. His passport and gold identity bracelet were secure in an inside pocket.

If there was any chase, he reckoned he was ahead of it.

It had been dark for about four hours when he reached the cottage. It was a warm summer night. The countryside was dry and brittle, needing rain. Although the occasional car had flashed past on the narrow local roads, he had not met any pedestrians.

There was a meagre slice of moon which showed him enough to dash another hope. In the back of his mind had lurked the possibility that Mostyn, in spite of his constant assertions of poverty, lived in luxury and would prove as well-fleshed a body as Lydia to batten on. But the crumbling exterior of the cottage told him that the long-term solution to his problems would have to lie elsewhere. The building had hardly changed at all through many generations of peasant owners.

And when Mostyn came to the door, he could have been the latest representative of that peasant dynasty. His wig was off, he wore a shapeless sort of nightshirt and clutched a candle-holder out of a Dickens television serial. The toothless lips moved uneasily and in his eye was an old peasant distrust of outsiders.

That expression vanished as soon as he recognized his visitor.

"Larry. I hoped you'd come to me. I read about it in the papers. Come inside. You'll be safe here."

Safe he certainly was. Mostyn's limited social round meant that there was no danger of the newcomer being recognized. No danger of his even being seen. For three days the only person Larry Renshaw saw was Peter Mostyn.

And Peter Mostyn still hadn't changed at all. He remained a pathetic cripple, rendered even more pathetic by his cringing devotion. For him Renshaw's appearance was the answer to a prayer. Now at last he had the object of his affections in his own home. He was in seventh heaven.

Renshaw wasn't embarrassed by the devotion; he knew Mostyn was far too diffident to try and force unwelcome attentions on him. For a little while at least he had found sanctuary, and was content for a couple of days to sit and drink his host's brandy and assess his position.

The assessment wasn't encouraging. Everything had turned sour. All the careful plans he had laid for Lydia's death now worked against him. The elaborate fixing of the time of his arrival at the flat no longer established his alibi; it now pointed the finger of murder at him. Even after he'd shot her, he might have been able to sort something out, but for that bloody sister of hers, ringing the bell and making him panic. Everything had turned out wrong.

On the third evening, as he sat silent at the table, savagely drinking brandy while Mostyn watched him, Renshaw shouted out against the injustice of it all. "That bloody bitch!"

"Lydia?" asked Mostyn hesitantly.

"No, you fool. Her sister. If she hadn't turned up just at that moment, I'd have got away with it. I'd have thought of something."

"At what moment?"

"Just after I'd shot Lydia. She rang the bell."

"What—about eight-thirty?"

"Yes."

Mostyn paled beneath his toupee. "That wasn't Lydia's sister."

"What? How do you know?"

"It was me." Renshaw looked at him. "It was me. I was flying back the next morning. You hadn't *rung*. I so wanted to see you before I left. I came to the flats. I didn't *intend* to go in. But I just asked the porter if you were there and he said you'd just arrived . . ."

"It was you! You bloody fool, why didn't you say?"

"I didn't know what had happened. I just—"

"You idiot! You bloody idiot!" The frustration of the last few days and the brandy came together in a wave of fury. Renshaw seized Mostyn by the lapels and shook him. "If I had known it was you. . . . You could have saved my life. You bloody fool! You . . ."

"I didn't know. I didn't know," the Little Boy whimpered. "When there was no reply, I just went back to the hotel. Honestly, if I'd known what was happening . . . I'd do anything for you, you *know*. Anything . . ."

Renshaw slackened his grasp on Mostyn's lapels and returned to Mostyn's brandy.

It was the next day that he took up the offer. They sat over the debris of lunch. "Peter, you said you'd do anything for me . . ."

"Of course, and I meant it. My life hasn't been much, you're the only person that matters to me. I'd do anything for you. I'll look after you here for as long as—"

"I'm not staying here. I have to get away."

Mostyn's face betrayed his hurt. Renshaw ignored it and continued, "For that I need money."

"I've told you, you can have anything that I—"

"No, I know you haven't got any money. Not real money. But I have. In the Left Luggage office at Liverpool Street Station I have over twelve thousand pounds in cash and jewellery." Renshaw looked at Mostyn with the smile he had always believed to be charming. "I want you to go to England to fetch it for me."

"What? But I'd never get it back over here."

"Yes, you would. You're the ideal smuggler. You put the stuff in your crutches. They'd never suspect someone like you."

"But I—"

Renshaw looked hurt. "You said you'd do anything for me . . ."

"Well, I would, but—"

"You can go into Cahors tomorrow and fix the flight."

"But . . . but that means you'll leave me again."

"For a little while, yes. I'd come back," Renshaw lied.

"I . . ."

"Please do it for me, please . . ." Renshaw put on an expression he knew to be vulnerable.

"All right, I will."

"Bless you, bless you. Come on, let's drink to it."

"I don't drink much. It makes me sleepy. I haven't got the head for it. I—"

"Come on, drink."

Mostyn hadn't got the head for it. As the afternoon progressed he became more and more embarrassingly devoted. Then he fell into a comatose sleep.

The day after next the plane ticket was on the dining-room table, next to Peter Mostyn's passport. Upstairs his small case was packed ready. He was to fly from Paris in three days' time, on the Wednesday. He would be back at the cottage by the weekend. With the money and jewels which would be Renshaw's lifeline.

Renshaw's confidence started to return. With money in his pocket, everything would once more become possible. Twelve thousand pounds was plenty to buy a new identity and start again. Talent like his, he knew, could not be kept down for long.

Mostyn was obviously uneasy about the task ahead of him, but he had been carefully briefed and he'd manage it all right. The Big Boy was entrusting him with a mission and the Little Boy would see that it was efficiently discharged.

A new harmony came into their relationship. Now that his escape had a date on it, Renshaw could relax and even be pleasant to his protector, Mostyn glowed with gratitude for the attention. It did not take much to make him happy, Renshaw thought contemptuously. Once again, as he looked at the prematurely aged and crippled figure, he found it incongruous that their bodies had ever touched. Mostyn had never been other than pathetic.

Still, he was useful. And, though it was making huge inroads into his carefully husbanded wealth, he kept the supply of brandy flowing. Renshaw topped up his tumbler again after lunch on the Monday afternoon.

It was then that there was a knock at the door. Mostyn leapt nervously to the window to check out the visitor. When he looked back at Renshaw, his face had even less colour under its thatch. "It's a gendarme."

Moving quickly and efficiently, Larry Renshaw picked up his dirty plate, together with the brandy bottle and tumbler, and went upstairs. His bedroom window was above the sloping roof of the porch. If anyone came up, he would be able to make a quick getaway.

He heard conversation downstairs, but it was too indistinct and his knowledge of French too limited for him to understand it. Then he heard the front door shut. From the window he saw the gendarme go to his bike and cycle off towards Montaigu-de-Quercy.

He gave it five minutes and went downstairs. Peter Mostyn sat at the table, literally shaking.

"What the hell's the matter?"

"The gendarme . . . he asked if I had seen you."

"So you said you hadn't."

"Yes, but . . ."

"But what? That's all there is to it, surely. There's been an Interpol alert to check out any contacts I might have abroad. They got your name from my address book back at the flat. So now the local bobby here has done his bit and will report back that you haven't seen me since last week in London. End of story. I'm glad it's happened; at least now I don't have to wait for it."

"Yes, but, Larry, look at the state I'm in."

"You'll calm down. Come on. Okay, it was a shock, but you'll get over it."

"That's not what I mean. What I'm saying is, if I'm in this state now, I just won't be able to go through with what I'm supposed to be doing on Wednesday."

"Look, for Christ's sake, all you have to do is to catch a plane to London, go to the Liverpool Street Left Luggage office, get the case, go to somewhere conveniently quiet, load the stuff into your crutches and come back here. There's no danger."

"I can't do it, Larry. I *can't*. I'll crack up. I'll give myself away somehow. If I were like you, I could do it. You've always had a stronger nerve for that sort of thing. I wish it were you who was going to do it, because I know you *could*. But I just . . ."

He petered out. Anger invaded Renshaw. "Listen, you little worm, you've got to do it! Good God, you've said enough times you'd do anything for me; and now, the first time I ask for something, you're bloody chicken."

"Larry, I would do anything for you, I would. But I just don't think I *can* go through with this. I'd mess it up somehow. Honestly, Larry, if there were anything *else* I could do . . ."

"Anything else? How about getting me off the murder charge? Maybe you'd like to do that instead?" Renshaw asked with acid sarcasm.

"If I could . . . Or if I had enough money to be any use . . . Or if—"

"Oh, shut up, you useless little queen!" Larry Renshaw stomped savagely upstairs with the brandy bottle.

They did not speak to each other for over 24 hours.

But the next evening, as he lay on the bed drinking brandy, watching the declining sun tinge the scrubby oak trees of the hillside with gold, Renshaw's instinct started to take over again. It was a warm feeling. Once more he felt protected. His instinct was an Almighty Big Boy, looking after him, guiding him, showing him the way forward, as it always had done before.

After about an hour, he heard the front door and saw Mostyn setting off down the road that led to Montaigu-de-Quercy. Again. He'd been out more than once since their row. No doubt going to buy more brandy as a peace offering. Poor little sod. Renshaw chuckled to himself at the aptness of the description.

Alone in the cottage, he dozed. The bang of the door on Mostyn's return woke him. And he was not surprised to wake up with his plan of campaign worked out in every detail.

Peter Mostyn looked up like a mongrel fearing a kick, but Larry Renshaw smiled at him and was amused to see how gratefully the expression changed. Mostyn had all the weakness of the sort of women Renshaw had spent his life avoiding.

"Larry, look, I'm terribly sorry about yesterday afternoon. I was just a coward. Look, I really *do* want to do something for you. You know I'd give my life for you if I thought it'd be any use. It's been a pretty wasted life, I'd like it to do *something* valuable."

"But not go to London and pick up my things?" Renshaw asked lightly.

"I just don't think I *could*, Larry, I don't think I have it *in me*. But I will go to London tomorrow. There is something else that I can do for you. I *can* help you. I *have* helped you already. I—"

"Never mind." Renshaw spread his hands in a magnanimous gesture of forgiveness. "Never mind. Listen, Peter," he went on intimately, "I behaved like a swine yesterday and I want to apologize. I'm sorry, this whole thing's been a dreadful strain, and I just haven't been appreciating all you're doing for me. Please forgive me."

"You've been fine. I . . ." Mostyn's expression hovered between surprise and delight at his friend's change of behaviour.

"No, I've been being a swine. Peace offering." He drew his hand out of his pocket and held it towards Mostyn.

"But you don't want to give me that. It's your identity bracelet, it's got your name on. And it's gold. I mean, you'd—"

"Please . . ."

Mostyn took the bracelet and slipped it on to his thin wrist.

"Listen, Peter, I've been so screwed up that I just haven't been thinking straight. Forget the money in London. Maybe I'll get it some day, maybe I won't. The important thing is that I'm safe at the moment, with a *friend*. A very good friend. Peter, what I want to ask is, can I stay here for a bit?" He looked up humbly. "If you don't mind."

"Mind? Look, you know, Larry, I'd be delighted. *Delighted.* You don't have to ask that."

"Bless you, Peter." Renshaw spoke softly, as if choked by emotion. Then he perked up. "If that's settled then, let's drink on it."

"I won't, thank you, Larry. You know it only makes me sleepy."

"Oh, come on, Peter. If we're going to live together, we've got to learn to enjoy the same hobbies." And he filled two tumblers with brandy.

The prospect opened up by the words "live together" was too much for Mostyn. There were tears in his eyes as he drained his first drink.

It was about an hour and a half later when Renshaw judged the moment to be right. Mostyn was slurring his words and yawning, but still conscious. His eyes focused in pleasure for a moment when Renshaw murmured, "Why don't we go upstairs?"

"Whaddya mean?"

"You know what I mean." He giggled.

"Really? Really?"

Renshaw nodded.

Mostyn rose, swaying, to his feet. "Where are my crutches?"

"They won't help you stand up straight in the state you're in." Renshaw giggled again, and Mostyn joined in. Renshaw ruffled his Little Boy's hair, and the toupee came off in his hand.

"Gimme thaback."

"When I come upstairs," Renshaw murmured softly. Then, in an even lower whisper, "Go up to my room, get my pyjamas, put them on and get into my bed. I'll be up soon."

Mostyn smiled with fuddled pleasure, and started off up the stairs. Renshaw heard the uneven footsteps in his room above, then the hobbling noises of undressing, the thump of a body hitting the bed and soon, predictably, silence.

He sat for about a quarter of an hour finishing his drink. Then, whistling softly, he started to make his preparations.

He moved slowly, but efficiently, following the infallible dictates of his instinct. First he went into the little bathroom and shaved off his remaining hair. It took a surprisingly short time. Then he removed his false teeth and put them in a glass of water.

He went cautiously up the stairs and inched open the door of his bedroom. As expected, Mostyn lay unconscious from the unaccustomed alcohol.

Unhurriedly, Renshaw placed the glass of teeth on the bedside table. Then he changed into the clothes Mostyn had just abandoned on the floor. He went into the other bedroom, picked up the overnight case that had been packed, and returned downstairs.

He picked up the air ticket and passport, which still lay accusingly on the dining table. He put on the toupee and compared his reflection with the passport photograph. The picture was ten years old and the resemblance quite sufficient. He picked up the crutches and tried them until he could reproduce the limp that appeared in the "Special Peculiarities" section.

Then he picked up the half-full brandy bottle, another unopened one and the candle on the table, and went upstairs.

The Little Boy lay on his Big Boy's bed, in his Big Boy's pyjamas, even wearing his Big Boy's gold identity bracelet, but was in no state to appreciate this longed-for felicity. He did not stir as his Big Boy sprinkled brandy over the bedclothes, the rush matting and the wooden floor boards. Nor did he stir when his Big Boy laid the lighted candle on the floor and watched its flames spread.

Larry Renshaw felt the usual confidence that following his instinct produced, as he travelled back to London in the identity of Peter Mostyn. He even found that there were compensations in being a pathetic, toothless cripple on crutches. People made way for him at the airport and helped him with his bags.

On the plane he mused comfortably about his next movements. Certainly his first port of call must be the Left Luggage office at Liverpool Street. . . . And then probably one of the fences he already knew, to turn the jewellery into cash. . . . Then, who could say? Possibly abroad again. . . . Certainly a new identity. . . .

But there was no hurry. That was the luxury his instinct

had achieved for him. In Mostyn's identity he was safe for as long as he could stand being such a pathetic figure. There was no hurry.

He felt tense as he approached Passport Control at Heathrow. Not frightened—he was confident his instinct would see him through—but tense. After all, if there was a moment when his identity was most likely to be questioned, this was it. But if he was accepted here as Peter Mostyn, then he had nothing more to worry about.

It was slightly unnerving, because the Passport Officer seemed to be expecting him. "Ah, Mr Mostyn," he said. "If you'd just take a seat here for a moment, I'll tell them you've arrived."

"But I—" No, better not to make a scene. Reserve righteous indignation for later. Must be some minor mix-up. He imagined how feebly Peter Mostyn would whine at the nuisances of bureaucracy.

He didn't have long to wait. Two men in raincoats arrived and asked him to go with them to a small room. They did not speak again until they were all seated.

"Now," said the man who seemed to be senior, "let's talk about the murder of Mrs Lydia Renshaw."

"Mrs Lydia Renshaw?" echoed Larry Renshaw, bemused. "But I'm Peter Mostyn."

"Yes," said the man, "we know that. There's no question about that. And that's why we want to talk to you about the murder of Mrs Lydia Renshaw."

"But . . . why?" Larry Renshaw asked, quite as pathetically as Peter Mostyn would have done.

"Why?" The man seemed puzzled. "Well, because of your letter of confession that arrived this morning."

It was some time before he actually saw the document that had incriminated him, but it didn't take him long to imagine its contents.

Because of his long-standing homosexual attraction to Larry Renshaw, Peter Mostyn had gone round to see him the evening before he was due to return to his home in France. At the block of flats in Abbey Road (where he was seen by the porter) he had found, not Renshaw, but Renshaw's wife, the woman who, in his eyes, had irrevocably alienated the affections of his friend. An argument had ensued, in the course of which he had shot his rival. Larry Renshaw, returning to his flat, seeing his wife's body and guessing what had happened, had immediately set off for France in pursuit of the murderer. It was Renshaw's arrival at his home that had prompted Peter Mostyn to make a clean breast of what he had done.

This put Larry Renshaw in a rather difficult position. Since he was now innocent, he could in theory claim back his own identity. But he had a nasty feeling that that would raise more questions than it would answer.

His instinct, now diminished to a limping, apologetic, pathetic thing, advised him to remain as Peter Mostyn, the Little Boy who had made the supreme sacrifice to protect his Big Boy.

So it was as Peter Mostyn that he was charged with, and found guilty of, the murder of Mrs Lydia Renshaw.

And it was as Peter Mostyn that he was later charged with, and found guilty of, the murder of Larry Renshaw.

DOUBLE GLAZING

THE FIREPLACE WAS rather splendid, a carved marble arch housing a black metal grate. The curves of the marble supports echoed the elaborate sweep of the coving and the outward spread of petals from the central ceiling rose. The white emulsion enthusiastically splashed over the room by the Housing Trust volunteers could not disguise its fine Victorian proportions. The old flooring had been replaced by concrete when the damp course was put in and the whole area was now snugly carpeted. This was one of the better conversions, making a compact residence for a single occupant, Jean Collinson thought as she sat before the empty grate opposite Mr Morton. A door led off the living-room to the tiny kitchen and bathroom. Quite sufficient for a retired working man.

She commented on the fireplace.

"Oh yes, it's very attractive," Harry Morton agreed. His voice still bore traces of his Northern upbringing. "Nice workmanship in those days. Draughty, mind, if you don't have it lit."

"Yes, but there's no reason why you shouldn't use it in the winter. When they did the conversion, the builders checked that the chimney wasn't blocked. Even had it swept, I think."

"Oh yes. Well, I'll have to see about that when the winter comes. See how far the old pension stretches."

"Of course. Do you find it hard to make ends meet?"

"Oh no. I'm not given to extravagance. I have no vices, so far as I know." The old man chuckled. He was an amiable soul; Jean found him quite restful after most of the others. Mrs Walker with her constant moans about how her daughter and grandchildren never came to visit, Mr Kitson with his incontinence and unwillingness to do anything about it, Mrs Grüber with her conviction that Jean was part of an international conspiracy of social workers devoted to the cause of separating her from a revoltingly smelly little Yorkshire terrier called Nimrod. It was a relief to meet an old person who seemed to be coping.

Mr Morton had already made his mark on the flat although he

had only moved in the week before. It was all very clean and tidy, no dust on any of the surfaces. (He had refused the Trust's offer of help with the cleaning, so he must have done it himself.) His few possessions were laid out neatly, the rack of pipes spotless on the mantelpiece, the pile of Do-It-Yourself magazines aligned on the coffee table, the bed squared off with hospital corners.

Mr Morton had taken the same care with his own appearance. His chin was shaved smooth, without the cuts and random tufts of white hair which Jean saw on so many of the old men she dealt with. His shirt was clean, tie tight in a little knot, jacket brushed, trousers creased properly and brown shoes buffed to a fine shine. And there didn't linger about him the sour smell which she now almost took for granted would emanate from all old people. If there was any smell in the room, it was an antiseptic hint of carbolic soap. Thank God, Jean thought, her new charge wasn't going to add too much to her already excessive workload. Just the occasional visit to check he was all right but, even from this first meeting, she knew he would be. Harry Morton could obviously manage. He'd lived alone all his life and had the neatness of an organized bachelor. But without that obsessive independence which so many of them developed. He didn't seem to resent her visit, nor to have complicated feelings of pride about accepting the Housing Trust's charity. He was just a working man who had done his bit for society and was now ready to accept society's thanks in the reduced circumstances of retirement. Jean was already convinced that the complaints which had led to his departure from his previous flat were just the ramblings of a paranoid neighbour.

She stifled a yawn. It was not that she was bored by Harry Morton's plans for little improvements to the flat. She had learned as a social worker to appear interested in much duller and less coherent narratives. But it was stuffy. Like a lot of old people, Harry Morton seemed unwilling to open the windows. Still, it was his flat and his right to have as much or as little ventilation as he wanted.

Anyway, Jean knew that the lack of air was not the real reason for her doziness. Guiltily, she allowed herself to think for a moment about the night before. She felt a little glow of fragile pleasure and knew she mustn't think about it too much, mustn't threaten it by inflating it in her mind beyond its proper proportions.

But, without inflation, it was still the best thing that had happened to her for some years, and something that she had thought, at thirty-two, might well never happen again. It had all been so straightforward, making nonsense of the agonizing and worry about being an emotional cripple which had seemed an inescapable part of her life ever since she'd broken up with Roger five years earlier.

It had not been a promising party. Given by a schoolfriend who had become a teacher, married a teacher and developed a lot of friends who were also teachers. Jean had anticipated an evening of cheap Spanish plonk, sharp French bread and predictable cheese, with conversation about how little teachers were paid, how much more everyone's contemporaries were earning, how teaching wasn't really what any of them had wanted to do anyway, all spiced with staff-room gossip about personalities she didn't know, wasn't likely to meet and, after half an hour of listening, didn't want to meet.

And that's how it had been, until she had met Mick. From that point on, the evening had just made sense. Talking to him, dancing with him (for some reason, though they were all well into their thirties, the party was still conducted on the lines of a college hop), then effortlessly leaving with him and going back to his flat.

And there it had made sense too. All the inhibitions she had carried with her so long, the knowledge that her face was strong rather than beautiful, that her hips were too broad and her breasts too small, had not seemed important. It had all been so different from the one-sided fumblings, the humourless groping and silent embarrassments which had seemed for some years all that sex had to offer. It had worked.

And Mick was coming straight round to her place after school. She was going to cook him a meal. He had to go to some Debating Society meeting and would be round about seven. Some days she couldn't guarantee to be back by then, the demands of her charges were unpredictable, but this time even that would be all right. Harry Morton was the last on her round and he clearly wasn't going to be any trouble. Covertly, with the skill born of long practice, she looked at her watch. A quarter to five. Good, start to leave in about five minutes, catch the shops on the way home, buy something special, maybe a bottle of wine. Cook a good dinner and then . . .

She felt herself blushing and guiltily pulled her mind back to listen to what Harry Morton was saying. Fantasizing never helped, she knew, it only distanced reality. Anyway, she had a job to do.

"I've got a bit of money saved," Harry was saying, "some I put aside in the post office book while I was still working and I've even managed to save a bit on the pension, and I reckon I'm going to buy some really good tools. I want to get a ratchet screwdriver. They're very good, save a lot of effort. Just the job for putting up shelves, that sort of thing. I thought I'd put a couple of shelves up over there, you know, for magazines and that."

"Yes, that's a very good idea." Jean compensated for her lapse into reverie by being bright and helpful. "Of course, if you need a hand with any of the heavy stuff, the Trust's got a lot of volunteers who'd be only too glad to—"

"Oh no, no, thank you. I won't need help. I'm pretty good with my hands. And, you know, if you've worked with your hands all your life, you stay pretty strong. Don't worry, I'll be up to building a few shelves. And any other little jobs around the flat."

"What did you do before you retired, Mr Morton?"

"Now please call me Harry. I was a warehouse porter."

"Oh."

"Working up at Granger's, don't know if you know them?"

"Up on the main road?"

"Yes. We loaded the lorries. Had trolleys, you know. Had to go along the racks getting the lines to put in the lorries. Yes, I did that for nearly twenty year. They wanted me to be a checker, you know, checking off on the invoices as the goods were loaded on to the lorries, but I didn't fancy the responsibility. I was happy with my trolley."

Suddenly Jean smiled at the old man, not her professional smile of concern, but a huge, genuine smile of pleasure that broke the sternness of her face into a rare beauty. Somehow she respected his simplicity, his content. It seemed to fit that the day after she met Mick, she should also meet this happy old man. She rose from her chair. "Well, if you're sure there's nothing I can do for you . . ."

"No, I'll be fine, thank you, love."

"I'll drop round again in a week or two to see how you're getting on."

"Oh, that'll be very nice. I'll be fine, though. Don't you worry about me."

"Good." Jean lingered for a moment. She felt something missing, there was something else she had meant to mention, now what on earth was it?

Oh yes. His sister. She had meant to talk to him about his sister, sympathize about her death the previous year. Jean had had the information from a social worker in Bradford where the sister had lived. They tried to liaise between different areas as much as possible. The sister had been found dead in her flat. She had died of hypothermia, but her body had not been discovered for eleven days, because of the Christmas break.

Jean thought she should mention it. There was always the danger of being thought to intrude on his privacy, but Harry Morton seemed a sensible enough old bloke, who would recognize her sympathy for what it was. And, in a strange way, Jean felt she ought to raise the matter as a penance for letting her mind wander while Harry had been talking.

"Incidentally, I heard about your sister's death. I'm very sorry."

"Oh, thank you." Harry Morton didn't seem unduly perturbed by the reference. "I didn't see a lot of her these last few years."

"But it must have been a shock."

"A bit, maybe. Typical, though. She always was daft, never took care of herself. Died of the cold, she did. Hyper . . . hyper-something they called it."

"Hypothermia."

"That's it. Silly fool. I didn't see her when I went up for the funeral. Just saw the coffin. Closed coffin. Could have been anyone. Didn't feel nothing, really."

"Anyway, as I say, I'm sorry."

"Oh, don't think about it. I don't. And don't you worry about me going the same way. For one thing, I always had twice as much sense as she did—from a child on. And then I can look after myself."

Jean Collinson left, feeling glad she had mentioned the sister. Now there was nothing nagging at her mind, nothing she felt she should be doing. Except looking forward to the evening. She wondered what she should cook for Mick.

Harry Morton closed the door after her. It was summer, but the corridor outside felt chilly. He shivered slightly, then went to his notebook and started to make a list.

He had always made lists. At the warehouse he had soon realized that he couldn't remember all the lines the checker gave him unless he wrote them down. The younger porters could remember up to twenty different items for their loads, but Harry recognized his limitations and always wrote everything down. It made him a little slower than the others, but at least he never got anything wrong. And the Head Checker had said, when you took off the time the others wasted taking back lines they had got wrong, Harry was quite as fast as any of them.

He headed the list "Things to do". First he wrote "Ratchet screwdriver". Then he wrote "Library".

Harry knew his own pace and he never tried to go any faster. When he was younger he had occasionally tried to push himself along a bit, but that had only resulted in mistakes. Now he did everything steadily, methodically. And now there was no one to push him. The only really miserable time of his life had been when a new checker had been appointed who had tried to increase Harry's work-rate. The old man still woke up sometimes in the night in the sweat of panic and confusion that the pressure had put on him. Unwillingly he'd remember the afternoon when he'd thrown a catering-size tin of diced carrots at his tormentor's head. But then he'd calm down, get up and make himself a cup of tea. That was all over. It hadn't lasted very long. The checker had been ambitious and soon moved on to an office job.

And now he wasn't at work, Harry had all the time in the world anyway. Time to do a good job. The only pressure on him was to get it done before the winter set in. And the winter was a long way off.

He read through all the Do-It-Yourself books he had got from the library, slowly, not skipping a word. After each one he would make a list, a little digest of the pros and cons of the methods discussed. Then he sent off for brochures from all the companies that advertised in his Do-It-Yourself magazines and subjected them to the same punctilious scrutiny. Finally, he made a tour of the local home-care shops, looked at samples and discussed the various systems with the proprietors. After six weeks he reckoned he knew everything there was to know about double glazing.

And by then he had ruled out quite a few of the systems on the market. The best method, he realized, was to replace the existing windows with new factory-sealed units, but, even if the Housing Trust would allow him to do this, it would be far too expensive and also too big a job for him to do on his own.

The next possible solution was the addition of secondary sashes, fixing a new pane over the existing window, leaving the original glass undisturbed. There were a good many proprietory sub-frame systems on the market, but again these would be far too expensive for his modest savings. He did some sums in his notebook, working out how long it would take him to afford secondary sashes by saving on his pension, but he wouldn't have enough till the spring. And he had to get the double glazing installed before the winter set in. He began to regret the generous proportions on which the Victorians had designed their windows.

He didn't worry about it, though. It was still only September. There was going to be a way that he could afford and that he could do on his own. That social worker was always full of offers of help from her network of volunteers, but he wasn't reduced to that yet.

Then he had the idea of going through the back numbers of his Do-It-Yourself magazines. He knew it was a good idea as soon as he thought about it. He sat in his armchair in front of the fireplace which was now hidden by a low screen, and, with notebook and pencil by his side, started to thumb through the magazines. He did them in strict chronological order, just as he kept them stacked on their new shelf. He had a full set for seven and a half years, an unbroken sequence from the first time he had become interested in Do-It-Yourself. That had been while he was being harassed by the new checker. He chuckled to remember that he'd bought the first magazine because it had an article in it about changing locks and he'd wanted to keep the checker out of his flat. Of course, the checker had never come to his flat.

He started on the first magazine and worked through, reading everything, articles and advertisements, in case he should miss what he was looking for. Occasionally he made a note in his notebook.

It was on the afternoon of the third day that he found it. The article was headed, "Cut the Costs of Double Glazing". His heart quickened with excitement, but he still read through the text at his regular, unvarying pace. Then he read it a second time, even more slowly, making copious notes.

The system described was a simple one, which involved sticking transparent film on the inside of the windows and thus creating the required insulation gap between the panes and the film. There were, the writer observed slyly, kits for this system available on the market, but the shrewd Do-It-Yourself practitioner would simply go to his local supermarket and buy the requisite number of rolls of kitchen clingfilm and then go to his hardware store to buy a roll of double-sided Sellotape for fixing the film, and thus save himself a lot of money. Harry Morton chuckled out loud, as this cunning plot was confided to him. Then he wrote on his list "Kitchen Clingfilm" and "Double-Sided Sellotape".

As always, in everything he did, he followed the instructions to the letter. At first, it was more difficult than it sounded. The kitchen film tended to shrivel up on itself and stretch out of true when he tried to extend it over the window frames. And it caught on the stickiness of the Sellotape before it was properly aligned. He had to sacrifice nearly a whole roll of clingfilm before he got the method right. But he pressed on, working with steady care, perched on the folding ladder he had bought specially for the purpose, and soon was rewarded by the sight of two strips stretched parallel and taut over the window frame.

He was lining up the third when the doorbell rang. He was

annoyed by the interruption to his schedule and opened the door grudgingly to admit Jean Collinson. Then he almost turned his back on her while he got on with the tricky task of winding the prepared film back on to its cardboard roll. He would have to start lining the next piece up again after she had gone.

Still, he did his best to be pleasant and offered the social worker a cup of tea. It seemed to take a very long time for the kettle to boil and the girl seemed to take a very long time to drink her tea. He kept looking over her shoulder to the window, estimating how many more strips it would take and whether he'd have to go back to the supermarket for another roll to make up for the one he'd ruined.

Had he taken any notice of Jean, he would have seen that she looked tired, fatigue stretching the skin of her face to show her features at their sharpest and sternest. Work was getting busy. She had ahead of her a difficult interview with Mrs Grüber, whose Yorkshire terrier Nimrod had developed a growth between his back legs. It hung there, obscene and shiny, dangling from the silky fur. The animal needed to go to the vet, but Mrs Grüber refused to allow this, convinced that it would have to be put down. Jean feared this suspicion was correct, but knew that the animal had to make the trip to find out one way or the other. It was obviously in pain and kept up a thin keening whine all the time while Mrs Grüber hugged it piteously to her cardigan. And Jean knew that she was going to have to be the one who got the animal to the vet.

Which meant she'd be late again. Which would mean another scene with Mick. He'd become so childish recently, so demanding, jealous of the time she spent with her old people. He had become moody and hopeless. Instead of the support in her life which he had been at first, he was now almost another case on her books. She had discovered how much he feared his job, how he couldn't keep order in class, and, though she gave him all the sympathy she could, it never seemed to be enough.

And then there were the logistics of living in two separate establishments an awkward bus-ride apart. Life seemed to have degenerated into a sequence of late-night and early-morning rushes from one flat to the other because one of them had left something vital in the wrong place. Jean had once suggested that they should move in together, but Mick's violent reaction of fear against such a commitment had kept her from raising the matter again. So their relationship had become a pattern of rows and making up, abject self-recrimination from Mick, complaints that she didn't really care about him and late-night reconciliations of desperate, clinging sex. Always too late. She had forgotten what a good night's sleep was by the time one end had been curtailed by arguments and coupling and the other by leaving at half-past six to get back to her place to pick up some case notes. Everything seemed threatened.

But it was restful in Harry's flat. He seemed to have his life organized. She found it an oasis of calm, of passionless simplicity, where she could recharge her batteries before going back to the difficulties of the rest of her life.

She was unaware of how he was itching for her to go. She saw the evidence of the double glazing and asked him about it, but he was reticent. He didn't want to discuss it until it was finished. Anyway, it wasn't for other people's benefit. It was for him.

Eventually Jean felt sufficiently steeled for her encounter with Mrs Grüber and brought their desultory conversation to an end. She did not notice the alacrity with which Harry Morton rose to show her out, nor the speed with which he closed the door after her.

Again he felt the chill of the corridor when the door was open. And even after it was closed there seemed to be a current of air from somewhere. He went across to his notebook and wrote down "Draught Excluder".

It was late October when she next went round to see the old man. She was surprised that he didn't immediately open the door after she'd rung the bell. Instead she heard his voice hiss out, "Who is it?"

She was used to this sort of reception from some of her old ladies, who lived in the conviction that every caller was a rapist at the very least, but she hadn't expected it from such a sensible old boy as Harry Morton.

She identified herself and, after a certain amount of persuasion, he let her in. He held the door open as little as possible and closed it almost before she was inside. "What do you want?" he asked aggressively.

"I just called to see how you are."

"Well, I'm fine." He spoke as if that ended the conversation and edged back towards the door.

"Are you sure? You look a bit pale."

He did look pale. His skin had taken on a greyish colour.

"You look as if you haven't been out much recently. Have you been ill? If you're unwell, all you have to do is—"

"I haven't been ill. I go out, do my shopping, get the things I need." He couldn't keep a note of mystery out of the last three words.

She noticed he was thinner too. His appearance hadn't suffered; he still dressed with almost obsessive neatness; but he had definitely lost weight. She wasn't to know that he was cutting down on food so that his pension would buy the "things he needed".

The room looked different too. She only took it in once she was inside. There was evidence of recent carpentry. No mess—all the sawdust was neatly contained on newspaper and offcuts of wood were leant against the kitchen table which Harry had used as a sawing bench—but he had obviously been busy. The ratchet screwdriver was prominent on the table top. The artefact which all this effort had produced was plain to see. The fine marble fireplace had been neatly boxed in. It had been a careful job. Pencil marks on the wood showed the accuracy of measurement and all of the screws were tidily countersunk into their regularly spaced holes.

Jean commented on the workmanship.

"When I do a job, I like to do it properly," Harry Morton said defensively.

"Of course. Didn't you . . . like the fireplace?"

"Nothing wrong with it. But it was very draughty."

"Yes." She wondered for a moment if Harry Morton were about to change from being one of her easy charges to one of her problems. He was her last call that day and she'd reckoned on just a quick visit. She'd recently made various promises to Mick about spending less time with her work. He'd suddenly got very aggressively male, demanding that she should look after him, that she should have a meal ready for him when he got home. He also kept calling her "woman", as if he were some character out of the blues songs he was always listening to. He didn't manage this new male chauvinism with complete conviction; it seemed only to accentuate his basic insecurity; but Jean was prepared to play along with it for a bit. She felt there was something in the relationship worth salvaging. Maybe when he relaxed a bit, things would be better. If only they could spend a little time on their own, just the two of them, away from outside pressures. . . .

She stole a look at her watch. She could spend half an hour with Harry and still be back at what Mick would regard as a respectable hour. Anyway, there wasn't anything really wrong with the old boy. Just needed a bit of love, a feeling that someone cared. That was what most of them needed when it came down to it.

"Harry, it looks to me like you may have been overdoing it with all this heavy carpentry. You must remember, you're not as young as you were and you do have to take things a bit slower."

"I take things at the right pace," he insisted stubbornly. "There's nothing wrong with me."

But Jean wasn't going to have her solicitude swept aside so easily. "No, of course there isn't. But look, I'd like you just to sit down for a moment in front of the . . . by the fireplace, and I'll make you a cup of tea."

Grumbling, he sat down.

"And why don't you put the television on? I'm sure there's some nice relaxing programme for you to see."

"There's not much I enjoy on the television."

"Nonsense, I'm sure there are lots of things to interest you." Having started in this bulldozing vein, Jean was going to continue. She switched on the television and went into the kitchen.

It was some children's quiz show, which Harry would have switched off under normal circumstances. But he didn't want to make the girl suspicious. If he just did as she said, she would go quicker. So he sat and watched without reaction.

It was only when the commercials came that he took notice.

There was a commercial for double glazing. A jovial man was demonstrating the efficacy of one particular system. A wind machine was set in motion the other side of an open window. Then the double-glazed window was closed and, to show how airtight the seal was, the man dropped a feather by the joint in the panes. It fluttered straight downwards, its course unaffected by any draughts.

From that moment Harry Morton was desperate for Jean to leave. He had seen the perfect way of testing his workmanship. She offered to stay and watch the programme with him, she asked lots of irrelevant questions about whether he needed anything or whether there was anything her blessed volunteers could do, but eventually she was persuaded to go. In fact she was relieved to be away. Harry had seemed a lot perkier than when she had arrived and now she would be back in time to conform to Mick's desired image of her.

Harry almost slammed the door. As he turned, he felt a shiver of cold down his back. Right, feathers, feathers. It only took a moment to work out where to get them from.

He picked up his ratchet screwdriver and went over to the bed. He drew back the candlewick and stabbed the screwdriver deeply into his pillow. And again, twisting and tearing at the fabric. From the rents he made a little storm of feathers flurried.

It was cold as she walked along towards Harry's flat and the air stung the rawness of her black eye. But Jean felt good. At least they'd got something sorted out. After the terrible fight of the night before, in the sobbing reconciliation, after Mick had apologized for hitting her, he had suggested that they go away together for Christmas. He hated all the fuss that surrounded the festival and always went off to stay in a cottage in Wales, alone, until it all died down. And he had said, in his ungracious way, "You can come with me, woman."

She knew it was a risk. The relationship might not stand the proximity. She was even slightly afraid of being alone with Mick for so long, now that his behaviour towards her had taken such a violent turn. But at bottom she thought it would work. Anyway, she had to try. They had to try. Ten days alone together would sort out the relationship one way or the other. And Christmas was only three weeks off.

As so often happened, her new mood of confidence was reflected in her work. She had just been to see Mrs Grüber. Nimrod had made a complete recovery after the removal of his growth and the old lady had actually thanked Jean for insisting on the visit to the vet. That meant Mrs Grüber could be left over the Christmas break without anxiety. And most of the others could manage. As Mick so often said, thinking you're indispensable is one of the first signs of madness. Of course they'd all be all right if she went away. And, as Mick also said, then you'll be able to concentrate on me for a change, woman. Yes, it was going to work.

Again her ring at the doorbell was met by a whispered "Who is it?" from Harry Morton. It was Jean—could she come in? "No," he said.

"Why not, Harry? Remember, I do have a duplicate key. The Housing Trust insists that I have that, so that I can let myself in if—"

"No, it's not that, Jean love," his old Northern voice wheedled. "It's just that I've got a really streaming cold. I don't want to breathe germs all over you."

"Oh, don't worry about that."

"No, no, really. I'm in bed. I'm just going to sleep it off."

Jean wavered. Now she came to think of it, she didn't fancy breathing in germs in Harry's stuffy little flat. "Have you seen the doctor?"

"No, I tell you it's just a cold. Be gone in a day or two, if I just stay in bed. No need to worry the doctor."

The more she thought about it, the less she wanted to develop a cold just before she and Mick went away together. But it was her job to help. "Are you sure there isn't anything I can do for you? Shopping or anything?"

"Oh. Well . . ." Harry paused. "Yes, I would be grateful, actually, if you wouldn't mind getting me a few things."

"Of course."

"If you just wait a moment, I'll write out a list."

Jean waited. After a couple of minutes a page from his notebook was pushed under the door. Its passage was impeded by the draught-excluding strip on the inside, but it got through.

Jean looked at the list. "Bottle of milk. Small tin of baked beans. Six packets of Polyfilla."

"Is that Polyfilla?" she asked, bewildered.

"Yes. It's a sort of powder you mix with water to fill in cracks and that."

"I know what it is. You just seem to want rather a lot of it."

"Yes, I do. Just for a little job needs doing."

"And you're quite sure you don't need any more food?"

"Sure. I've got plenty," Harry Morton lied.

"Well, I'll probably be back in about twenty minutes."

"Thank you very much. Here's the money." A few crumpled notes forced their way under the door. "If there's no reply when you get back, I'll be asleep. Just leave the stuff outside. It'll be safe."

"Okay. If you're sure there's nothing else I can do."

"No, really. Thanks very much."

Harry Morton heard her footsteps recede down the passage and chuckled aloud with delight at his own cunning. Yes, she could help him. First useful thing she'd ever have done for him.

And she hadn't noticed the windows from the outside. Just thought the curtains were drawn. Yes, it had been a good idea to board them up over the curtains. He looked with satisfaction at the wooden covers, with their rows of screws, each one driven securely home with his ratchet screwdriver. Then he looked at the pile of new wood leaning against the door. Yes, with proper padding that would be all right. Mentally he earmarked his bedspread for the padding and made a note of the idea on the "Jobs to Do" list in his notebook.

Suddenly he felt the chill of a draught on his neck. He leapt up to find its source. He had long given up using the feather method. Apart from anything else, he had used his pillows as insulation in the fireplace. Now he used a lighted candle. Holding it firmly in front of him, he began to make a slow, methodical circuit of the room.

★

It was two days before Christmas, two o'clock in the afternoon. Jean and Mick were leaving at five. "Five sharp, woman," he had said. "If you ain't here then, woman, I'll know you don't give a damn about me. You'd rather spend your life with incontinent old men." Jean had smiled when he said it. Oh yes, she'd be there. Given all that time together, she knew they could work something out.

And, when it came to it, it was all going to be remarkably easy. All of her charges seemed to be sorted out over the holiday. Now Nimrod was all right, Mrs Grüber was in a state of ecstasy, full of plans for the huge Christmas dinner she was going to cook for herself and the dog. Mrs Walker was going to stay with her daughter, which meant that she would see the grandchildren, so she couldn't complain for once. Even smelly old Mr Kitson had been driven off to spend the holiday with his married sister. Rather appropriately, in Bath. The rest of her cases had sorted themselves out one way or the other. And, after all, she was only going to be away for ten days. She felt she needed the break. Her Senior Social Worker had wished her luck and told her to have a good rest, and this made Jean realize how long it was since she had been away from work for any length of time.

She just had to check that Mr Morton was all right, and then she was free.

Harry was steeping his trousers in mixed-up Polyfilla when he heard the doorbell. It was difficult, what he was doing. Really, the mixture should have been runnier, but he had not got out enough water before he boarded up the door to the kitchen and bathroom. Never mind, though, the stuff would still work and soon he'd be able to produce more urine to mix it with. He was going to use the Polyfilla-covered trousers to block the crevice along the bottom of the front door. His pyjamas and pullover were already caulking the cracks on the other one.

He congratulated himself on judging the amount of Polyfilla right. He was nearly at the end of the last packet. By the time he'd blocked in the plug sockets and the ventilation grille he'd found hidden behind the television, it would all be used up. Just the right amount.

He froze when he heard the doorbell. Lie doggo. Pretend there's no one there. They'll go away.

The bell rang again. Still he didn't move. There was a long pause, so long he thought the challenge had gone. But then he heard an ominous sound, which at once identified his caller and also raised a new threat.

It was the sound of a key in his lock. That bloody busybody of a social worker had come round to see him.

There was nothing for it. He would have to let her in. "Just a minute. Coming," he called.

"Hurry up," the girl's voice said. She had told him to hurry up. Like the new checker, she had told him to hurry up.

He picked up his ratchet screwdriver and started to withdraw the first of the screws that held the large sheet of chipboard and its padding of bedclothes against the front door. At least, he thought, thank God I hadn't put the sealing strips along here.

Jean's voice sounded quite agitated by the time he removed the last screw. "What's going on? Can't you hurry up?"

She had said it again. He opened the door narrowly and she pushed in, shouting, "Now what the hell do you think you're—"

Whether she stopped speaking because she was taken aback by the sight of the room and her half-naked host, or because the ratchet screwdriver driven into her back near the spine had punctured her heart, it is difficult to assess. Certainly it is true that the first blow killed her; the subsequent eleven were unnecessary insurance.

Harry Morton left the body on the floor and continued methodically with his tasks. He replaced the chipboard and padding over the door and sealed round it with his trousers, sports jacket, shirt and socks, all soaked in Polyfilla. Then he blocked up the plugs and ventilator grille.

He looked round with satisfaction. Now that was real insulation. No one could die of cold in a place like that. Always had been daft, his sister. But he didn't relax. One more final check-round with the candle, then he could put his feet up.

He went slowly round the room, very slowly so that the candle wouldn't flicker from his movement, only from genuine draughts.

Damn. It had moved. He retraced a couple of steps. Yes, it fluttered again. There was a draught.

By the fireplace. That fireplace had always been more trouble than it was worth.

It needed more insulating padding. And more Polyfilla to seal it.

But he'd used everything in the room and there was no water left to mix the Polyfilla with. He felt too dehydrated to urinate. Never mind, there was a solution to everything. He sat down with his notebook and pencil to work it out.

Well, there was his underwear, for a start. That was more insulation. He took it off.

Then he looked down at Jean Collinson's body and saw the solution. To both his problems. Her body could be crammed into the chimney to block out the draughts and her blood (of which there was quite a lot) could mix with the Polyfilla.

He worked at his own pace, unscrewing the boxwork he had put around the marble fireplace with his ratchet screwdriver. Then he pulled out the inadequate insulation of pillows and Do-It-Yourself magazines and started to stuff the body up the chimney.

It was hard work. He pushed the corpse up head first and the broad hips stuck well in the flue, forming a good seal. But he had to break the legs to fit them behind his boxwork when he replaced it. He crammed the crevices with the pillows and magazines and sealed round the edges with brownish Polyfilla.

Only then did he feel that he could sit back with the satisfaction of a job well done.

They found his naked body when they broke into the flat after the Christmas break.

He would have died from starvation in time, but in fact, so good was his insulation, he was asphyxiated first.

THE NUGGY BAR

MURDER, LIKE ALL great enterprises, repays careful planning; and, if there was one thing on which Hector Griffiths prided himself, it was his planning ability.

It was his planning ability which had raised him through the jungle of the domestic cleaning fluids industry to be Product Manager of the GLISS range of indispensable housewives' aids. His marriage to Melissa Wintle, an attractive and rich widow with a teenage daughter, was also a triumph of planning. Even his wife's unfortunate death three years later, caused by asphyxiation from the fumes of a faulty gas heater while he was abroad on business, could be seen as the product of, if not necessarily planning, then at least serendipity.

But no amount of planning could have foreseen that Melissa's will would have left the bulk of her not inconsiderable wealth to Janet, daughter of her first marriage, rather than to Hector, her second husband.

So when, at the age of fifty-two, Hector Griffiths found himself reduced to his GLISS salary (generous, but by no means sufficient to maintain those little extras—the flat in Sloane Street, the cottage in Cornwall, the Mercedes, the motor-boat—which had become habitual while his wife was alive) and saddled with the responsibility of an unforthcoming, but definitely rich, step-daughter, he decided it was time to start planning again.

Hector Griffiths shared with Moses, Matthew, Mark, Luke, John and other lesser prophets and evangelists the advantage of having written his own Bible. It was a series of notes which he had assembled during the planning build-up to the launch of NEW GREEN GLISS—WITH AMMONIA, and he was not alone in appreciating its worth. No less a person than the company's European Marketing Director (Cleaning Fluids) had congratulated him on the notes' cogency and good sense after hearing Hector use them as the basis of a Staff Training Course lecture.

Hector kept the notes, which he had had neatly typed up by his secretary, in a blue plastic display folder, of which favoured Management Trainees were occasionally vouchsafed a glimpse. On its title page were two precepts, two precepts which provided a dramatic opening to Hector's lectures and which, he had to admit, were rather well put.

A. EVEN AT THE COST OF DELAYING THE LAUNCH OF YOUR PRODUCT, ALWAYS ALLOW SUFFICIENT TIME FOR PLANNING. IMPATIENCE BREEDS ERROR, AND ERROR IS EXPENSIVE.
B. ONCE YOU HAVE MADE YOUR MAJOR DECISIONS ABOUT THE PRODUCT AND THE TIMING OF ITS LAUNCH, DO NOT INDULGE SECOND THOUGHTS. A DELAYED SCHEDULE IS ALSO EXPENSIVE.

A third precept, equally important but unwritten, dictated that before any action was taken on a new product, there should be a period of Desk Work, of sitting and thinking, looking at the project from every angle, checking as many details as could be checked, generally familiarizing oneself with every aspect of the job in hand. Thinking at this earlier, relaxed stage made it easier to deal with problems that arose later, when time for thought was a luxury and one had to act on impulse.

It was nearly three months after Melissa's death before Hector had time to settle down to the Desk Work for his new project. He had been busy with the European launch of GLISS SCOURING PADS and had also found that clearing a deceased's belongings and sorting out a will, even such a simple and unsatisfactory one as Melissa's, took a surprising amount of time. Janet had also needed attention. Her mother's death had taken place at Easter, which meant that the girl had been home from her Yorkshire boarding school. Janet, now a withdrawn fifteen-year-old, had unfortunately been asleep at the time of Melissa's accident, had heard nothing and so been unable to save her. Equally unfortunately, from her step-father's point of view, she had not been in the bathroom with her mother when the gas fumes started to escape, which would have solved his current difficulties before they arose.

But, as Hector always told the eager young men in beige suits and patterned ties on the Staff Training Courses, success rarely comes easily, and the wise manager will distrust the solution that arrives too readily.

No, Janet was still with him, and he did not regret the time he had devoted to her. His plans for her future had not yet crystallized but, whatever it was to be, prudence dictated that he should take on the role of the solicitous step-father. Now she was such a wealthy young woman, it made sense that he should earn at least her goodwill.

He smiled wryly at the thought. Something told him he would require more of her than goodwill for the occasional handout. The flat in London, the cottage in Cornwall, the motor-boat and the Mercedes demanded a less erratic income. He needed permanent control of Janet's money.

But he was jumping to conclusions. He always warned Management Trainees against prejudging issues before they had done their Desk Work.

Hector Griffiths opened the blue folder on his desk. He turned over the page of precepts and looked at the next section.

1. NEED FOR PRODUCT (FILLING MARKET VOID, INCREASING BRAND SHARE)

It took no elaborate research to tell him that the product was needed. Now Melissa was dead, there was a market void, and the product required to fill it was money.

Unwilling to reject too soon any possibility, he gave thought to various methods of money-making. His prospects at GLISS were healthy, but not healthy enough. Even if, when the Marketing Director (U.K.) retired and was replaced by the European Marketing Director (Cleaning Fluids), Hector got the latter's job (which was thought likely), his salary would only rise by some 25 per cent, far off parity with the wealth he had commanded as Melissa's husband. Even a massive coincidence of coronaries amongst the senior management of GLISS which catapulted Hector to the Managing Director's office would still leave him worse off.

Career prospects outside GLISS, for a man of fifty-two, however good a planner, offered even less. Anyway, Hector didn't want to struggle and graft. What he had had in mind had been a few more years of patronizing his underlings in his present job and then an early, dignified and leisured retirement, surrounded by all the comforts of Melissa (except for Melissa herself).

So how else did people get money? There was crime, of course—theft, embezzlement and so on—but Hector thought such practices undignified, risky and positively immoral.

No, it was obvious that the money to ease his burdens should be Melissa's. Already he felt it was his by right.

But Janet had it.

On the other hand, if Janet died, the trust that administered the money for her would have to be broken, inevitably to the benefit of her only surviving relation, her poor step-father, desolated by yet another bereavement.

The real product for which there was a market void, and which would undeniably increase Hector Griffiths' brand share, was Janet's death.

2. SPECIFIC DESCRIPTION OF PRODUCT

Fifteen-year-old girls rarely die spontaneously, however convenient and public-spirited such an action might be, so it was inevitable that Janet would have to be helped on her way.

It didn't take a lot of Desk Work to reach the conclusion that she would have to be murdered. And, following unhappy experiences with the delegation of responsibility over the European launch of GREEN GLISS SCOURING PADS, Hector realized he would have to do the job himself.

3. TIMING OF LAUNCH

This was the crucial factor. How many products, Hector would rhetorically demand of the ardent young men who dreamt of company Cortinas and patio doors, how many products have been condemned to obscurity by too hasty a schedule? Before deciding on the date of your launch, assess the following three points:

A. HOW SOON CAN THE PRODUCTION, PUBLICITY AND SALES DEPARTMENTS MAKE THE PRODUCT A VIABLE COMMERCIAL PROPOSITION?

B. HOW LONG WILL IT BE BEFORE THE MARKET FORCES WHICH REVEALED A NEED FOR THE PRODUCT ALTER? (N.B. OR BEFORE A RIVAL CONCERN ALSO NOTES THE NEED AND SUPPLIES IT WITH THEIR OWN PRODUCT?)

C. WHAT SPECIAL FACTORS DOES YOUR PRODUCT HAVE WHICH CREATE SPECIAL NEEDS IN TIMING? (e.g. YOU DO NOT LAUNCH A TENNIS SHOE CLEANER IN THE WINTER.)

Hector gave quite a lot of Desk Work to this section. The first question he could not answer until he had done some serious Research and Development into a murder method. That might take time.

But, even if the perfect solution came within days, there were many arguments for delaying the launch. The most potent was Melissa's recent death. Though at no point during the police investigations or inquest had the slightest suspicion attached to him, the coincidence of two accidents too close together might prompt unnecessarily scrupulous inquiry. It also made sense that Hector should continue to foster his image of solicitude for his step-daughter, thus killing the seeds of any subsequent suspicion.

The answer to Question A, therefore, was that the launch should be delayed as long as possible.

But the length of this delay was limited by the answer to Question B. Though with a sedately private matter like the murder of Janet, Hector did not fear, as he would have done in the cut-throat world of cleaning fluids, a rival getting in before him, there was still the strong pressure of market forces. The pittance Melissa had accorded him in her will would maintain his current lifestyle (with a conservative allowance for inflation) for about eighteen months. That set the furthest limit on the launch (though prudence suggested it would look less suspicious if he didn't run right up against bankruptcy).

In answer to Question C (what he humorously referred to to his Management Trainees as the "tennis shoe question"), there was a significant special factor. Since Janet was at boarding school in Yorkshire, where his presence would be bound to cause comment, the launch had to be during the school holidays.

Detailed consideration of these and other factors led him to a date of launch during the summer of the following year, some fifteen months away. It seemed a long time to wait, but, as Hector knew, IMPATIENCE BREEDS ERROR.

4. RESEARCH AND DEVELOPMENT OF PRODUCT
(A. THEORETICAL)

He was able, at his desk, to eliminate a number of possible murder methods. Most of them were disqualified because they failed to meet one important specification: that he should not be implicated in any way.

Simplified, this meant either a) that Janet's death should look like an accident, b) that her step-father should have a cast-iron alibi for the time of her death, or, preferably, c) both.

He liked the idea of an accident. Even though he would arrange things so that he had nothing to fear from a murder inquiry, it was better to avoid the whole process. Ideally, he needed an accident which occurred while he was out of the country.

A wry instinct dissuaded him from any plan involving faulty gas heaters. A new product should always be genuinely original.

Hector went through a variety of remotely-controlled accidents that could happen to teenage girls, but all seemed to involve faulty machinery and invited uncomfortably close comparisons with gas heaters. He decided he might have to take a more personal role in the project.

But if he had to be there, he was at an immediate disadvantage. Anyone present at a suspicious death becomes a suspicious person. What he needed was to be both present and absent at the same time.

But that was impossible. Either he was there or he wasn't. His own physical presence was immovable. The time of the murder was immovable. And the two had to coincide.

Or did they?

It was at this moment that Hector Griffiths had a brainwave.

They did sometimes come to him, with varying force, but this one was huge, bigger even, he believed, than his idea for the green tear-off tag on the GLISS TABLE-TOP CLEANER sachets.

He would murder Janet and then change the time of her murder.

It would need a lot of research, a lot of reading books of forensic medicine, but, just as Hector had known with the green tag, he knew again that he had the right solution.

4. RESEARCH AND DEVELOPMENT OF PRODUCT (B. PRACTICAL)

One of Hector's favourite sentences from his Staff Training lecture was: "The true Genesis of a product is forged by the R and D boys in the white heat of the laboratory." Previously, he had always spoken it with a degree of wistfulness, aware of the planner's distance from true creativity, but with his new product he experienced the thrill of being the real creator.

He gave himself a month, the month that remained before Janet would return for her summer holidays, and at the end of that time he wanted to know his murder method. There would be time for refinement of details, but it was important to get the main outline firm.

He made many experiments which gave him the pleasure of research, but not the satisfaction of a solution, before he found the right method.

He found it in Cornwall. Janet had agreed to continue her normal summer practice of spending the month of August at the cottage, and early in July Hector went down for a weekend to see that the place was habitable and to take the motor-boat for its first outing of the season. While Melissa had been alive, the cottage had been used most weekends from Easter onwards and, as he cast off his boat from the mooring in front of his cottage and breathed the tangy air, Hector decided to continue the regular visits.

He liked it down there. He liked having the boat to play with, he liked the respect that ownership of the cottage brought him. Commander Donleavy, with whom he drank in the Yacht Club, would often look out across the bay to where it perched, a rectangle of white on the cliff, secluded but cunningly modernized, and say, "Damned fine property, that."

The boat was a damned fine property, too, and Hector wasn't going to relinquish either of them. Inevitably, as he powered through the waves, he thought of Melissa. But without emotion, almost without emotion now. Typical of her to make a mistake over the will.

She came to his mind more forcibly as he passed a place where they had made love. During the days of their courtship, when he had realized that her whimsical nature would require a few romantic gestures before she consented to marry him, he had started taking her to unlikely settings for love-making.

The one the boat now chugged past was the unlikeliest of all. It was a hidden cave, only accessible at very low tide. He had found it by accident the first time he had gone out with Melissa in the boat. His inexperience of navigation had brought their vessel dangerously close to some rocks and, as he leant out to fend off, he had fallen into the sea. To his surprise, he had found sand beneath his feet and caught a glimpse of a dark space under an arch of rock.

Melissa had taken over the wheel and he had scrambled back on board, aware that the romantic lover image he had been fostering was now seriously dented by his incompetence. But the cave he had seen offered a chance for him to redeem himself.

Brusquely ordering Melissa to anchor the boat, he had stripped off and jumped back into the icy water. (It was May.) He then swam to the opening he had seen and disappeared under the low arch. He soon found himself on a sandy beach in a small cave, eerily lit by reflection of the sun on the water outside.

He had reappeared in the daylight and summoned Melissa imperiously to join him. Enjoying taking orders, she had stripped off and swum to the haven, where, on the sand, he had taken her with apparent, but feigned, brutality. When doing the Desk Work on his project for getting married to Melissa, he had analysed in her taste for Gothic romances an ideal of a dominant, savage lover, and built up the Heathcliff in himself accordingly.

It had worked, too. It was in the cave that she had agreed to marry him. Once the ceremony was achieved, he was able to put aside his Gothic image with relief. Apart from anything else, gestures like the cave episode were very cold.

When, by then safely married, they next went past the cave opening, Melissa had looked at him wistfully, but Hector had pretended not to see. Anyway, there had been no sign of the opening; it was only revealed at the lowest spring tide. Also by then it was high summer and the place stank. The council spoke stoutly of rotting seaweed, while local opinion muttered darkly about a sewage outlet, but, whatever the cause, a pervasively offensive stench earned the place the nickname of "Stinky Cove" and kept trippers away when the weather got hot.

As he steered his boat past the hidden opening and wrinkled his nose involuntarily, all the elements combined in Hector's head, and his murder plan began to form.

4. RESEARCH AND DEVELOPMENT OF PRODUCT
(C. EXPERIMENTAL)

Commander Donleavy was an inexhaustible source of information about things nautical, and he loved being asked, particularly by someone as ignorantly appreciative as Hector Griffiths. He had no problem explaining to the greenhorn all about the 28-day cycle of the tides, and referring him to the tide tables, and telling him that yes, of course it would be possible to predict the date of a spring tide a year in advance. Not for the first time he marvelled that the government didn't insist on two years in the regular Navy as the minimum qualification for anyone wishing to own a boat.

Still, Griffiths wasn't a bad sort. Generous with the pink gins, anyway. And got that nice cottage over the bay. "Damned fine property, that," said Commander Donleavy, as he was handed another double.

The cycle of the tides did not allow Hector Griffiths to become an "R and D boy" and get back into "the white heat of the laboratory" again until his step-daughter was established in the cottage for her summer holiday. Janet was, he thought, quieter than ever; she seemed to take her mother's death hard. Though not fractious or uncooperative, she seemed listless. Except for a little sketching, she appeared to have no interests, and showed no desire to go anywhere. Better still, she did not seem to have any friends. She wrote duty postcards to two elderly aunts of Melissa in Stockport, but received no mail and made no attempt to make new contacts. All of which was highly satisfactory.

So, on the day of the spring tide, she made no comment on her step-father's decision to take the boat out, and Hector felt confident that, when he returned, he would still find her stretched lethargically in her mother's armchair.

He anchored the motor-boat in shallow water outside the cave entrance, took off his trousers (beneath which he wore swimming trunks), put on rubber shoes, and slipped over the side. The water came just above his knee, and more of the entrance arch was revealed. On his previous visit the tide cannot have been at its very lowest. But the entrance remained well hidden; no one who didn't know exactly where it was would be likely to find it by chance.

He had a flashlight with him, but switched it off once he was inside the cave. The shifting ripples of reflection gave enough light.

It was better than he remembered. The cave was about the size, and somehow had the atmosphere, of a small church. There was a high pile of fallen rocks and stones up the altar end, which, together with the stained glass window feel of the filtered light, reinforced the image.

But it was an empty church. There was no detritus of beer-cans, biscuit packets or condoms to suggest that anyone else shared Hector's discovery.

Down the middle of the cave a seeping stream of water traversed the sand. Hector trod up this with heavy footsteps, and watched with pleasure as the marks filled in and became invisible.

The pile of rubble was higher than it had at first appeared. Climbing it was hard, as large stones rocked and smaller ones scuttered out under the weight of his feet. When he stood precariously on the top and looked down fifteen feet to the unmarked sand below, he experienced the sort of triumph that the "R and D boys" must have felt when they arrived at the formula for the original GLISS CLEANING FLUID.

In his pocket he found a paper bag and blew it up. Inflated, it was about the size of a human head. He let it bounce gently down to the foot of the rubble pile, and picked up a large stone.

It took three throws before he got his range, but the third stone hit the paper bag right in the middle. The target exploded with a moist thud. Shreds of it lay plastered flat against the damp sand.

Hector Griffiths left the cave and went back to get his step-daughter's lunch.

5. PACKAGING (WHAT DO YOU WANT THE PRODUCT TO LOOK LIKE? WHAT DOES THE PUBLIC WANT THE PRODUCT TO LOOK LIKE?)

"The appearance of your product is everything," the diligent young men who worried about their first mortgages and second babies would hear. "Packaging can kill a good product and sell a bad one. It can make an original product look dated, and an old one look brand new."

It could also, Hector Griffiths believed, make the police believe a murder to be an accident and an old corpse to be a slightly newer one.

As with everything, he planned well ahead. The first component in his murder machine was generously donated by its proposed victim. Listless and unwilling to go out, Janet asked if he would mind posting her cards to Melissa's aunts in Stockport. She didn't really know why she was writing to them, she added mournfully; they were unlikely ever to meet again now Mummy was dead.

Hector took the cards, but didn't post them. He did not even put stamps on them. You never knew how much postal rates might go up in a year. He put them away in a blue folder.

There wasn't a lot more that could be done at that stage, so he spent the rest of his time in Cornwall being nice to Janet and drinking with Commander Donleavy at the Yacht Club.

He listened to a lot of naval reminiscences and sympathized with the pervading gloom about the way the world was going. He talked about the younger generation. He said he had nothing to complain of with his step-daughter, except that she was so quiet. He said how he tried to jolly her along, but all she seemed to want to do was mope around the cottage or go off on long walks on her own. Oh yes, she did sketch a bit. Wasn't that her in a blue smock out by the back door of the cottage? Commander Donleavy looked through his binoculars and said he reckoned it must be—too far to see her clearly, though.

If he was in the Yacht Club in the evening, Hector might draw the Commander's attention to the cottage lights going off as Janet went to bed. Always turned in by ten-thirty—at least he couldn't complain about late hours. She was a strange child.

Commander Donleavy laughed and said there was no accounting for the ways of women. Good Lord, within a year that little mouse could have turned into a regular flapper, with boyfriends arriving every hour of the day and night.

Hector said he hoped not (without as much vigour as he felt) and laughed (without as much humour as he manifested). So the holidays passed.

When he got back behind his desk at GLISS, he found a letter telling him that an international domestic cleaning exhibition, INTERSAN, would be held in Hamburg from the 9th to the 17th of September the following year.

This was better than he had dared hope. He called in his assistant, a former Management Trainee, who was in charge of the undemanding and unexciting GLISS SPOT-REMOVER range and who constantly complained about his lack of responsibility, and asked him to represent the company at the exhibition. Hector knew it was a long way off, but he thought it would give the young man something to look forward to. He was beginning to feel his age, he added tantalizingly, and thought there might be other responsibilities he would soon wish to delegate.

On 14 September, Hector Griffiths set aside that day's copy of the *Daily Telegraph*. He put it with the postcards in the blue folder.

There was little more he could do for the time being, except to go over his planning in detail and check for flaws. He found none, but he still thought there was something missing. He needed one more element, one clinching piece of evidence. Still, no need to panic; it'd come. Just a matter of patient Desk Work. So, while he devoted most of his energies to the forthcoming launch of GLISS HANDY MOPPITS (IDEAL FOR THE KITCHEN, NURSERY OR HANDBAG), he kept a compartment of his mind open to receive another inspiration.

So the months passed. He and Janet Christmassed quietly in

London. To his relief, she did not appear to be fulfilling Commander Donleavy's prognostications; if anything, she was quieter still. The only change was that she said she hated school, was getting nowhere there, and wanted to leave. Her indulgent step-father suppressed his glee, thought about the matter seriously, and finally agreed that she should leave at the end of the summer term, then join him for August at the cottage, so that they could decide on her future.

6. PUBLICITY (MAKE SURE EVERYONE KNOWS ABOUT YOUR PRODUCT EXACTLY WHEN *YOU* WANT THEM TO.)

This was the only one of Hector Griffiths' headings which might, while vital for any GLISS product, seem to be less applicable in the case of a murder.

But publicity is not only making things public; it is also keeping things secret until the time is right, and Hector's experience at GLISS had taught him a great deal about this art. Though lacking the glamour of military secrets, cleaning fluid secrets were still valuable and had been the subjects of espionage. So Hector was trained to keep his plans to himself.

And, anyway, there was going to come a time when publicity of the conventional sort was necessary, indeed essential. If the police never found Janet's body, then the plan was incomplete. Not only might there be difficulties in releasing her money to her step-father, he might also have to suffer the stigma of suspicion. As with the launch of a product, what was important was the moment of public revelation. And the timing of that, with this product as with any other, Hector would dictate personally.

It was, incidentally, while he was thinking of publicity that he came upon the missing element in his campaign. Some months before the launch of GLISS HANDY MOPPITS (IDEAL FOR THE KITCHEN, NURSERY OR HANDBAG) Hector had to go to his advertising agency to agree the publicity campaign for the new product. He enjoyed these occasions, because he knew that he, as Product Manager, was completely in command, and loved to see his account executive fawn while he deliberated.

One particular ploy, which gave him a great deal of satisfaction, was simply delaying his verdict. He would look at the artwork, view the television commercial or listen to the campaign outline, then, after remaining silent for a few minutes, start talking about something completely different. The executive presenting to him, fearful above all else of losing the very lucrative GLISS account, would sweat his way up any conversational alley the Product Manager wished to lead him, until finally Hector relented and said what he thought.

After seeing the television commercial for GLISS HANDY MOPPITS (IDEAL FOR THE KITCHEN, NURSERY OR HANDBAG), Hector started playing his game and asked what else the executive was working on.

The young man, a fine sweat lending his brow a satisfying sheen, answered sycophantically. His next big job was for one of the country's biggest confectionery firms, the launch of a brand new nut and nougat sweet—the NUGGY BAR. It was going to be a huge nationwide campaign, newspapers, cinema, television, radio, the lot. The product was already being tested in the Tyne-Tees area. Look, would Mr Griffiths like to try one? Nice blue and gold wrapper, wasn't it? Yes, go on, try—we've got plenty—the office is full of them.

Well, what did Mr Griffiths think of it? Pretty revolting? Hmm. Well, never mind. Yes, take one by all means. Well, anyway, whatever Mr Griffiths thought of them, he was going to be hard put to avoid them. After the launch on 10 September, he would see them in every shop in the country.

Hector Griffiths glowed inwardly. Yes, of course there was skill and there was planning, but there was also luck. Luck, like the fact that the old GLISS FLOOR POLISH tin had adapted so easily to metric standards. Luck, like suddenly coming across the NUGGY BAR. It was a magnetism for luck that distinguished a great Product Manager from a good Product Manager.

The NUGGY BAR was secure in his pocket. His mind raced on, as he calmly told the account executive that he found the GLISS HANDY MOPPITS (IDEAL FOR THE KITCHEN, NURSERY OR HANDBAG) commercial too flippant, and that it would have to be remade, showing more respect for the product.

7. RUN-UP TO LAUNCH (ATTEND TO DETAILS. CHECK, CHECK
AND RECHECK.)

Hector Griffiths checked, checked and rechecked.

In June he went to an unfamiliar boat dealer in North London and bought, for cash, an inflatable dinghy and outboard motor.

The next weekend he went down to Cornwall and, after much consultation with Commander Donleavy, bought an identical dinghy and outboard from the boatyard that serviced his motor-boat.

Three days later he bought some electrical time-switches in an anonymous Woolworths.

Then, furtively, in a Soho sex shop, he bought an inflatable woman.

In another anonymous Woolworths, he bought a pair of rubber gloves.

At work, the GLISS HANDY MOPPITS (IDEAL FOR THE KITCHEN, NURSERY OR HANDBAG) were successfully launched. Hector's assist-ant, in anticipation of his exciting trip to Hamburg for INTERSAN, took his holiday in July. One of his last actions before going away was to prepare the authorization for the continued production of GLISS SPOT-REMOVER. This was the formal notice to the production department which would ensure sufficient supplies of the product for November orders. It was one of those boring bits of paperwork that had to be prepared by the individual Product Manager and sent to the overall GLISS Product Manager for signature.

Hector's assistant did it last thing on the day he left, deposited it in his out-tray, and set off for two weeks in Hunstanton, cheered by the fact that Griffiths had said he was going to take a longer holiday that summer, all of August plus two weeks of September. Another indication, like INTERSAN, that the old man was going to sit back a bit and give others a chance.

So Hector's assistant didn't see the old man in question remove the GLISS SPOT-REMOVER authorization from his out-tray. Nor did he see it burnt to nothing in an ash-tray in the Sloane Street flat.

Janet left her Yorkshire boarding school as quietly as she had done everything else in her life, and joined her step-father in London. At the beginning of August they went down to Cornwall.

She remained as withdrawn as ever. Her step-father encouraged her to keep up her sketching, and to join him in occasional trips in the motor-boat or his new rubber dinghy. He spoke with some concern to Commander Donleavy in the Yacht Club about her listlessness. He pointed her out sketching outside the cottage, and the Commander almost saw her figure through his binoculars. Once or twice in the evening, Hector commented to the Commander about the early hour at which she switched the lights out.

On 16 August, Hector Griffiths went out fishing on his own and unfortunately cut both his hands when a nylon line he was reeling in pulled taut.

That evening he tried to talk to his step-daughter about a career, but found it hard going. Hadn't she discussed it with friends? With teachers at the school? Wasn't there someone he could ring and talk to about it?

After a lot of probing, she did give him the name of her French mistress, who was the only person she seemed to have been even slightly close to at the school. Had she got her phone number? asked Hector. Yes. Would she write it down for him? Here, on this scrap of paper.

Reluctantly she did. She didn't notice that the scrap of paper was a piece torn from a copy of the *Daily Telegraph*. Or that the only printing on it was most of the date—"14 September, 19 . . ."

Her step-father continued his uphill struggle to cheer her up. Look, here was something he'd been given. A new sort of chocolate bar, nut and nougat, called the NUGGY BAR. Not even on the market yet. Go on, try a bit, have a bite. She demurred, but eventually, just to please him, did take a bite.

She thought it was "pretty revolting".

8. THE LAUNCH

The spring tide was to be at its lowest at 1941 on 17 August, but Hector Griffiths didn't mention this when he persuaded his step-daughter to come out for a trip in the motor-boat at half-past six that evening. Janet wasn't keen, but nor was she obstructive, so soon the boat, with its rubber dinghy towed behind, was chugging along towards "Stinky Cove". Her step-father's hands on the wheel wore rubber gloves, to prevent dirt from getting into the wounds made by his fishing line the previous day.

Janet seemed psychologically incapable of enthusiasm for anything, but Hector got very excited when he thought he saw an opening in the rocks. He steered the boat in close and there, sure enough, was an archway. The stench near the rocks was strong enough to deter any but the most ardent speleologist—in fact, there were no other vessels in sight—but Hector still seemed keen to investigate the opening. He anchored the motor-boat and urged Janet into the dinghy. They cast off and puttered towards the rocks.

Instructing his step-daughter to duck, Hector lined the boat up, cut the motor, and waves washed the dinghy through on to the sand of a hidden cave.

With expressions of wonder, Hector stepped out into a shallow stream, gesturing Janet to follow him. She did so with her usual lethargy. Her step-father pulled the dinghy some way up on to the sand. Crowing with childlike excitement about the discovery they'd made, he suggested exploring. Maybe this little cave led to a bigger one. Wasn't that an opening there at the top of the pile of rubble? He set off towards it. Without interest, but co-operative to the last, Janet followed.

It was on the precarious top of the pile that Hector Griffiths appeared to lose his balance and fall heavily against his step-daughter. She fell sideways down the loose surface to the sand of the cave floor. Fortunately she fell face down, so she didn't see the practised aim of the rock that went flying towards her head.

The damp thud of its impact was very similar to that an earlier missile had made against a paper bag, but louder. The commotion was sufficient to dislodge a shower of small stones from the roof of the cave, which gave very satisfactory credibility to the idea that Janet had been killed by a rockfall.

Hector also found it a source of satisfaction that she had landed away from the stream. When her body was finally discovered, he didn't want her clothes to be soaked through; it must be clear that she had entered the cave in the dinghy, in other words, at the lowest ebb of a spring tide.

Hector stepped carefully down the rubble. Keeping his feet in the stream, he inspected Janet. A little blood and brain from her crushed skull marked the sand. She was undoubtedly dead.

With his gloved hands, he slipped the scrap of *Daily Telegraph* with her French mistress's phone number and the opened NUGGY BAR with its blue and gold wrapper into Janet's pocket.

He then walked down the stream to the opening, already slightly smaller with the rising tide, waded into the sea and swam out to the motor-boat.

On board he removed a tarpaulin from his second rubber dinghy, attached its painter to the back of the larger boat and cast it behind. Then he chugged back to his mooring near the cottage, as the tide continued to rise.

9. THE VITAL FIRST MONTH (YOUR PRODUCT IS YOUR BABY— NURSE IT GENTLY.)

Hector Griffiths still had nearly a month of his six-week holiday in Cornwall to go, and he passed it very quietly and peacefully. Much of the time he was in the Yacht Club drinking with Commander Donleavy.

There he would complain to the Commander, and anyone else who happened to be listening, about his step-daughter's reticence and ask advice on what career he should guide her towards. Now and then at lunchtime he would point out the blue smock-clad figure sitting sketching outside the back door of the cottage. At night he might comment on her early hours as he saw the cottage lights go off.

In the mornings, before he went out, he would check the time-switches and decide whether or not to use the inflatable woman. He didn't want the sketching to become too predictable, so he varied the position of the dummy in its smock and frequently just left it indoors. Once or twice, at dusk, he took it out in the dinghy past the harbour and waved to the fishermen on the quay.

At the end of August he posted Janet's cards to Melissa's aunts in Stockport. Their messages had the timeless banality of all postcard communications.

In the first week of September he continued his nautical rounds and awaited the explosion from GLISS.

Because the cottage wasn't on the telephone, the explosion, when it came, on 5 September, was in the form of a telegram. (Hector had kept the sketching dummy out of the way for a few days in anticipation of its arrival.) It was from his assistant, saying a crisis had arisen, could he ring as soon as possible.

He made the call from the Yacht Club. His assistant was defiantly guilty. Something had gone wrong with the production authorization for GLISS SPOT-REMOVER. The factory hadn't received it and now there would be no stock to meet the November orders.

Hector Griffiths swore—a rare occurrence—and gave his assistant a lavish dressing-down. The young man protested he was sure he had done the paperwork, but received an unsympathetic hearing. Good God, couldn't he be trusted with the simplest responsibility? Well, there was nothing else for it, he'd have to go and see all the main buyers and apologize. No, letters wouldn't do, nor would the telephone. GLISS's image for efficiency was at stake and the cock-up had to be explained personally.

But, the young man whimpered, what about his forthcoming trip to INTERSAN in Hamburg?

Oh no! Hector had forgotten all about that. Well, it was out of the question that his assistant should go now, far too much mopping-up to be done. Damn, he'd have to go himself. GLISS must be represented. It was bloody inconvenient, but there it was.

After a few more demoralizing expletives, Hector put the phone down and, fuming, joined Commander Donleavy at the bar. Wasn't it bloody typical? he demanded rhetorically, can't trust anyone these days—now he was going to have to cut his holiday short just because of the incompetence of his bloody assistant. Young people had no sense of responsibility.

Commander Donleavy agreed. They should bring back National Service.

Hector made a few more calls to GLISS management people, saying how he was suddenly going to have to rush off to Hamburg. He sounded aggrieved at the change of plan.

On his last day in Cornwall, the 6th of September, he deflated the dinghy and the woman. He went a long way out to sea in the motor-boat, weighted them with the outboard motor and a few stones, and cast them overboard. The electrical time-switches and the rubber gloves followed.

That evening he said goodbye to Commander Donleavy in the Yacht Club. He confessed to being a little worried about Janet. Whereas previously she had just seemed listless, she now seemed deeply depressed. He didn't like to leave her in the cottage alone, though she spoke of going up to London, but he wasn't sure that he'd feel happier with her there. Still, he had to go on this bloody trip and he couldn't get her to make up her mind about anything. . . .

Commander Donleavy opined that women were strange fish.

As he drove the Mercedes up to London on 7 September, Hector Griffiths reviewed the necessary actions on his return from Hamburg. Because of the GLISS SPOT-REMOVER crisis, he could legitimately delay going back to Cornwall for a week or two. And, since the cottage wasn't on the phone and she hadn't contacted him, he'd have to write to Janet. Nice, fatherly, solicitous letters.

Only after he had received no reply to two of these would he start to worry and go down to Cornwall. That would get him past the next low tide when the cave was accessible.

On arriving and finding his letters unopened on the mat (he would first search the cottage for a copy of the *Daily Telegraph* for 14 September and, if he found one, destroy it), he would drive straight back to London, assuming that he must somehow have missed his step-daughter there. He would ring her French mistress and Melissa's aunts in Stockport and only after drawing blanks there would he call the police.

When they spoke to him, he'd mention Janet's talk of going up to London. He'd also mention her depressed state. He would delay as long as possible mentioning that his rubber dinghy appeared to be missing.

Then, preferably as much as four months after her murder on 17 August, by which time, his reading of forensic medicine told him, it would be difficult to date the death with more than approximate accuracy, he would remember her once mentioning to him a hidden cave she'd found at low tide round "Stinky Cove".

The body would then be discovered.

Because of the lack of accurate timing from its state of decomposition, the police would have to date her death from other clues. The presence of the dinghy and the dryness of her clothes would indicate that she had entered the cave at a spring tide, which at once limited the dates.

Local people would have seen the dinghy, if not the girl, around until shortly before Hector's departure on 7 September. But other clues would be found in the girl's pocket. First, a NUGGY BAR, a new nut and nougat confection which was not available in the shops until 10 September. And, second, a phone number written on a scrap of newspaper dated 14 September. Since that was the date of a spring tide, the police would have no hesitation in fixing the death of Janet Wintle on 14 September.

On which date her step-father was unexpectedly, through a combination of circumstances he could not have foreseen, in Hamburg at INTERSAN, an international domestic cleaning exhibition.

So Hector Griffiths would have to come to terms with a second accidental death in his immediate family within two years.

And the fact that he would inherit his step-daughter's not inconsiderable wealth could only be a small compensation to him in his bereavement.

10. IS YOUR PRODUCT A SUCCESS? (ARE YOU SURE THERE'S NOTHING YOU'VE FORGOTTEN?)

On the day before he left for Hamburg, Hector Griffiths had a sudden panic. Suppose one of Melissa's aunts in Stockport had died? They were both pretty elderly and, if it had happened, it was the sort of thing Janet would have known about. She'd hardly have sent a postcard to someone who was dead.

He checked by ringing the aunts with some specious inquiry about full names for a form he had to fill in. Both were safely alive. And both had been so glad to get Janet's postcards. When they hadn't heard from her the previous year, they were afraid she had forgotten them. So it was lovely to get the two postcards.

Two postcards? What, they'd got two each?

No, no, that would have been odd. One each, two in all.

Hector breathed again. He thought it fairly unlikely, knowing Janet's unwillingness to go out, that she'd sent any other postcards, but it was nice to be sure.

So everything was happily settled. He could go abroad with a clear conscience.

He couldn't resist calling GLISS to put another rocket under his assistant and check if there was anything else urgent before he went away.

There was a message asking him to call the advertising agency about the second wave of television commercials for GLISS HANDY MOPPITS (IDEAL FOR THE KITCHEN, NURSERY OR HANDBAG). He rang through and derived his customary pleasure from patronizing the account executive. Just as he was about to ring off, he asked, "All set for the big launch?"

"Big launch?"

"On the tenth. The NUGGY BAR."

"Oh God. Don't talk to me about NUGGY BARS. I'm up to here with NUGGY BARS. The bloody Product Manager's got cold feet."

"Cold feet?"

"Yes. He's new to the job, worried the product's not going to sell."

"What?"

"They've got the report back from the Tyne-Tees area where they tested it. Apparently forty-seven per cent of the sample thought it was 'pretty revolting'."

"So what's going to happen?"

"Bloody Product Manager wants to delay the launch."

"Delay the launch?"

"Yes, delay it or cancel the whole thing. He doesn't know what he wants to do."

"But he can't pull out at this stage. The television time's been contracted and the newspapers and—"

"He can get out of most of it, if he doesn't mind paying off the contracts. He's stuck with the magazine stuff, because they go to press so far ahead, but he can stop the rest of it. And, insofar as he's capable of making a decision, he seems to have decided to stop it. Call came through just before lunch—Hold everything—The NUGGY BAR will not be launched on the tenth of September!''

The Mercedes had never gone faster than it did on the road down to Cornwall. In spite of the air-conditioning, its driver was drenched in sweat.

The motor-boat, too, was urged on at full throttle until it reached "Stinky Cove". Feverishly Hector Griffiths let out the anchor cable and, stripping off his jacket and shoes, plunged into the sea.

The water was low, but not low enough to reveal the opening. Over a week to go to the spring tide. He had to dive repeatedly to locate the arch, and it was only on the third attempt that he managed to force his way under it. Impelled by the waves, he felt his back scraped raw by the rocks. He scrambled up on to the damp sand.

Inside all seemed dark. He cursed his stupidity in not bringing a flashlight. But, as he lay panting on the sand, he began to distinguish the outlines of the church-like interior. There was just enough glow from the underwater arch to light his mission. Painfully, he picked himself up.

As he did so, he became aware of something else. A new stench challenged the old one that gave the cove its name. Gagging, he moved towards its source.

Not daring to look, he felt in her clothes. It seemed an age before he found her pocket, but at last he had the NUGGY BAR in his hand.

Relief flooded his body and he tottered with weakness. It'd be all right. Back through the arch, into the boat, back to London, Hamburg tomorrow. Even if he'd been seen by the locals, it wouldn't matter. The scrap of *Daily Telegraph* and the dry state of Janet's clothes would still fix the date of her death a week ahead. It'd all be all right.

He waded back into the cold waves. They were now splashing higher up the sand, the tide was rising. He moved out as far as he could and leant against the rock above the arch. A deep breath, and he plunged down into the water.

First, all he saw was a confusion of spray, then a gleam of diluted daylight ahead, then he felt a searing pain against his back and, as his breath ran out, the glow of daylight dwindled.

The waves had forced him back into the cave.

He tried again and again, but each time was more difficult. Each time the waves were stronger and he was weaker. He wasn't going to make it. He lay exhausted on the sand.

He tried to think dispassionately, to recapture the coolness of his planning mind, to imagine he was sitting down to the Desk Work on a cleaning fluid problem.

But the crash of the waves distracted him. The diminishing light distracted him. And, above all, the vile smell of decomposing flesh distracted him.

He controlled his mind sufficiently to work out when the next low tide would be. His best plan was to conserve his strength till then. If he could get back then, there was still a good chance of making the flight to Hamburg and appearing at INTERSAN as if nothing had happened.

In fact, that was his only possible course.

Unless . . . He remembered his lie to Janet. Let's climb up the pile of rubble and see if there's an opening at the top. It might lead to another cave. There might be another way out.

It was worth a try.

He put the NUGGY BAR in his trouser pocket and climbed carefully up the loose pile of rocks. There was now very little light. He felt his way.

At the top he experienced a surge of hope. There was not a solid wall of rock ahead, just more loose stones. Perhaps they blocked another entrance . . . a passage? Even an old smugglers' tunnel?

He scrabbled away at the rocks, tearing his hands. The little ones scattered, but the bigger ones were more difficult. He tugged and worried at them.

Suddenly a huge obstruction shifted. Hector jumped back as he heard the ominous roar it started. Stones scurried, pattered and thudded all around him. He scrambled back down the incline.

The rockfall roared on for a long time and he had to back nearer and nearer the sea. But for the darkness he would have seen Janet's body buried under a ton of rubble.

At last there was silence. Gingerly he moved forward.

A single lump of rock was suddenly loosed from above. It landed squarely in the middle of his skull, making a damp thud like an exploded paper bag, but louder.

Hector Griffiths fell down on the sand. He died on 8 September.

Outside his motor-boat, carelessly moored in his haste, dragged its anchor and started to drift out to sea.

It was four months before the police found Hector Griffiths' body. They were led to it eventually by a reference they found in one of his late wife's diaries, which described a secret cave where they had made love. It was assumed that Griffiths had gone there in his dinghy because of the place's morbidly sentimental associations, been cut off by the rising tide and killed in a rockfall. His clothes were soaked with salt water because he lay so near the high tide mark.

It was difficult to date the death exactly after so long, but a check on the tide tables (in which, according to a Commander Donleavy, Griffiths had shown a great interest) made it seem most likely that he had died on 14 September. This was confirmed by the presence in his pocket of a NUGGY BAR, a nut and nougat confection which was not available in the shops until 10 September.

Because the Product Manager of NUGGY BAR, after cancelling the product's launch, had suddenly remembered a precept that he'd heard in a lecture when he'd been a Management Trainee at GLISS. . . .

ONCE YOU HAVE MADE YOUR MAJOR DECISIONS ABOUT THE PRODUCT AND THE TIMING OF ITS LAUNCH, DO NOT INDULGE SECOND THOUGHTS.

So he'd rescinded his second thoughts and the campaign had gone ahead as planned. (It may be worth recording that the NUGGY BAR was not a success. The majority of the buying public found it "pretty revolting".)

The body of Hector Griffiths' step-daughter, Janet Wintle, was never found. Which was a pity for two old ladies in Stockport who, under the terms of a trust set up in her mother's will, stood to inherit her not inconsiderable wealth.

THE GIRLS IN VILLA COSTAS

THERE WAS ONLY one girl worth looking at in that planeload. I'd been doing the job for two months, since May, and I'd got quicker at spotting them.

She was tall, but then I'm tall, so no problem there. Thin, but the bits that needed to be round were good and round. Dress: expensive casual. Good jeans, white cotton shirt, artless but pricey. Brown eyes, biscuit-coloured hair pulled back into a rubber band knot, skin which had already seen a bit of sun and just needed Corfu to polish up the colour. (Have to watch that. With a lot of the girls—particularly from England—they're so pale you daren't go near them for the first week. Lascivious approaches get nothing but a little scream and a nasty smell of Nivea on your hands.)

The girl's presence moved me forward more keenly than usual with my little spiel. "Hello, Corforamic Tours, Corforamic Tours. I am your Corforamic representative, Rick Lawton. Could you gather up your baggage please, and proceed outside the arrivals hall to your transport."

I ignored the puffing English matrons and homed in on the girl's luggage.

It was then that I saw the other one. She looked younger, shorter, dumpier; paler brown hair, paler eyes, a sort of diluted version, as if someone had got the proportions wrong when trying to clone from the dishy one.

They were obviously together, so I had to take one bag for each. They thanked me in American accents. That in itself was unusual. Most of the girls who come on these packages are spotty typists from Liverpool.

But then their destination was unusual, too. The majority of the Corforamic properties are tiny, twin-bedded apartments in Paleokastritsa and Ipsos. But there's one Rolls-Royce job near Aghios Spiridion—converted windmill, sleeps eight, swimming pool, private beach, live-in maid, telephone. And that was where they were going. They'd booked for a month.

I read it on their labels. "Miss S. Stratton" (the dishy one). "Miss C. Stratton" (the other one). And underneath each name, the destination—"Villa Costas".

By six I'd seen all the ordinary punters installed, answered the questions about whether it was safe to drink the water, given assurances that the plumbing worked, given the names of doctors to those with small children, told them which supermarkets sold Rice Krispies, quoted the minimal statistics for death by scorpion sting, and tried to convince them that the mere fact of their having paid for a fortnight's holiday was not going automatically to rid the island of mosquitoes.

Villa Costas was a long way to the north of the island. I'd pay a call there the next day.

I drove to Niko's, on the assumption that none of my charges would venture as far as his disco on their first evening. You get to value your privacy in this job. I sat under the vine-laden shelter of the bar and had an ouzo.

As I clouded the drink with water and looked out over the glittering sea, I felt low. Seeing a really beautiful woman always has that effect. Seems to accentuate the divide between the sort of man who gets that sort of girl and me. I always seem to end up with the ugly ones.

It wasn't just that. There was money, too, always money. Sure I got paid as the Corforamic rep., but not much. Winter in England loomed, winter doing some other demeaning selling job, earning peanuts. Not the sort of money that could coolly rent the Villa Costas for a month. Again there was the big divide. Rich and poor. And I knew which side I really belonged. Poor, I was cramped and frustrated. Rich, I could really be myself.

Niko's voice cut into my gloom. "Telephone, Rick."

She identified herself as Samantha Stratton. The dishy one. Her sister had seen a rat in the kitchen at Villa Costas. Could I do something about it?

I said I'd be right out there. Rats may not be dragons, but they can still make you feel knight-errantish. And, as any self-respecting knight-errant knows, there is no damsel so susceptible as one in distress.

Old Manthos keeps a kind of general store just outside Kassiope. It's an unbelievable mess, slabs of soap mixed up with dried fish, oil lamps, saucepans, tins of powdered milk, brooms, faded postcards, coils of rope, tubes of linament, deflated beach-balls, dusty Turkish Delight, and novelty brandy bottles shaped like Ionic columns. Most of the stock appears to have been there since the days of his long-dead father, whose garlanded photograph earnestly surveys the chaos around him.

But, in spite of the mess, Manthos usually has what you want. May take a bit of time and considerable disturbance of dust, but he'll find it.

So it proved on this occasion. With my limping Greek, it took a few minutes for him to understand the problem, but once he did, he knew exactly where to go. Two crates of disinfectant were upturned, a bunch of children's fishing nets knocked over, a pile of scouring pads scattered, and the old man triumphantly produced a rusty tin, whose label was stained into illegibility.

"Very good," he said, "very good. Kill rats, kill anything." He drew his hand across his throat evocatively.

I paid. As I walked out of the shop, he called out, "And if that doesn't work . . ."

"Yes?"

"Ask the priest. The Papas is sure to have a prayer for getting rid of rats."

It was nearly eight o'clock when I got to Villa Costas, but that's still hot in Corfu in July. Hot enough for Samantha to be on the balcony in a white bikini. The body fulfilled, or possibly exceeded, the promise I had noted at the airport.

"Candy's in bed," she said. "Shock of seeing the rat on top of all that travelling brought on a migraine."

"Ah. Well, let's see if we can put paid to this rat's little exploits," I said, in a business-like and, to my mind, rather masculine manner.

"Sure."

I filled some little paper dishes with poison and laid them round the kitchen floor. Then I closed the tin and washed my hands. "Shall I leave the poison with you, so you can put down more if you want to?"

She was standing in the kitchen doorway. The glow of the dying sun burnt away her bikini. Among other things, I saw her head shake. "No, thanks. Dangerous stuff to have around. You take it."

"Okay."

"Like a drink?"

She was nice. Seemed very forthcoming with me, too. But I didn't want to queer anything up by moving too fast.

Still, when she asked where one went for fun on the island, I mentioned Niko's disco. And, by the time I left—discreetly, didn't lay a finger on her, play it cool, play it cool—we'd agreed to meet there the next evening.

And as I drove back to my flat in Corfu Town, I was beginning to wonder whether maybe after all I was about to become the sort of man who gets that sort of girl.

When I arrived at nine, there were quite a lot of people at the disco. But no tall, beautiful American girl. Come to that, no less tall, less beautiful American girl.

I could wait. Niko signalled me over to where he was sitting, and I ordered an ouzo.

The group drinking at the table was predictable. Niko's two brothers (the one who drove a beer lorry and the one who rented out motor-scooters) were there, along with his cousin the electrician, and Police Inspector Kantalakis, whose relaxed interpretation of government regulations about overcrowding, noise and hygiene always ensured him a generous welcome at the bar.

There was also a new face. Wiry black hair thinning on top, thick black moustache draped over the mouth, healthy growth of chest hair escaping from carefully faded denims. Solid, mid-thirties maybe, ten years older than me. "Rick, this is Brad," said Niko.

He stretched out a hairy hand. "Hi." Another American. "We were just talking about Niko's wife," he said with a grin.

They all laughed, Niko slightly ruefully. Whereas some people have bad backs or business worries to be tenderly asked after, Niko always had wife problems. It was a running joke and, from the way Brad raised it, he seemed to know the group well. "How are things at home, Niko?" he continued.

The proprietor of the bar shrugged that round-shouldered gesture that encompasses the whole world of marital misery.

Brad chuckled. "Sure beats me why people get married at all."

Inspector Kantalakis and the others gave man-of-the-world laughs, siding with him and conveniently forgetting their own tenacious little wives. The American turned to me. "You married?"

I shook my head. "Never felt the necessity."

"Too right. There is no necessity."

The married men laughed again, slightly less easily. Brad called their bluff. "Now come on, all you lot got wives. Give me one good reason *why*, one argument in favour of marriage."

Inspector Kantalakis guffawed. "Well, there's sex . . ."

"You don't have to get married for that," I said.

The Inspector looked at me with distaste. For some reason he never seemed to like me much.

"Come on, just one argument for marriage," insisted Brad.

They looked sheepish. Faced by this transatlantic sophisticate, none of them was going to show himself up by mentioning love, children, or religion. They wanted to appear modern, and were silent.

"You think of any reason, Rick?"

"Money," I said, partly for the laugh I knew the word would get, but also because the idea had been going through my mind for some years. Marriage remains one of the few legal ways that someone without exceptional talents can make a quick and significant change in his material circumstances. I reinforced the point, playing for another laugh. "Yes, I reckon that's the only thing that'd get me to the altar. I'm prepared to marry for money."

As the laugh died, Brad looked at me shrewdly. "If that's so, then you ought to set your cap at what's just arriving."

I turned to see the girls from Villa Costas getting out of a hire car. "Those two," Brad continued, "are the daughters of L. K. Stratton of Stratton Petrochemicals. When the old man goes, the elder one gets the lot."

I was feeling sore. The two girls had joined us at the table and had a couple of drinks. Seeing them together again had only reinforced my previous impression. Miss S. (Samantha) Stratton was not only beautiful, but also poised and entertaining. Miss C. (Candice, to give her full name) Stratton was not only drab in appearance, but mouselike and tentative in conversation. I waited for a lull in the chat, so that I could ask Samantha to dance. If she had needed any recommendation other than that body, Brad's words had just supplied it.

But the minute I was about to suggest a dance, damn me if Brad, who seemed to know the girls quite well, didn't say, "C'mon, Sam, let's bop," and lead her off into the flashing interior of the disco. The way they started dancing suggested that they knew each other *very* well.

Within minutes, Niko and his relations and Inspector Kantalakis had melted away, leaving me in a role I had suffered too often in double dates from schooltime onwards—stuck with the ugly one.

And what made it worse was that I gathered in this case she was also the poor one.

I stole a look across at her. The sun had already started its work on her pale flesh. The nose glowed; in a couple of days the skin would be coming off like old wallpaper.

She caught my eye and gave a gauche little smile, then looked wistfully to the thundering interior.

No, no, I wasn't going to be caught that way. That terrible old feeling that you *ought* to ask a girl to dance. Hell, I was twenty-six, not some creepy little adolescent.

Still, I had to say something, or just leave. "Your big sister seems to be enjoying herself," I commented sourly.

"Half-sister, actually. And only big in the sense that she's taller than I am."

"You mean you're older than she is?"

"Two years and four months older."

"Would you like to dance?"

Candice was very shy and I played with her exemplary tact. Met her every evening for most of the next week. Picked her up at the Villa Costas and took her down to Niko's. She was too shy to go there on her own, and Sam and Brad (who turned out to be engaged, for God's sake) seemed anxious to be off on their own most of the time.

So I courted Candice like a dutiful boy-next-door. Looked at her soulfully, danced close, kissed her goodbye, nothing more. I was the kind of young man every mother would like their daughter to meet—serious, respectful, with intentions honourable even to the point of matrimony.

And, once I'd written off any chance with Samantha, Candice really didn't seem too bad. Not unattractive at all. Any personal lustre she lacked I could readily supply by thinking of her father's millions.

The fourth night, as I kissed her goodbye with boyish earnestness, I explained that a new planeload of tourists was arriving the next day and I wouldn't have time to pick her up. She looked disappointed, which showed I was getting somewhere. Rather than not see me, she agreed to go under her own steam to Niko's, meet me there at nine. That was a big step for her. I promised I wouldn't be late.

By the middle of the following afternoon it was clear I was going to be. The flight from London was delayed by an hour and a half.

Never mind. Still the dutiful, solicitous boy-next-door, I rang the Villa Costas. Brad answered. Sorry, would he mind telling Candice I couldn't get to Niko's till half-past ten? Either I'd see her there or pick her up usual time the next evening.

Sure, Brad'd see she got the message.

*

When I saw her face at ten-twenty that night at Niko's, it was clear she hadn't got the message. She was sitting at the same table as, but somehow not with, Niko's relations and Inspector Kantalakis. And she looked furious.

It didn't surprise me. Greek men don't really approve of women, even tourists, going to bars alone, and that lot wouldn't have made any secret of their feelings. I moved forward with smiling apologies on my lips.

But I didn't get a chance to make them. Candice rose to her feet. "I only stayed," she spat out, "to tell you that I think you're contemptible, and that we will not meet again."

"Look, I left a message with Brad. I said I'd be late and . . ."

"It's not just your lateness I'm talking about. Goodbye." And she swept off to the hire car.

I sat down, shaken. Inspector Kantalakis was looking at me with a rather unpleasant smile. "What the hell did you say to her?" I asked.

He shrugged. "I may have mentioned your views on marriage."

"What? Oh shit—you mean about marrying for money?"

"I may have mentioned that, yes."

"But when I said it, it was only a joke."

"You sounded pretty serious to me," said the Inspector, confirming my impression that he didn't like me one bit.

But that evening wasn't over. I started hitting the local paint-stripper brandy. I was furious. The Inspector and the others sauntered off, as if satisfied by their evening's destruction. I gazed bitterly across the black sea to the few mysterious lights of Albania.

"Rick." I don't know how long had passed before the sound broke into my gloom. I looked up.

It was Samantha. And she was crying.

"What's the matter?"

"It's that bastard, Brad . . ."

"Oh. I've got a bone to pick with him too. What's he done?"

"Oh, he's just . . . It's always the same. He treats me badly and he goes off with some other girl and always reckons he can just pick up again as if nothing has happened and . . . Well, this is the last time, the last time . . ." She was crying a lot by then.

"Can I get you a drink or . . . ?"

"No, I just want to go back to the villa. I was looking for Candy. I wanted a lift. Brad's driven off in his car and . . ."

"Candy's gone, I'm afraid."

"Oh."

"I'll give you a lift."

When we were in the car park, she was seized by another burst of crying and turned towards me. Instinctively my arms were round her slender, soft, soft body and I held her tight as the spasms subsided.

"Doesn't take you long," said a voice in Greek.

I saw Inspector Kantalakis' sardonic face in the gloom.

"Mind your own business," I said. At least, that would be a paraphrase. The expression on the Inspector's face showed that I was making great strides with my colloquial Greek.

"She's upset," I continued virtuously. "I'm just comforting her, as a friend."

But I wasn't, I wasn't.

Amazing how quickly things can change. Actually, since by "things" I mean women, I suppose it's not so amazing.

I got to know a lot more about Samantha on that drive back, and I discovered that appearances can be distinctly deceptive. For a start, the great engagement with Brad was not, as it appeared, the marriage of true minds, but a kind of possessive blackmail exerted on an unwilling girl by a selfish and violent man. She had been trying to break it off for years.

Also—and this was the bit I enjoyed hearing—the reason for the quarrel of that night had been her admitting she fancied someone else. Me.

"But if you're so keen to get rid of him, why did you mind his going off with another girl?"

"Only because I know he'll be back. He never stays away for long. And then he thinks he can just pick up where he left off."

"Hmm. But he couldn't do that if he found you'd got someone else."

"That's true."

The car had stopped outside Villa Costas. We were suddenly in each other's arms. Her body spoke its clear message to mine, while our tongues (when free) mumbled meaningless nothings. Yes, she wanted me. Yes, I was the only man who she'd ever felt like that about.

But no, I'd better not come into the villa now. Because of Candy . . . And she didn't really fancy the beach. Tomorrow. Tomorrow afternoon at three. She'd see that Candy was out. And then . . .

The way she kissed me, and where she kissed me, left me in no doubt as to what would happen then.

I arrived sharp at three the following afternoon in a state of . . . well, let's say in a predictable state of excitement.

But things weren't initially as private as I had hoped. Theodosia, the live-in maid, was sitting on the verandah under the shade of an olive tree. (Corfiots, unlike the tourists, regard sun as a necessary evil, and avoid it when possible.) She grinned at me in a way that I found presumptuously knowing.

And then, as if that wasn't enough, Candice Stratton appeared from the villa and stood for a moment blinded by the sun. She wore a bikini in a multi-coloured stripe that accentuated her dumpiness; she carried a box of Turkish Delight that would no doubt, in time, accentuate it further. The other hand held a striped towel and an Agatha Christie.

When her eyes had accommodated to the brightness, they saw me, and an expression of loathing took over her face. "You bastard! I said I never wanted to see you again. So don't think you can come crawling back."

Any intentions I might have had to be nice to her vanished at that. "I didn't come to see *you*," I said, and walked past her into the villa. I felt Theodosia's inquisitive eyes follow me.

Samantha was on the balcony in the white bikini. Momentarily I played the aggrieved lover. "I thought you were going to see Candy was out."

"Sorry, we got delayed. Brad came round."

I hadn't reckoned on that.

"Don't worry, Rick. I sent him off with a flea in his ear." She looked at me levelly. "I haven't changed my mind."

I relaxed. "How'd he take it?"

"Usual arrogance. Said he'd be back. Even tried his old trick of making up to Candy to make me jealous. Brought her a big box of Turkish Delight and all that. He ought to know by now it doesn't work."

"On you or on her?"

"On me, you fool." She rose and put an arm round my waist. Together we watched Candy across the little private bay, settling on her towel for further ritual peeling.

I looked into Samantha's brown eyes, screwed up against the glare of the sun. I was aware of the tracery of fine lines around them as her body pushed against mine.

"Candy be out there for some time?" I murmured.

"You betcha. She'll eat her way right through that box of Turkish Delight. Always eats when she's unhappy."

My hand glided up the curve of her back and gave the bikini strap a gentle twang. "Shall we go inside?"

There was a double bed (a rarity in the world of Corforamic, another luxury feature of the Villa Costas). We lay on it and I reached more purposefully for the strap.

"Oh damn," said Samantha.

"What?"

"Candy didn't take her drink."

"Hmm?"

"There's a large Coca-Cola in the fridge. She was going to take it with her."

"So?" I shrugged.

"So . . . if she hasn't got it, she'll be back here as soon as she's thirsty. And the Turkish Delight's going to make her very thirsty."

"Ah."

"You take it over to her."

"But she doesn't want to see me . . ."

"Then we won't be disturbed." There was a kind of logic in that. "Go on, Rick. And while you're away, I'll slip out of these heavy clothes."

When I got back, Samantha had slipped out of her few milligrams of clothes. She had on nothing but a bottle of Remy Martin and two glasses on the flat table of her stomach.

Candy had been predictably annoyed to see me, but had accepted the bottle of Coke wordlessly. And Theodosia's beady little eyes had followed me all the way across the beach and back.

But I soon forgot both of them. Samantha's body would have cleaned out the memory bank of a computer.

With the body and the brandy, time telescoped and distorted. We caressed and made love and dozed and caressed and made love and dozed . . . Sam's hands had the softness of a mouth and her mouth the versatility of fingers, so that after a time I ceased trying to work out which bit was doing what and succumbed to the bliss of anatomical confusion.

Darkness came and we didn't notice it. Through the sea-breathing blackness our bodies found new games to play, and as dawn started its first grey probings, we still found the possibilities had not been exhausted.

I didn't hear whether Candice came in or not. Quite honestly, I had other things on my mind. Not only on my mind, either.

Sleep eventually claimed us, but in my dreams the ecstasy seemed to continue.

It was therefore an unpleasant shock to be woken by the sight of Inspector Kantalakis at the foot of the bed, and by the sound of his voice saying, in English, "Still furthering your marriage plans, Mr Lawton?"

We both sat up. Samantha raised a sheet to cover her breasts, and I was pleased about that. I felt a proprietary interest; they weren't there to be drooled over by Greek policemen.

She was still half-asleep. "Marriage?" she echoed. "You did mean it, Rick, what you said last night, about wanting to marry me?"

"Uh?" I was still pretty much asleep too.

"I have bad news," said Inspector Kantalakis.

We looked at him blearily.

"Miss Stratton, your sister was found this morning on the beach. Dead."

"What?"

"She appears to have been poisoned."

I don't know if you've ever been involved in a murder inquiry in Greece, but let me tell you, it is something to be avoided. Questions, questions, questions, endlessly repeated in hot concrete police cells. And expressions on the cops' faces that show they don't subscribe to the old British tradition of people being innocent until proved guilty.

I was with them for about 24 hours, I suppose, and the first thing I did when I got out was to go up to the Villa Costas. Sam looked shaken. She'd had quite a grilling too, though some connection of her father's had pulled strings through the American Embassy in Athens and it hadn't taken as long as mine.

"And now the bastard's disappeared," were her first words.

"Who?" My mind wasn't working very well.

"Brad."

"What do you mean?"

"Brad must have poisoned her."

"Why?" I couldn't catch up with all this.

"Because of the money."

"Uh?"

"He wanted me *and* Daddy's money. With Candy dead, I inherit."

"Good Lord, that never occurred to me."

"Well, it's true."

"But how did he do it?"

"Obvious. The Turkish Delight."

"Are you sure?"

"The Inspector says he hasn't had the forensic analysis yet—everything takes that much longer on an island—but I'd put money on the results."

"Brad'll never get away with it."

"Oh, he'll have sorted out some sort of alibi. He's devious. He will get away with it, unless we can find some proof of his guilt."

"But it will all have been for nothing if he doesn't get you."

"Yes." She sounded listless.

"And he hasn't got you, has he?"

She pulled herself together and looked at me with a little smile. "No, he hasn't. You have."

"So that's all right."

She nodded, but still seemed troubled. "The only thing that worries me . . ."

"Yes?"

"Is that he does still have power over me when I see him."

"Then we must ensure you don't see him. If he's disappeared, that doesn't sound too difficult. Anyway, as soon as the analysis of the Turkish Delight comes through, the police'll be after him."

"But suppose they're not. Suppose he's sorted out some kind of alibi . . ."

"Don't worry." Suddenly I was full of crusading spirit. "If the police won't do it, I'll prove myself that he poisoned Candy."

"Oh, thank you, Rick. Thank God I've got you."

I tried all the contacts I had on the island, but none of them had seen Brad. I didn't give up, though. I wanted to do it for Sam, to prove Brad's crime and see to it that he was put behind bars where he belonged.

It was the next day she told me she was going to have to fly back to the States. Her father, L. K. Stratton, had had a mild stroke when he heard the news of his elder daughter's death, and the younger one had to fly back to be by his side. Inspector Kantalakis had cleared her from his inquiries, and she was free to go. Apparently, he was near to an arrest; just needed the results of the forensic analysis to clinch it.

Though I was depressed about her going, the news of the investigation front was promising. The police were obviously near to nailing Brad, just needed proof of the poison in the Turkish Delight.

All they had to do then was find him.

Unless I could find him first.

I arranged that I'd see Sam off at the airport.

It was less than two weeks since I'd first seen her when I kissed her goodbye. A lot had happened in less than two weeks. When I first saw that splendid body I hadn't dared hope that it would ever be pressed to mine with such trust and hope.

"I'll come back as soon as I can, Rick. Really."

"I know. Let's hope you're back to give evidence at a murder trial."

"I will be. Don't worry."

Her baggage was checked in through to Kennedy via London. There didn't seem much more to say. Our togetherness didn't need words.

Not many, anyway. "And then, Sam, we'll get married, huh?"

She nodded gently and gave me another kiss. Then she turned and went off towards the Departure Lounge. Tall, beautiful, and mine.

Not only mine, it occurred to me, but also very rich. Suddenly I had got it all, suddenly I was the sort of man who got that sort of girl.

I watched her into the Departure Lounge. She didn't turn round. We didn't need that sort of clinging farewell.

Suddenly I got a shock. A dark, denim-clad figure had appeared beside her in the Lounge.

Brad.

I couldn't go through ticket control to save her. I had to find the police. And fast.

I was in luck. As I rushed into the dazzle of sunlight, I saw Inspector Kantalakis leaning against my car, with his hands behind his back.

"The man who murdered Candy—I know who it is," I panted.

"So do I," said the Inspector.

"He intended to marry Sam, but he wanted the money too, so he poisoned Candy."

"Exactly."

"Well, why don't you arrest him?"

"I've been waiting for a forensic report for final proof. Now I have it. Now there will be an arrest."

"Good. He's in the airport building. The plane leaves in half an hour."

"Yes." The Inspector made no move.

Fine, he must have the place staked out. We could relax; there was plenty of time. I grinned. "So the poison *was* in the Turkish Delight."

He shook his head. "No."

"No?"

"It was really a very straightforward case. Our murderer, who made no secret of his intention to marry for money, tried first with the older sister, the heiress. Unfortunately they quarrelled, so he took up with the younger one. But she would only inherit if her elder sister died. So . . ." He shrugged.

"I didn't realize Brad had ever made a play for Candy."

"He hadn't. Nor did he kill her. After he saw the girls in the Villa Costas, he spent the rest of the day of the murder with me."

"Then who are we talking about?" I asked blankly.

Inspector Kantalakis drew one hand from behind his back. It held a rusty tin, a tin which had been bought from Manthos' shop. "I found this in the trunk of your car."

"Yes, I bought it to deal with the rats at the Villa Costas."

"Really? It was this poison that killed Candice Stratton. It was put in the bottle of Coca-Cola."

"The Coca-Cola!"

"Yes. The Coca-Cola you gave to the murder victim. Do you deny you gave it to her? The maid Theodosia saw you."

"No, I gave it all right. I see! Brad must have dosed it, knowing Candy'd drink it sooner or later. He must have fixed it when he came round that morning with the Turkish Delight. Sam may have seen him go to the fridge. Ask her."

"I have asked her, Mr Lawton. According to Miss Samantha Stratton, there never was any Coca-Cola in the Villa Costas. Nor, incidentally, were there any rats," Inspector Kantalakis added portentously.

Then he arrested me.

And I realized that, after all, I wasn't the sort of man who got that sort of girl.

I don't know. Maybe I'm just stupid.

HOW'S YOUR MOTHER?

"IT'S ALL RIGHT, Mother. Just the postman," Humphrey Partridge called up the stairs, recognizing the uniformed bulk behind the frosted glass of the front door.

"Parcel for you, Mr Partridge." As he handed it over, Reg Carter the postman leant one arm against the door-frame in his chatting position. "From some nurseries, it says on the label."

"Yes—"

"Bulbs, by the feel of it."

"Yes." Humphrey Partridge's hand remained on the door, as if about to close it, but the postman didn't seem to notice the hint.

"Right time of year for planting bulbs, isn't it? November."

"Yes."

Again Reg was impervious to the curtness of the monosyllable. "How's your mother?" he asked chattily.

Partridge softened. "Not so bad. You know, considering."

"Never seem to bring any letters for her, do I?"

"No. Well, when you get to that age, most of your friends have gone."

"Suppose so. How old is she now?"

"Eighty-six last July."

"That's a good age. Doesn't get about much."

"No, hardly at all. Now if you'll excuse me, I do have to leave to catch my train."

Humphrey Partridge just restrained himself from slamming the door on the postman. Then he put his scarf round his neck, crossed the ends across his chest and held them in position with his chin while he slipped on his raincoat with the fleecy lining buttoned in. He picked up his brief-case and called up the stairs, "Bye, bye, Mother. Off to work now. Be home usual time."

In the village post office Mrs Denton watched the closing door with disapproval and shrugged her shawl righteously around her. "Don't like that Jones woman. Coming in for *The Times* every morning. Very lah-di-dah. Seems shifty to me. Wouldn't be surprised if there was something going on there."

"Maybe." Her husband didn't look up from his morbid perusal of the *Daily Mirror*. "Nasty business, this, about the woman and the R.A.F. bloke."

"*The Red Scarf Case*," Mrs Denton italicized avidly.

"Hmm. They say when the body was found—" He broke off as Humphrey Partridge came in for his *Telegraph*. "Morning. How's the old lady?"

"Oh, not too bad, thank you. Considering . . ."

Mrs Denton gathered her arms under her bosom. "Oh, Mr Partridge, the vicar was in yesterday, asked me if I'd ask you. There's a jumble sale in the Institute tomorrow and he was looking for some able-bodied helpers just to shift a few—"

"Ah, I'm sorry, Mrs Denton, I don't like to leave my mother at weekends. She's alone enough with me being at work all week."

"It wouldn't be for long. It's just—"

"I'm sorry. Now I must dash or I'll miss my train."

They let the silence stand for a moment after the shop door shut. Then Mr Denton spoke, without raising his eyes from his paper. "Lives for his mother, that one."

"Worse things to live for."

"Oh yes. Still doesn't seem natural in a grown man."

"Shouldn't think it'd last long. Old girl must be on the way out. Been bedridden ever since they moved here. And how long ago's that? Three years?"

"Three. Four."

"Don't know what he'll do when she goes."

"Move maybe. George in the grocer said something about him talking of emigrating to Canada if only he hadn't got the old girl to worry about."

"I expect he'll come into some money when she goes." When Mrs Denton expected something, it soon became fact in the village.

Humphrey Partridge straightened the ledgers on his desk, confident that the sales figures were all entered and his day's work was done. He stole a look at his watch. Five twenty-five. Nearly time to put his coat on and . . .

The phone rang. Damn. Why on earth did people ring up at such inconvenient times? "Partridge," he snapped into the receiver.

"Hello, it's Sylvia in Mr Brownlow's office. He wondered if you could just pop along for a quick word."

"What, now? I was about to leave. Oh, very well, Miss Simpson. If it's urgent."

Mr Brownlow looked up over his half-glasses as Partridge entered. "Humphrey, take a pew."

Partridge sat on the edge of the indicated chair, poised for speedy departure.

"Minor crisis blown up," said Brownlow languidly. "Know I was meant to be going to Antwerp next week, for the conference?"

"Yes."

"Just had a telex from Parsons in Rome. Poor sod's gone down with some virus and is stuck in an Eyetie hospital, heaven help him. Means I'll have to go out to Rome tomorrow and pick up the pieces of the contract. So there's no chance of my making Antwerp on Monday."

"Oh dear."

"Yes, it's a bugger. But we've got to have someone out there. It's an important conference. Someone should be there waving the flag for Brownlow and Potter."

"Surely Mr Potter will go."

"No, he's too tied up here."

"Evans?"

"On leave next week. Had it booked for yonks. No, Partridge, you're the only person who's free to go."

"But I'm very busy this time of year."

"Only routine. One of the juniors can keep it ticking over."

"But surely it should be someone whose standing in the company—"

"Your standing's fine. Be good experience. About time you took some more executive responsibility. Bound to be a bit of a reshuffle when Potter retires and you're pretty senior on length of service. . . . Take that as read then, shall we? I'll get Sylvia to transfer the tickets and hotel and—"

"No, Mr Brownlow. You see, it's rather difficult."

"What's the problem?"

"It's my mother. She's very old and I look after her, you know."

"Oh come on, it's only three days, Partridge."

"But she's very unwell at the moment."

"She always seems to be very unwell."

"Yes, but this time I think it's . . . I mean I'd never forgive myself if . . ."

"But this is important for the company. And Antwerp's not the end of the earth. I mean, if something happened, you could leap on to a plane and be back in a few hours."

"I'm sorry. It's impossible. My mother . . ."

Mr Brownlow sat back in his high swivel chair and toyed with a paper knife. "You realize this would mean I'd have to send someone junior to you . . ."

"Yes."

"And it's the sort of thing that might stick in people's minds if there were a question of promotion or . . ."

"Yes."

"Yes. Well, that's it." Those who knew Mr Brownlow well would have realized that he was extremely annoyed. "I'd better not detain you any longer or I'll make you late for your train."

Partridge looked gratefully at his watch as he rose. "No, if I really rush, I'll just make it."

"Oh terrific," said Mr Brownlow, but his sarcasm was wasted on Partridge's departing back.

"Mother, I'm home. Six thirty-five on the dot. Had to run for the train, but I just made it. I'll come on up."

Humphrey Partridge bounded up the stairs, went past his own bedroom and stood in the doorway of the second bedroom. There was a smile of triumph on his lips as he looked at the empty bed.

★

Partridge put two slices of bread into his toaster. He had had the toaster a long time and it still worked perfectly. Better than one of those modern pop-up ones. Silly, gimmicky things.

He looked out of the kitchen window with satisfaction. He felt a bit stiff, but it had been worth it. The earth of the borders had all been neatly turned over. And all the bulbs planted. He smiled.

The doorbell rang. As he went to answer it, he looked at his watch. Hmm, have to get his skates on or he'd miss the train. Always more difficult to summon up the energy on Monday mornings.

It was Reg Carter the postman. "Sorry, couldn't get these through the letter box." But there was no apology in his tone: no doubt he saw this as another opportunity for one of his interminable chats.

Partridge could recognize that the oversize package was more brochures and details about Canada. He would enjoy reading those on the train. He restrained the impulse to snatch them out of the postman's hand.

"Oh, and there was this letter too."

"Thank you."

Still the postman didn't hand them over. "Nothing for the old lady today neither."

"No, as I said last week, she doesn't expect many letters."

"No. She all right, is she?"

"Fine, thank you." The postman still seemed inclined to linger, so Partridge continued, "I'm sorry. I'm in rather a hurry. I have to leave for work in a moment."

The next thing Reg Carter knew, the package and letter were no longer in his hands and the door was shut in his face.

Inside Humphrey Partridge put the unopened brochures into his brief-case and slid his finger along the top of the other envelope. As he looked at its contents, he froze, then sat down at the foot of the stairs, weak with shock. Out loud he cried, "This is it. Oh, Mother, this is it!"

Then he looked at his watch, gathered up his brief-case, scarf and coat and hurried out of the house.

★

"There's more about that Red Scarf Case in *The Sun*," said Mr Denton with gloomy relish.

"It all comes out at the trial. Always does," his wife observed sagely.

"Says here he took her out on to the golf links to look at the moon. Look at the moon—huh!"

"I wouldn't be taken in by something like that, Maurice. Serves her right in a way. Mind you, he must have been a psychoparth. Sergeant Wallace says nine cases out of ten—"

Partridge entered breezily. "*Telegraph*, please. Oh, and a local paper, please."

"Local paper?" Mrs Denton, starved of variety, pounced on this departure from the norm.

"Yes, I just want a list of local estate agents."

"Thinking of buying somewhere else?"

"Maybe not buying," said Partridge, coyly enigmatic.

He didn't volunteer any more, so Mr Denton took up the conversation with his habitual originality. "Getting colder, isn't it?"

Partridge agreed that it was.

Mrs Denton added her contribution. "It'll get a lot colder yet."

"I'm sure it will," Partridge agreed. And then he couldn't resist saying, "Though with a bit of luck I won't be here to feel it."

"You are thinking of moving then?"

"Maybe. Maybe." And Humphrey Partridge left the shop with his newspapers, unwontedly frisky.

"I think," pronounced Mrs Denton, focusing her malevolence, "there's something going on there."

"You wanted to see me, Partridge?"

"Yes, Mr Brownlow."

"Well, make it snappy. I've just flown back from Rome. As it turns out I could have made the Antwerp conference. Still, it's giving young Dyett a chance to win his spurs. What was it you wanted, Partridge?" Mr Brownlow stifled a yawn.

"I've come to give in my notice."

"You mean you want to leave?"

"Yes."

"This is rather unexpected."

"Yes, Mr Brownlow."

"I see." Mr Brownlow swivelled his chair in irritation. "Have you had an offer from another company?"

"No."

"No, I hardly thought . . ."

"I'm going abroad. With my mother."

"Of course. May one ask where?"

"Canada."

"Ah. Reputed to be a land of opportunity. Are you starting a new career out there?"

"I don't know. I may not work."

"Oh, come into money, have we?" But he received no answer to the question. "Okay, if you'd rather not say, that's your business. I won't inquire further. Well, I hope you know what you're doing. I'll need a month's notice in writing."

"Is it possible for me to go sooner?"

"A month's notice is customary." Mr Brownlow's temper suddenly gave. "No, sod it, I don't want people here unwillingly. Just go. Go today!"

"Thank you."

"Of course, we do usually give a farewell party to departing staff, but in your case . . ."

"It won't be necessary."

"Too bloody right it won't be necessary." Mr Brownlow's eyes blazed. "Get out!"

Partridge got home just before lunch in high spirits. Shamelessly using Brownlow and Potter's telephones for private calls, he had rung an estate agent to put his house on the market and made positive enquiries of the Canadian High Commission about emigration. He burst through the front door and called out his customary, "Hello, Mother. I'm home."

The words died on his lips as he saw Reg Carter emerging from his kitchen. "Good God, what are you doing here? This is private property."

"I was doing my rounds with the second post."

"How did you get in?"

"I had to break a window."

"You had no right. That's breaking and entering. I'll call the police."

"It's all right. I've already called them. I've explained it all to Sergeant Wallace."

Partridge's face was the colour of putty. "Explained what?" he croaked.

"About the fire." Then again, patiently, because Partridge didn't seem to be taking it in. "The fire. There was a fire. In your kitchen. I saw the smoke as I came past. You'd left the toaster on this morning. It had got the tea towel and the curtains were just beginning to go. So I broke in."

Partridge now looked human again. "I understand. I'm sorry I was so suspicious. It's just . . . Thank you."

"Don't mention it," said Reg Carter, with an insouciance he'd learned from some television hero. "It was just I thought, what with your mother upstairs, I couldn't afford to wait and call the fire brigade. What with her not being able to move and all."

"That was very thoughtful. Thank you." Unconsciously Partridge was edging round the hall, as if trying to usher the postman out. But Reg Carter stayed firmly in the kitchen doorway. Partridge reached vaguely towards his wallet. "I feel I should reward you in some way . . ."

"No, I don't want no reward. I just did it to save the old lady."

Partridge gave a little smile and nervous nod of gratitude.

"I mean, it would be awful for her to be trapped. Someone helpless like that."

"Yes."

Up until this point the postman's tone had been tentative, but, as he continued, he became more forceful. "After I'd put the fire out, I thought I ought to see if she was all right. She might have smelt burning or heard me breaking in and been scared out of her wits. . . . So I called up the stairs to her. She didn't answer."

The colour was once again dying rapidly from Partridge's face. "No, she's very deaf. She wouldn't hear you."

"No. So I went upstairs," Reg Carter continued inexorably. "All the doors were closed. I opened one. I reckon it must be your room. Then I opened another. There was a bed there. But there was no one in it."

"No."

"There was no one in the bathroom. Or anywhere. The house was empty."

"Yes."

The postman looked for a moment at his quarry, then said, "I thought that was rather strange, Mr Partridge. I mean, you told us all your mother was bedridden and lived here."

"She does—I mean she did." The colour was back in his cheeks in angry blushes.

"Did?"

"Yes, she died," said Partridge quickly.

"Died? When? You said this morning when I asked after her that—"

"She died a couple of days ago. I'm sorry, I've been in such a state. The shock, you know. You can't believe that it's happened and—"

"When was the funeral?"

A new light of confusion came into Partridge's eyes as he stumbled to answer. "Yesterday. Very recently. It's only just happened. I'm sorry, I'm not thinking straight. I don't know whether I'm coming or going."

"No." Reg Carter's voice was studiously devoid of intonation. "I'd better be on my way. Got a couple more letters to deliver, then back to the post office."

Humphrey Partridge mumbled more thanks as he ushered the postman out of the front door. When he heard the click of the front gate, he sank trembling on to the bottom stair and cried out loud, "Why, why can't they leave us alone?"

Sergeant Wallace was a fat man with a thin, tidy mind. He liked everything in its place and he liked to put it there himself. The one thing that frightened him was the idea of anyone else being brought in to what he regarded as his area of authority, in other words, anything that happened in the village. So it was natural for him, when the rumours about Humphrey Partridge reached unmanageable proportions, to go and see the man himself rather than reporting to his superiors.

It was about a week after the fire. Needless to say, Reg Carter had talked to Mr and Mrs Denton and they had talked to practically everyone who came into the post office. The talk was now so wild that something had to be done.

Humphrey Partridge opened his front door with customary lack of welcome, but Sergeant Wallace forced his large bulk inside, saying he'd come to talk about the fire.

Tea chests in the sitting-room told their own story. "Packing your books I see, Mr Partridge."

"Yes. Most of my effects will be going to Canada by sea." Partridge assumed, rightly, that the entire village knew of his impending departure.

"When is it exactly you're off?"

"About a month. I'm not exactly sure."

Sergeant Wallace settled his uninvited mass into an armchair. "Nice place, Canada, I hear. My nephew's over there."

"Ah."

"You'll be buying a place to live . . . ?"

"Yes."

"On your own?"

"Yes."

"Your mother's no longer with you?"

"No. She . . . she died."

"Yes. Quite recently, I hear." Sergeant Wallace stretched out, as if warming himself in front of the empty grate. "It was to some extent about your mother that I called."

Partridge didn't react, so the Sergeant continued. "As you know, this is a small place and most people take an interest in other people's affairs . . ."

"Can't mind their own bloody business, most of them."

"Maybe so. Now I don't listen to gossip, but I do have to keep my ear to the ground—that's what the job's about. And I'm afraid I've been hearing some strange things about you recently, Mr

Partridge." Sergeant Wallace luxuriated in another pause. "People are saying things about your mother's death. I realize, being so recent, you'd probably rather not talk about it."

"Fat chance I have of that. Already I'm getting anonymous letters and phone calls about it."

"And you haven't reported them?"

"Look, I'll be away soon. And none of it will matter."

"Hmm." The Sergeant decided the moment had come to take the bull by the horns. "As you'll probably know from these letters and telephone calls then, people are saying you killed your mother for her money."

"That is libellous nonsense!"

"Maybe. I hope so. If you can just answer a couple of questions for me, then I'll know so. Tell me first, when did your mother die?"

"Ten days ago. The eleventh."

"Are you sure? It was on the eleventh that you had the fire and Reg Carter found the house empty."

"I'm sorry. A couple of days before that. It's been such a shock, I . . ."

"Of course." Sergeant Wallace nodded soothingly. "And so the funeral must have been on the tenth?"

"Some time round then, yes."

"Strange that none of the local undertakers had a call from you."

"I used a firm from town, one I have connections with."

"I see." Sergeant Wallace looked rosier than ever as he warmed to his task. "And no doubt it was a doctor from town who issued the death certificate?"

"Yes."

"Do you happen to have a copy of that certificate?" the Sergeant asked sweetly.

Humphrey Partridge looked weakly at his tormentor and murmured, "You know I don't."

"If there isn't a death certificate," mused Sergeant Wallace agonizingly slowly, "then that suggests there might be something unusual about your mother's death."

"Damn you! Damn you all!" Partridge was almost sobbing with

passion. "Why can't you leave me alone? Why are you always prying?"

The Sergeant recovered from his surprise. "Mr Partridge, if a crime's been committed—"

"No crime's been committed!" Partridge shouted in desperate exasperation. "I haven't got a mother. I never saw my mother. She walked out on me when I was six months old and I was brought up in care."

"Then who was living upstairs?" asked Sergeant Wallace logically.

"Nobody. I live on my own, I always have lived on my own. Don't you see, I hate people." The confession was costing Partridge a lot, but he was too wound up to stop its outpouring. "People are always trying to find out about you, to probe, to know you. They want to invade your house, take you out for drinks, invade your privacy. I can't stand it. I just want to be on my own!"

Sergeant Wallace tried to interject, but Partridge steam-rollered on. "But you can't be alone. People won't let you. You have to have a reason. So I invented my mother. I couldn't do things, I couldn't see people, because I had to get back to my mother. She was ill. And my life worked very well like that. I even began to believe in her, to talk to her. She never asked questions, she didn't want to know anything about me, she just loved me and was kind and beautiful. And I loved her. I wouldn't kill her—I wouldn't lay a finger on her—it's you, all of you who've killed her!" He was now weeping uncontrollably. "Damn you, damn you."

Sergeant Wallace took a moment or two to organize this new information in his mind. "So what you're telling me is, there never was any mother. You made her up. You couldn't have killed her, because she never lived."

"Yes," said Partridge petulantly. "Can't you get that through your thick skull?"

"Hmm. And how do you explain that you suddenly have enough money to emigrate and buy property in Canada?"

"My premium bond came up. I got the letter on the morning of the fire. That's why I forgot to turn the toaster off. I was so excited."

"I see." Sergeant Wallace lifted himself ponderously out of his chair and moved across to the window. "Been digging in the garden, I see."

"Yes, I put some bulbs in."

"Bulbs, and you're about to move." The Sergeant looked at his quarry. "That's very public-spirited of you, Mr Partridge."

The post office was delighted with the news of Partridge's arrest. Mrs Denton was firmly of the opinion that she had thought there was something funny going on and recognized Partridge's homicidal tendencies. Reg Carter bathed in the limelight of having set the investigation in motion and Sergeant Wallace, though he regretted the intrusion of the C.I.D. into his patch, felt a certain satisfaction for his vital groundwork.

The Dentons were certain Reg would be called as a witness at the trial and thought there was a strong possibility that they might be called as character witnesses. Mrs Denton bitterly regretted the demise of the death penalty, feeling that prison was too good for people who strangled old ladies in their beds. Every passing shopper brought news of developments in the case, how the police had dug up the garden, how they had taken up the floorboards, how they had been heard tapping the walls of Partridge's house. Mrs Denton recommended that they should sift through the ashes of the boiler.

So great was the community interest in the murder that the cries of disbelief and disappointment were huge when the news came through that the charges against Partridge had been dropped. The people of the village felt that they had been robbed of a pleasure which, by any scale of values, was rightfully theirs.

But as the details seeped out, it was understood that Partridge's wild tale to Sergeant Wallace was true. There had been no one else living in the house. He had had a large premium bond win. And the last record of Partridge's real mother dated from four years previously when she had been found guilty of soliciting in Liverpool and sentenced to two months in prison.

The village's brief starring role in the national press was over and its people, disgruntled and cheated, returned to more domestic scandals. Humphrey Partridge came back to his house, but no one saw him much as he hurried to catch up on the delay to his emigration plans which his wrongful arrest had caused him.

It was two days before his departure, in the early evening, when he had the visitor. It was December, dark and cold. Everyone in the village was indoors.

He did not recognize the woman standing on the doorstep. She was dressed in a short black and white fun-fur coat, which might have been fashionable five years before. Her hair was fierce ginger, a strident contrast to scarlet lipstick, and black lashes hovered over her eyes like bats' wings. The stringiness of her neck and the irregular bumps of veins under her black stockings denied the evidence of her youthful dress.

"Hello, Humphrey," she said.

"Who are you?" He held the door, as usual, ready to close it.

The woman laughed, a short, unpleasant sound. "No, I don't expect you to recognize me. You were a bit small when we last met."

"You're not . . . ?"

"Yes, of course I am. Aren't you going to give your mother a kiss?"

She thrust forward her painted face and Partridge recoiled back into the hall. The woman took the opportunity to follow him in and shut the front door behind her.

"Nice little place you've got for yourself, Humphrey." She advanced and Partridge backed away from her into the sitting-room. She took in the bareness and the packing cases. "Oh yes, of course, leaving these shores, aren't you? I read in the paper. Canada, was it? Nice people, Canadians. At least, their sailors are." Another burst of raucous laughter.

"'Cause of course you've got the money now, haven't you, Humphrey? I read about that too. Funny, I never met anyone before what'd won a premium bond. Plenty who did all right on the horses, but not premium bonds."

"What do you want?" Partridge croaked.

"Just come to see my little boy, haven't I? Just thinking, now you're set up so nice and cosy, maybe you ought to help your Mum in her old age."

"I don't owe you anything. You never did anything for me. You walked out on me."

"Ah, that was ages ago. And he was a nice boy, Clinton. I had to have a fling. I meant to come back to you after a week or two. But then the council moved in and Clinton got moved away and—"

"What do you want?"

"I told you. I want to be looked after in my old age. I read in the paper about how devoted you were to your old mother." Again the laugh.

"But you aren't my mother." Partridge was speaking with great care and restraint.

"Oh yes, I am, Humphrey."

"You're not."

"Yes. Ooh, I've had a thought—why don't you take your old mother to Canada with you?"

"You are not my mother!" Partridge's hands were on the woman's shoulders, shaking out the emphasis of his words.

"I'm your mother, Humphrey."

His hands rose to her neck to silence the taunting words. They tightened and shuddered as he spoke. "My mother is beautiful and kind. She is nothing like you. She always loved me. She still loves me!"

The spasm passed. He released his grip. The woman's body slipped down. As her head rolled back, her false teeth fell out with a clatter on to the floor.

Sergeant Wallace appeared to be very busy with a ledger when Humphrey Partridge went into the police station next morning. He was embarrassed by what had happened. It didn't fit inside the neat borders of his mind and it made him look inefficient. But eventually he could pretend to be busy no longer. "Good morning, Mr Partridge. What can I do for you?"

"I leave for Canada tomorrow."

"Oh. Well, may I wish you every good fortune in your new life there."

"Thank you." A meagre smile was on Partridge's lips. "Sergeant, about my mother . . ."

Sergeant Wallace closed his ledger with some force. "Listen, Mr Partridge, you have already had a full apology and—"

"No, no, it's nothing to do with that. I just wanted to tell you . . ."

"Yes?"

". . . that I *did* kill my mother."

"Oh yes, and then I suppose you buried her in the garden, eh?"

"Yes, I did."

"Fine." Sergeant Wallace reopened his ledger and looked down at the page busily.

"I'm confessing to murder," Partridge insisted.

The Sergeant looked up with an exasperated sigh. "Listen, Mr Partridge, I'm very sorry about what happened and you're entitled to your little joke, but I do have other things to do, so, if you wouldn't mind . . ."

"You mean I can just go?"

"Please."

"To Canada?"

"To where you bloody well like."

"Right then, I'll go. And . . . er . . . leave the old folks at home."

Sergeant Wallace didn't look up from his ledger as Partridge left the police station.

Outside, Humphrey Partridge took a deep breath of air, smiled and said out loud, "Right, mother, Canada it is."

PARKING SPACE

"YOUR WIFE TELLS me you're going to take up shooting," said Alex Paton, during a lull in the dinner party conversation.

Kevin Hooson-Smith flashed a look of annoyance at his wife, Avril, but smiled casually and responded, "Well, thought it might be rather fun. You know, at some point. When I've got time for a proper weekend hobby. Old Andersen keeps us at it so hard at the moment, I think that may be a few years hence."

He laughed heartily to dissipate the subject, but Alex Paton wasn't going to let it go. "But Avril said you'd actually bought a shotgun."

"Well . . ." Kevin shrugged uncomfortably. "Useful thing to have. You know, if the opportunity came up for a bit of shooting, one wouldn't want to say, No, sorry, no can do, no gun." He laughed again, hoping the others would join in. Surely he'd got the words right. If Alex Paton or Philip Wilkinson had said that, the other would certainly have laughed. But they didn't, so he had to continue. "You shoot at all, Alex?"

"Not much these days. Pop off the occasional rabbit if I go down to the country to see Mother. Father left me his pair of Purdey's, which aren't bad. What make was the gun you got, Kevin?"

"Oh, I forget the name. Foreign."

"Dear, dear. Some evil continental pop-gun." They all laughed at that.

"Absolutely," said Kevin. At least he'd got that right. "More wine, Alex?"

"Thank you."

"It's a seventy-one—Pommard."

"I noticed."

Kevin busied himself with dispensing wine to his guests, but Alex was still not deflected from the subject. "Avril said she thought you were going off shooting this weekend . . ."

"Oh, I don't know. Maybe. Will you have a little more, Elizabeth? Fine. No, I saw something about one of these weekend teaching courses, you know, in shooting. . . . We all have to learn some time, don't we?" Kevin laughed again.

"Oh yes," Alex agreed. "If we don't already know."

Philip Wilkinson came kindly into the pause. "You know, anyone who's keen on shooting ought to chat up that new girl who's just started cooking the directors' lunches. Davina Whatsername . . ."

"Entick," Kevin supplied.

"Yes. Her old man's Sir Richard Entick."

Alex Paton was impressed. "Really? I hadn't made that connection. Well, he's got some of the best shooting in the country. Yes, keep on chatting her up, Kevin."

Kevin laughed again, but again alone. They were silent, though there was quite a lot of noise from the cutlery. Avril hoped the steak wasn't too tough. She had done it exactly as the cordon bleu monthly part-work had said. Well, except that had said *best* grilling steak, but the best was so expensive. The stuff she had got had been expensive enough. She was sure it was all right.

Maybe they weren't talking because they were too busy eating. Enjoying it. The other two wives hadn't said much all evening. Maybe the wives of stockbrokers from Andersen Small weren't expected to say anything. Well, she wasn't going to be totally silent and submissive. Particularly with an empty wine glass. "Hey, Kev, you missed me out on your rounds. Could I have a bit more wine?"

Kevin somewhat ungraciously pushed the wine bottle towards her.

"Kev," Alex Paton repeated. "That's rather an attractive coining."

Kevin was immediately on the defensive. Though he smiled, Avril recognized the tension in his jaw muscles. "Actually, the name Kevin is quite old. Came across something about it the other day. Means 'handsome birth'. There was a St Kevin way back in the sixth century. A hermit, I think. In Ireland."

"Ah," murmured Alex Paton. "In Ireland."

They all laughed at that, though neither Kevin nor Avril could have said exactly why. Emboldened by his success, Alex Paton went on, "And tell me, what about Hooson-Smith? Does that name go back to the sixth century?"

After the laugh that greeted that one, they were all silent again. Kevin didn't start any new topic of conversation, so Avril decided it was her duty as hostess to speak. The sound of a car at the front of the house provided her cue.

"I bet that's our next door neighbour moving his car. You know, he's really strange. Very petty. He gets terribly upset if he can't park his car exactly outside his front door. And I mean exactly. We have known him to get up at three in the morning and move it, if he hears someone moving theirs and leaving a space. I mean, isn't that ridiculous? It's no trouble just to walk a couple of yards, but he always wants to be exactly outside. I hope we never get as petty as that."

They were all looking at her. She didn't know why. Maybe she had spoken rather louder than usual. She felt relaxed by the wine. It had been a long day. All the usual vexations of the children and tidying the house and then, on top of that, cooking this dinner party. Kevin insisted that everything had to be just so for his colleagues from Andersen Small. She didn't really see why. It was not as if they had ever been invited to them. And the wives didn't seem real, just exquisitely painted clothes-horses, not real women who you could have a good natter with.

Alex Paton broke the pause and responded to her speech. "Yes, well, fortunately that's a problem we don't have to cope with. We are blessed with a rather quaint, old-fashioned device called a garage."

After the laugh, Philip Wilkinson started talking about the intention of Andersen Small to open an office in Manila, and the attention moved away from Avril.

Only Kevin was still looking at her. She seemed to see him through a swimmy haze. And there was no love in his expression.

"I don't like to leave the washing-up till the morning, Kev."

"Well, do it now, if you feel that strongly about it." He was already out of his suit and unbuttoning the silk shirt that had been a special offer in the *Observer*. "All I know is, it's after one and I have a heavy day tomorrow. I have a long costing meeting with Andersen first thing."

"I've got a lot to do tomorrow too."

"Having coffee with some other under-employed woman, then tea with someone else."

"No, not that. I've hardly met anyone since we've been in Dulwich. Not like it was in Willesden."

"Equally the people here are rather different than those there were in Willesden. Better for the boys to grow up with." Kevin was now down to his underpants. He turned away from her to take them off, as if ashamed.

"But the boys don't grow up with them. They spend all their time travelling back and forth to that bloody private school and don't seem to make any friends."

"Don't say 'bloody'. It makes you sound more Northern than ever."

"Well, I am bloody Northern, aren't I?"

"There's no need to rub everyone's face in it all the time, though, is there?"

"Anyway, I'm no more Northern than you are. I just haven't tarted up my vowels and started talking in a phony accent that all my posh friends laugh at."

"They do not laugh at me!" Kevin was dangerously near the edge of violence.

Avril bit back her rejoinder. No, calm down. She hadn't wanted the evening to end like this. She lingered in front of the dressing table, unwilling to start removing her make-up. It had used to be a signal between them. Well, more than a signal. She would start to remove her make-up and he would say, "Come on, time enough for that. We've got more important things to do", and pull her down on to the bed. Now he rarely seemed to think they had more important things to do. Now, she felt, he wouldn't notice if she never even put on any make-up.

He was in his pyjamas and under the duvet, his back unanswerably turned to her side of the bed. (Why a duvet? She hated it. She loved the secure strapped-in feeling of sheets and blankets, the tight little cocoon their bed had been back in the flat in Willesden.)

Then she remembered their new chore. "Have you potted James?"

"No."

"But I thought we'd agreed you'd do it."

"You may have agreed that. I haven't agreed anything. Anyway, it's ridiculous, a child of six needing to be potted."

"If he isn't, he wets the bed."

"If he is, he still seems to wet it. It's ridiculous."

"It's only since he's been at that new school."

"I don't see what that has to do with it."

"It has everything to do with it. He hates it there. He hates how all the other boys make fun of him, hates how they imitate his accent."

"Perhaps that'll teach him to improve his accent."

"What, you want another phony voice in the family?"

"AVRIL! SHUT UP, SHUT UP, SHUT UP!" He was sitting up in bed, his face red with fury.

Avril again retreated and went and potted James. When she came back, Kevin was pretending to be asleep. The rigidity of his body showed he wasn't really. She knew his mind was working, rehearsing tiny humiliations, planning revenges, planning more success. He worked hard to make himself what he wanted to be.

She sat down at the dressing table and picked up a new jar of cream to remove her make-up. But she didn't open it. Somehow she felt something might still happen; he might get out of bed and put his arms round her. "Kevin . . ."

The totality of his silence again gave the lie to his appearance of sleep.

"Kev, did you mean that about not going away this weekend?"

"No, I'm going."

"On this shooting course?"

"Yes."

"But you told Alex you might not."

"Because it wasn't his business. I was bloody annoyed at you for starting talking about shooting anyway."

"But you only bought the gun this week. And they seemed to

know about it. I thought at last there was a common subject we could all talk about."

"Well, you were wrong. In future, stick to talking about cooking or children or the next door neighbour's car. And, for Christ's sake, let me go to sleep!"

"So you're definitely going this weekend?"

"Yes."

"Taking the car?"

"Yes. Why do you ask?"

"I was thinking, if you weren't here, I could take the kids up to see Mum."

"All the way to Rochdale?"

"It'd be a break. She'd love to see them. And now you've taken over the fourth bedroom, it's very difficult for her to come and stay down here."

"I need a study. But even more than that I need sleep."

"We could go up to Rochdale by train."

"What? Do you have any idea how much fares are these days?"

"I'd just like to see Mum. She's getting on and she was pretty knocked out by that bout of 'flu."

"If you can afford it out of the housekeeping, then go by all means."

"You know I can't. You'd have to pay."

"Well, I can't afford to."

"You can afford brand new shotguns and shooting courses and bottles of wine and—"

"Avril!" Kevin sat up again in bed. This time he was icy cool, even more potentially violent than he had been when he was shouting. "I make all the money that comes into this household, so will you please leave it to me to decide how it should be spent. From an early age I have tried to better myself and I intend to continue to do that. When I die, the boys will be left in a much better position than where I started. I know what I'm doing."

Avril sighed. "It depends on your definition of 'better'. From where I'm sitting, everything seems to be a lot worse than it ever was."

"I'm sorry, Avril. If you can't appreciate the improvements that

I have brought into our lives, then I'm afraid there is no point in continuing this rather fruitless discussion."

"Right." Avril opened the jar of cream. "Right, I am now going to remove my make-up."

"Fine." Kevin looked curiously at the jar. "What's that stuff? It's new."

"It's called rejuvenating cream."

"Left it a bit late, haven't you?" he said and turned back into the duvet.

By eight o'clock on the Saturday night Avril was exhausted. The boys were so highly-strung at the moment. They were so tensely on their best behaviour at the new school that the release of the weekend made them manically high-spirited and quarrelsome. Kevin's absence didn't make things any easier. Though Avril often resented, or even laughed at, his performance as the stern Victorian *paterfamilias*, it did curb the boys' worst excesses. Without him there, and having made no friends in the area, the boys put all their emotional pressure on to their mother. She had to be playleader, entertainer, referee and caterer.

By eight o'clock, when she had finally dragged them away from the television and got them into bed, largely by brute force, she was absolutely drained. She collapsed on the sofa in the sitting-room and once again everything seemed to swim before her eyes.

A pall of depression draped itself over her. She tried to lift it by using her mother's eternal remedy, counting her blessings. She could hear her mother's voice, with its warm Lancastrian vowels, saying, "Now come on, our Avril, cheer up. Remember, there's always someone worse off than yourself. You just count your blessings, young lady."

She felt a terrible lonely nostalgia and an urge to ring her mother immediately. But no, Mum needed her help now; she mustn't ring and burden the old lady with her troubles. That was giving in.

No, come on, our Avril, count your blessings.

Right, for a start, nice house, two lovely boys, husband very successful, making far more money than any of the other boys from

Rochdale you might have married. Okay, marriage going through a sticky patch at the moment, but that was only to be expected from time to time. Kevin's was an exacting job, and it was only to be expected that some of the tension he felt should be released at home. It was her job as a wife to make that home an attractive place for him to return to and relax in.

And if he needed to get out sometimes on his own, she mustn't make a fuss. This shooting weekend would probably do him a lot of good. Do them both a lot of good, give them a break from the claustrophobia of marriage.

And he'd been so excited about the gun. He seemed to have spent all his spare time that week cleaning it and oiling it, fiddling with all the little pads and brushes that he had bought with it. And this weekend was his chance to show it off. It was no different from James's desire to take his new Action Man to school on his birthday.

And at least it wasn't a woman. Let him fiddle with guns to his heart's content, so long as he wasn't fiddling with another woman. True, he hadn't been fiddling with her much recently, but that again was just a phase. It'd get better.

She started to feel more confident. Good God, they hadn't kept the marriage going from Rochdale, through all his time at college, the squalid flat in Willesden, his awful job in I.C.I., bringing up small children, all that pressure and aggravation, for it to fall apart now.

No, it'd be all right.

Good old Mum. It always worked. Count your blessings and you'll feel better. Come on, they breed them tough in Rochdale. Pick yourself up, get yourself a drink and cook yourself some supper.

The sherry bottle was empty.

Oh no. She couldn't really go out to the off-licence and leave the boys alone in the house. They'd never wake, but . . . No, she couldn't. Anyway, come to think of it, she hadn't got any cash. The housekeeping didn't seem to go far these days, and with that dinner party in the middle of the week, there was nothing left.

Damn. She could really use a drink.

On the other hand . . . Upstairs in Kevin's study there was a whole huge rack full of wine. All those bottles that involved so much correspondence with what he called his "shipper" and so much consultation of books on wine appreciation and tables of good years and . . .

Yes, Kevin could certainly spare her a bottle of wine. A small recompense for her letting him go off for the weekend on his own. She wouldn't take one of his most precious ones, not one of the dinner party specials, just something modest and warming.

His study was unlike the rest of the house. It was the spare bedroom, but he had moved the bed out and had the room decorated in dark green. There was an old (well, reproduction) desk and leather chairs. It sought to capture the look of a gentleman's club.

The boys were never allowed inside. Avril was discouraged from entering except to clean. The difference in décor seemed symbolic of a greater difference, as if the room had declared U.D.I. from the rest of the house.

The wine-rack covered one whole wall. The range was extensive. Kevin approached the purchase of wine as he did everything else, with punctilious attention to detail and a desire to do the correct thing.

Avril chose a bottle of 1977 Côtes du Rhône, which surely couldn't be too important. Anyway, he owed her at least that.

There was a corkscrew on his desk, so she opened it straight away. The presence of the corkscrew suggested that Kevin himself drank the occasional bottle up there, which in turn suggested that somewhere he must have glasses.

She opened the cupboard by the window. She didn't notice whether there were any glasses. Something else took her attention.

Standing upright in the cupboard, with all its cleaning materials ranged neatly beside it, was Kevin's new shotgun.

Avril swayed for a moment. This dizziness was getting worse. She supported herself against the window frame and looked out into the road.

Parked exactly in front of their house was a silver-grey Volkswagen Golf.

*

It was the Monday evening before she got a chance to confront him. He had arrived back late on the Sunday and Monday morning was the usual scrum of forcing breakfast into her three men and rushing the boys through heavy traffic to their distant private school.

All day she phrased and rephrased what she was going to say to him, and when the opportunity came, she was determined not to shirk it. He had bought some sherry and poured her a drink, a perfunctory politeness which he performed automatically every evening before retiring upstairs with his brief-case to work until told that his supper was ready.

She took the glass, and, before he could get out his "Just going up to do a bit of work", said, "I see you didn't take your shotgun away with you for your shooting weekend."

He looked first surprised, then very annoyed. "You've been up rooting round my study." When he was angry, his voice lapsed back into Lancastrian. The "u" in "study" sounded as in "stood".

"I went up there."

"Well, I wish you bloody wouldn't! I've got a lot of important papers up there and I don't like the thought of getting them all out of order."

But she wasn't going to be deflected so easily. "Stop changing the subject. I want to know why you didn't take your precious brand-new shotgun with you when you went off on this shooting weekend."

He smiled patronizingly. "Oh really, Avril. You don't know the first thing about shooting. It isn't just something you can step straight into. You have to learn a lot of theoretical stuff first—you know, safety drill and so on. You don't start handling guns straight away. I knew that, so I left the gun this time."

"This time? You mean there will be more weekends?"

"Oh yes. As I say, it's not something you can pick up over-night."

She looked downcast. He put his arms round her. "Why don't we go upstairs?"

She looked up into his eyes gratefully.

The phone rang.

"You get it. It's bound to be for you. Join me upstairs." And he went up.

After the phone-call, she found him in the study rather than the bedroom, but she was too upset to register his change of intention. "It was Mrs Eady."

"Mrs Eady?"

"Who lives next door to Mum. Kev, Mum's had a stroke."

"Oh no. Is she . . . I mean, how is she?"

"Mrs Eady says it wasn't a bad one, but I don't know what that means. I'll have to go up there."

"I suppose so."

"Straight away. I'll have to. Can I take the car?"

"It's not going to be very convenient. I've got one or—"

"Kev . . ."

He crumbled in the face of this appeal. "Of course. Are you really going to go straight off?"

"I must. I can't just leave her."

"What about the boys?"

"You can manage for a couple of days."

"But getting them to school? If you've got the car . . ."

"Oh God, yes. Look, there's Mrs Bentley. Lives round in Parsons Road. Her son goes to the school. I'm sure she'd take them too."

"How well do you know her?"

"Hardly at all. But this is an emergency."

"Will you ring her?"

"No, you do it, Kev. I've got to dash." She started looking round the room for a holdall to take with her.

"I think it'd be better if you rang, Avril. Avril. What are you looking at, Avril?"

It was nearly dark, but the study curtains were still open. The light from a street-lamp shone on the silver top of the Volkswagen Golf.

"That car. It's the third day it's been parked outside."

"So what? Lots of people park round here. It's near the station."

"But that car hasn't moved for three days."

"Perhaps someone's left it while they go on holiday."

"I don't think so."

"Well, what do you think?"

"I don't know, Kev." Abruptly she moved from the window. "I must go."

The cars on the M1 kept blurring, losing their shape and becoming little blobs of colour. Avril clenched her jaw and tensed the muscles round her eyes, fighting to keep them open. In three nights she couldn't have had more than half an hour's sleep. Driving through Monday night and then the worry about Mum.

The fact that the stroke had been so slight and Mum had seemed so little affected by it only made things worse. The incident became a divine admonition. It's nothing this time, but next time it could be serious, and there's you living over two hundred miles away.

Not that Mum had said that. She wouldn't. She was temperamentally incapable of using any sort of emotional blackmail. But Avril's mind supplied the pressure.

No, Mum had been remarkably cheerful. She fully expected to die soon and regarded this mild stroke as an unexpected bonus, a remission. And she was delighted to see Avril, though very apologetic at having "dragged her all this way".

Mum would be all right. Even if she were taken seriously ill, there would be no problem. She was surrounded by friends. Mrs Eady kept an eye on her and there were lots more ready at a moment's notice to perform any small service that might be required. That was what really upset Avril, the knowledge that her mother didn't need her. That, and the warmth that she encountered in her home town. The world of ever-open back doors and ever-topped-up teapots contrasted painfully with the frosty genteel anonymity of Dulwich.

And yet they'd all seemed impressed by her life, not envious, but respectful, as if she and Kevin were somehow their ambassadors in a more sophisticated world.

She'd met Tony Platt in the supermarket. Tony Platt, who she'd gone out with for nearly a year and even considered marrying. And there he was, looking just the same except balding, and with three kids. Three bouncing kids with cheerful, squabbling Lancastrian voices and not an inhibition between them.

Tony had been pleased to see her. Friendly and slow, as he'd always been. "Heard you were living down in the Smoke. Sorry we lost touch. You married Kevin Smith, didn't you?"

And he'd said she was looking grand, and she knew it wasn't true. She knew that strain reflected itself immediately in her face, pulling it down, etching deep lines in her skin. And make-up no longer seemed to smooth out the lines, but rather to highlight them. Still, if she could get some sleep, maybe she'd start to feel better. Yes, when she got home she'd get some sleep. Kevin had rung through each day and assured her that everything was all right.

The cars around her started to lose their outlines again. Must concentrate. Keep going. Only another seventy miles.

A car overtook her, fast, and then cut in in front of her. Too close. Far too close. She had to brake.

She focused on the car.

It was a silver-grey Volkswagen Golf.

I see, trying to get me now, she thought. Right, I'll show them.

She flattened her foot on the accelerator. They wouldn't get away with trying to frighten her.

Her car moved closer and closer to the large-windowed back of the Golf. It speeded up, but it couldn't get away from her. She was gaining.

Suddenly the Golf, pressed for space, swung out to overtake a lorry in front. Avril snatched her steering wheel to the right too.

There was a furious hooting and a scream of brakes as the Range Rover overtaking her had to slam on everything to avoid collision.

There was no collision. Avril swung back to the left and her car slowed down with a crunch on the hard shoulder. As she rubbed her swimming eyes, she could hear the voice of the Range Rover's driver ringing round her head. "You bloody fool! What the hell do you think you're doing?"

The car was still parked outside when she got back to the house. The silver-grey Volkswagen Golf.

Its number-plate was different from the one on the motorway, but she wasn't necessarily fooled by that. She still felt the bonnet to see if the engine was warm and listened for the tick of contracting metal. But there was nothing. It seemed that the car had not been used recently.

Inside the house was absolutely quiet. It was nearly half-past six. The boys should be back from school. She swayed with exhaustion as she stood in the hall.

No, must resist the temptation to go to bed. Must find where the boys were. Probably with Kevin. Perhaps he'd left work early to fetch them from school. Even Andersen Small must recognize emergencies.

Must be with Kevin. Nowhere else they could be. Unless they were with that Mrs Bentley. Anyway, better ring her to thank her for taking them to school.

"Oh, Mrs Hooson-Smith, I must say I'm very relieved you've rung. I was beginning to wonder if I was going to have to look after your sons for the rest of my life."

"I'm so sorry. I thought you wouldn't mind just taking them to and from school. My mother's been ill and—"

"No, I didn't mind that at all, but I must confess having them to stay for the past three days has been a bit of a strain."

"I'm so sorry. I didn't know."

"Your husband had to go away on business."

"Oh no."

"So on Tuesday afternoon I was faced with the alternatives of putting them up or turning them out on to the streets. I must say, I do regard it as something of an imposition. It's not as if they're even special friends of Nigel."

"I had no idea. I'm so grateful. I do hope they behaved themselves."

"To an extent. Of course, people have different standards. About a lot of things."

"Oh dear. Did my husband warn you about James's bed-wetting?"

"No, he didn't."

*

It was quarter past eight. The boys were finally in bed, though not asleep. Still arguing fiercely. They were upset and confused, and, as usual, expressed their confusion by fighting.

Avril fell on to her bed without taking any of her clothes off. Just sleep, sleep.

The phone rang. She answered it blearily.

"It's Philip Wilkinson. Is Kevin there?"

"No, he's away on business. I don't know when he'll be back."

"He's not away on business. I saw him in the office this morning. Then he went off after lunch."

"Then I've no idea where he is. All I know is that he's been away on business for the last three days."

"He hasn't."

"What?"

"He's been in the office for the last few days. On and off. A bit distracted, but he's been there."

"Oh. Well, I'm sorry, we've got our wires crossed somehow. As I say, I have no idea where he is. I'm absolutely shagged out and I'm going to sleep."

She put the phone down and lay back on the bed. But, in spite of her exhaustion, sleep didn't come. Her mind had started working.

Kevin came back about half-past eleven. She heard the front door, then his footsteps up the stairs. But he didn't come straight into the bedroom as usual. She heard him going into the bathroom, where he seemed to be going through some fairly extensive washing and teeth-cleaning.

Eventually he came into the bedroom. "Oh, I thought you'd be asleep."

"As you see, I'm not."

"No. How's your Mum?"

"Better."

"Good." He reached for his pyjamas. "Oh, I'm tired out."

"Kevin, what do you mean by leaving the boys with Mrs Bentley?"

"I had to do something. I was called away on business."

"You weren't."

"What do you mean?"

"That smoothie Philip Wilkinson rang to speak to you. In the course of conversation, he revealed that you have not been away on business for the past three days."

"Ah." Kevin put his pyjamas down again. Slowly he started to put his clothes back on. As he did so, he spoke. Flatly, without emotion. "Right, in that case I'd better tell you. You'd have to know soon, anyway. The fact is, I have fallen in love with someone else."

"What, you mean another woman?"

"Yes. I have spent most of the past week with her."

"Most of the past week? The shooting weekend . . ."

"There was no shooting weekend."

"But how could you? What about me?"

"I don't think there's much left between us now, Avril."

"Who is she?"

"Her name's Davina Entick. She works at Andersen Small."

Avril started laughing. "Oh God, Kevin, you're predictable. Clawing your grubby way up the social ladder. First you got the voice, then you got the job and the house. Then you looked around and you thought, what haven't I got? The right woman. I need a matching woman to make a set with my shotgun and my wine-rack and all my other phony status-symbols. So you start sniffing round some little feather-headed debutante.

"Well, let me tell you, Kevin Smith, it won't work. Okay, maybe you managed to get into bed with her. A man can usually manage that if he's sufficiently determined, and you've never lacked determination, Kevin Smith. But that's all you'll get out of her. You can't screw your way into the upper classes. You've always been as common as dirt, Kevin Smith. And about as wholesome."

He knotted his silk tie. "I didn't expect you to understand. I'm sure you've forgotten what love feels like."

"If I have, it's only because I've been living with you for the past fourteen years."

"I'm going now."

"Oh, back to the little lovenest in Mayfair?"

"Fulham, actually."

"Oh, Fulham—what a let-down. Couldn't you find a nice upper-class dolly-bird with the right address? Never mind, maybe you can trade them in at Harrods. Fix yourself up with a nice shop-soiled Duke's daughter, how about that?"

Kevin still spoke quietly. "I'm leaving, Avril. I won't come back, except to pick up my things."

"Oh yes, pick up your things." She rose from the bed and went across to the chest of drawers. "Why not take your things with you now? I'm sure Devonia won't want to soil her pretty little hands with washing sweaty shirts and horrid stained Y-fronts, will she?" As she spoke, she opened the drawers and started throwing clothes at Kevin. "Here, have your things. Have your clean shirts, and your socks, and your Y-fronts, and your vests, and your handkerchiefs and your bloody Aran sweaters and . . ."

Quite suddenly, she collapsed on the floor crying.

Kevin, who had stood still while all his clothes were flung at him, looked down at her contemptuously. "And you wonder why I'm leaving you."

She heard the car start. But when she looked out of the window, it was out of sight. All she could see, through the distorting film of her eyes, parked exactly outside the house, was the silver-grey Volkswagen Golf.

"Mummy, why have you drawn the curtains?"

"It's nearly night-time, James."

"But it's not dark. It's summer."

"Look, if I want to draw the curtains in my own house, I will bloody well draw them."

"But you must have a reason."

Oh yes, Avril had a reason. But not one she could tell. You can't tell your six-year-old son that you've drawn the front curtains because you can't bear another second looking at the car parked outside your house. You can't tell anyone that sort of thing. It doesn't make sense.

So, as usual, answer by going on to the attack. "Anyway, it's time you were in bed. Go on, upstairs."

"Am I going to have a bath?"

"No, you can have one tomorrow night."

"You said that last night."

"Look, I have not got the energy to give you a bath tonight. Now GO UPSTAIRS!"

"Can't I wait till Christopher comes home?"

"No. You go to bed." Avril didn't want to think where her ten-year-old son was. Mrs Bentley, who had very grudgingly picked up James from school, had brought back some message about Christopher's being off with some friends and making his own way home on the bus. Avril knew she should be worried about him, but her mind was so full of other anxieties that that problem would have to join the queue and be dealt with when its time came.

A new thought came into her head. A new thought, calming like a sedative injection. Yes, of course, that was the answer. She'd just have to go out and check. Then it would be easy. Just get James into bed and she could go. He'd be all right for a few minutes.

"Go on, James, upstairs, or I'll get really cross."

Her younger son looked stubborn and petulant, just like his father when he didn't get his own way. With an appalling shock, Avril realized that she could never be free of Kevin. She could remove his belongings, fumigate the house of his influence, even move somewhere else, but the boys would always be with her. Two little facsimiles of their father, two little memento moris.

"I need some clean pyjamas," objected James. "I haven't got any clean pyjamas in my drawer, because you haven't done any washing."

Now she had no control over her anger. "And you know why you need clean pyjamas every night, don't you? Because you wet your bloody bed like a six-month-old baby!"

She knew she shouldn't have said it. She knew all the child psychology books said shouting at them only made the problem worse. And, when she saw James's face disintegrate into tears, she knew how much she had hurt him. She was his defender. His father had told him off about it, but she was always the one who intervened, made light of it, said it'd soon be all right. And now she had turned against him.

At least it got him out of the room. He did go upstairs. Maybe, when all this was over, she'd have time to rebuild her relationship with her children. Now she was just too tired. It was the Thursday. Kevin had gone the previous Friday. Nearly a week ago. And still she had hardly slept at all. She lay back on the sofa. Strangely, she felt relaxed. Maybe now sleep would come.

But no, of course. Her good thought. Yes, her good peace-bringing thought. Yes, she must do that.

She stood up. The whole room seemed to sway insubstantially around her.

She went into the hall, then out of the front door. She averted her eyes from the thing parked in front of the house and set off briskly up the road.

A five-minute walk brought her to her objective. It was where she had remembered it would be, in the middle of the council estate.

It was an old Citroën DS. The tyres were flat and the back window smashed. Aerosols had passed comment on its bodywork.

But what she was looking for was affixed to the windscreen. It was a notice from the Council, saying that the car was dangerous rubbish and would have to be moved. She noted down the details of the department responsible.

Back outside the house, she forced herself to look at the car. It hadn't moved. It was in exactly the same position. Resin from a tree above it had dropped on to the bodywork and dust had stuck to this, dulling the silver-grey sheen.

But it was still a new car. This year's model. Some residual logic in her mind told her that no Council was going to come and tow this away as dangerous rubbish.

For a moment she wanted to cry. But then everything became clear.

She wondered why she hadn't seen it earlier. Yes, of course. The car had arrived on the supposed shooting weekend. The smart new car had arrived just at the time Kevin had gone off with his smart new girlfriend. At last she understood why she felt threatened by it.

She was so absorbed that she didn't hear the police car draw up behind her. It was only when the officer who got out of it spoke to her directly that she came back to life.

"Mrs Hooson-Smith?"

"Yes."

"I've brought your son Christopher back. I'm afraid he was caught shop-lifting from the supermarket."

Avril sat by the window in Kevin's study, looking down at the silver-grey Volkswagen Golf. Now she knew who it belonged to she could face it.

It was Saturday. People walked up and down the road loaded with shopping or planks and paint pots for the weekend's Do-It-Yourself. She had sent the boys out. She didn't know where they had gone. Probably the park. The policeman had said she must keep an eye on them, particularly Christopher until his appearance in the Juvenile Court on the Tuesday. But she couldn't yet. Not till all this was over.

It was sunny and very hot. But she didn't open the window. Her dressing-gown was hot, but she couldn't be bothered to take it off, still less to get dressed. A sickly smell of urine wafted from James's room, but she was too distracted to go and change his wet sheets. Even to close the study door and shut out the smell.

She had to watch the car.

The phone rang.

It was a dislocating intrusion. Like someone forgetting their lines in the middle of a good play, a reminder of another reality.

She lifted the receiver gingerly. "Hello."

"It's Kevin."

He sounded business-like. This was the way she had heard him speak into the phone on the rare occasions when she'd gone up to Andersen Small to meet him and had to wait in his office.

"Oh." She hadn't expected ever to hear from him again. He was a part of her life that she no longer thought about. It was strange to be reminded that he was still alive. He had no place in the weightless, transitional world she now inhabited.

"How are things, Avril?"

She didn't answer. She couldn't cope with the philosophical ramifications of the question.

"Listen, I've been thinking. I want to get things cut and dried."

Unaccountably she giggled. "You always did, Kevin."

"What I mean is, I want a divorce. I want to marry Davina."

"And does she want to marry you?"

"I haven't asked her yet, not in so many words. I wanted to get our end sorted out first, to feel free . . ."

"Free," she echoed colourlessly.

He ignored the interruption. "Then I'll speak to Davina. It'll be all right. We have an understanding."

"I'm sure you have." Suddenly anger animated Avril's lethargy. "It'll be easy enough for her to have an understanding of you. All she has to understand is selfishness and petty-mindedness and social-climbing. And I'm sure, from your point of view, she takes no understanding at all. You can't understand something when there's nothing there to understand."

"There's no need to be abusive. Particularly about someone you haven't met. Davina is in fact a highly intelligent girl."

Avril didn't think this assertion worthy of comment.

"Anyway, all I'm saying is that I will be starting proceedings for divorce, and it's going to be easier all round if you don't create any problems over it. I'll see that you and the boys are well looked after financially. By the way, how are the boys?"

"Fine," she replied. Why bother to tell him otherwise?

"Anyway, I'll be round at some point to pick up my things. I hope we'll be able to meet without too much awkwardness. We're both grown-up people and I hope we'll be able to deal with this whole business in a civilized, adult manner."

Avril put the phone down.

A civilized, adult manner. She laughed.

Pick up my things. She laughed further.

If, of course, you have any things to pick up.

She took a bottle out of the wine-rack and threw it against the opposite wall. It shattered satisfyingly.

She did the same with another bottle. And another and another, until the whole rack was empty.

It was enjoyable. She looked round for further destruction.

She opened the cupboard by the window.

And there it was. Of course. The brand-new shotgun.

Kevin had a book about shotguns on his desk. Good old Kevin. Never go into anything without buying lots of books to show you how to do it. Do your homework, you don't want to look a fool.

The book made it easy to load the gun and showed how to release the safety-catch. Avril slipped a cartridge into each barrel from Kevin's unopened box.

Then she opened the window a little and continued watching the silver-grey Volkswagen Golf parked outside.

It was early Sunday morning. Eight o'clock maybe. She had seen it get light a couple of hours earlier. All night she had watched the car outside. It would be terrible not to be there when they arrived.

She didn't know where the boys were. She vaguely recollected their coming back at lunchtime on the Saturday. But they had found there was no lunch prepared and had gone out again. She thought they had said something about spending the night in the park, but she couldn't be sure. It had been difficult to take in what they said. Her dizziness and the mobility of everything that surrounded her seemed to have grown. It was as if her head had levitated and floated above her body in some transparent viscous pool.

But she knew she would be all right. Her body would hold up as long as was necessary.

The phone rang. This time its intrusion didn't seem so incongruous. It now took on the ambivalence of everything else she saw and heard. It might be real, it might not. It didn't matter much one way or the other.

She answered it. As she did so, she thought to herself, "If it's real, then I'm answering it. If it's not, then I'm not." That was very funny, and she giggled into the receiver.

"Hello, is that Avril?"

"Yes. Almost definitely." She giggled again.

"It's Mrs Eady."

"Ah, Mrs Eady."

"It's about your Mum, Avril. I'm afraid she's had another stroke. Doctor's with her now."

"Ah."

"And I'm afraid this one's more serious. Doctor says he doesn't think she'll last long."

"Ah."

"Look, Avril, can you come up? I mean, she's still alive now, but I don't know how long it'll be. They're going to take her into hospital and . . . Avril, are you still there?"

"Oh yes," said Avril wisely.

"Can you come up?"

"Come up?"

"To Rochdale."

"Oh no, I'm very busy."

"But it's your Mum. I mean, she can still recognize me and—"

"No, I'm sorry. I can't do anything till they come."

She put the phone down.

It was nearly eleven o'clock when the girl arrived. She came up the road carrying two suitcases.

It was the suitcases that alerted Avril. Kevin had got a nerve. To send the girl to pick up his things. A bloody nerve.

The girl walked up the road slowly, giving Avril plenty of time to look at her. No, she wasn't that pretty. Not even as young as she'd expected. Looked about her age. Very brown, though, very tanned.

Avril knew she would stop by the car and, sure enough, she did. The two cases were put down, and the girl fumbled in her handbag for car-keys. I see, she'd load up with Kevin's things and then drive off in the car.

Avril could see everything very clearly now. The world around her had stabilized, in fact she could see it in sharper detail than usual. She sighted along the barrels of the shotgun.

The girl had found her key and was bending to open the car door. Avril felt the trigger with her finger. Just one trigger. Kevin wouldn't approve of waste. Just one cartridge would do it.

She squeezed the trigger.

She was totally unprepared for the recoil, which knocked her off her chair. But when she picked herself up and looked out of the window, she saw she had succeeded.

The girl seemed to be kneeling against the side of the car. Her back was a mass of red. The side windows were holed and frosted and there were small holes in the silver-grey bodywork of the Volkswagen Golf.

Kevin arrived in his car a moment later and parked behind the Golf. He was in a furious temper.

Davina had turned down his proposal. Not only that, she had laughed at him when he made it. She had let him know in no uncertain terms that at the moment she had no thoughts of marriage and was only looking for good sex. She had added as riders that, if she had been looking for a husband, she would have looked some way beyond him, and that she was beginning to have grave doubts about the quality of the sex he provided.

So he was coming home with his tail between his legs. Avril, he knew, would welcome him. She had no alternative.

As he got out of the car, he couldn't help noticing the bloody mess beside the Golf. He stared at the body with his back to his house.

So it was the back of his head that received the main blast of the second barrel of his new shotgun. Some more holes appeared in the bodywork of the silver-grey Volkswagen Golf.

The Detective-Inspector watched the police car drive off. "Well, she seemed to go docilely enough, Sergeant."

"Yes, sir. The only thing she seemed worried about was that the Golf would definitely get towed away. Said it was in her parking space. I assured her it would, and she seemed quite happy."

"Strange. I mean, not her shooting the husband. Apparently he'd left her and gone off with some other woman, so there's a motive there. But the other woman she shot . . . completely random."

"She's not hubby's girlfriend?"

"Oh, Sergeant, wouldn't that be nice and neat." The Detective-

Inspector smiled. "No, we've identified her from things in her handbag. Passport, airline ticket stubs—very well-documented. Just come back from a fortnight's package holiday in Sardinia."

"No connection with this family at all?"

The Detective-Inspector shook his head. "Not yet. I personally don't think we'll probably ever find one. I think that poor woman's only offence was to use someone else's parking space."

TICKLED TO DEATH

IF A DEAD body could ever be funny, this one was. Only intimations of his own mortality prevented Inspector Walsh from smiling at the sight.

The corpse in the greenhouse was dressed in a clown's costume. Bald plastic cranium with side-tufts of ropey orange hair. Red jacket, too long. Black and white check trousers suspended from elastic braces to a hooped waistband. Shoes three foot long pointing upwards in strange semaphore.

"Boy, he's really turned his toes up," said Sergeant Trooper, who was prone to such witticisms even when the corpse was less obviously humorous.

The clown's face could not be seen. The back of a plate supplied a moonlike substitute which fitted well with the overall image.

"Going to look good on the report," Sergeant Trooper continued. "Cause of death—suffocation. Murder weapon—a custard pie."

"I suppose that *was* the cause . . . Let the photographers and fingerprint boys do their bit and we'll have a look."

These formalities concluded, Inspector Walsh donned rubber gloves and cautiously prised the plate away. Over its make-up, the face was covered with pink goo. It was clogged in the nostrils and in the slack, painted mouth.

"Yes, Sergeant Trooper, it looks like suffocation."

"Course it does. What's your alternative? Poisoned custard in the pie?"

"Well, it's certainly not custard." The Inspector poked at the congealed mess. It was hard and crumbly. "Even school custard wasn't this bad. No, it's plaster of Paris or something. They don't usually use that for slapstick, do they?"

Sergeant Trooper shook his head. "Nope. Foam, flour and water, dough . . . not plaster of Paris."

"Hmm. Which probably means the crime was premeditated."

The Sergeant thought this too obvious to merit a response.

Inspector Walsh bent down and felt in the capacious pockets of the red jacket.

"What are you looking for? I don't think clowns carry credit cards or passports."

"No," Inspector Walsh agreed, producing a string of cloth sausages and a jointless rubber fish.

"Wonder if there's anything else." He felt again in the pockets. His rubber-gloved hand closed round a soft oval object. He squeezed it gently.

"Bloody hell," said Sergeant Trooper.

Thin jets of water found their way through the caked white beneath the clown's eyes. Inspector Walsh drew out a rubber bulb attached to a plastic tube.

"Old clown's prop—squirting eyes."

He reached into the other pocket and found what felt like a switch. He pressed it.

The two tufts of orange hair shot out at right angles from the clown's bald head. As they did so, the noise of a klaxon escaped from somewhere inside the jacket.

Inspector Walsh stood up. "I don't know," he said. "It's a funny business."

"The fact is," objected the Teapot, "it's damnably inconvenient. These people are our guests. We can't just keep them here against their will."

"No, we can't," the Pillar-box agreed shrilly. "What will they think of our hospitality?"

The Yorkshire terrier, scampering around the study, barked its endorsement of their anger.

"I'm sorry." Inspector Walsh leant coolly back against the leather-topped desk. "But a murder has been committed and we cannot allow anyone to leave the building until we have taken their statements."

"Well, I may be forced to speak to your superior," snapped the Teapot. "I am not without influence in this area."

"I'm sure you're not," the Inspector soothed. "Now why don't you take your lid off and sit down?"

The Teapot flounced angrily, but did remove its hatlike lid and, hitching up its wired body, perched on a low stool.

"You may as well sit down too, madam." The Inspector pointed to a second stool and the Pillar-box, with equally bad grace, folded on to it. Pale blue eyes flashed resentment through the posting slit.

"And can we get rid of that bloody dog?" A uniformed policeman ushered the reluctant Yorkshire terrier out of the study. "Oh, and get us some tea while you're at it, could you, Constable?" The Inspector smiled perfunctorily. "Now let's just get a few facts straight. You are Mr and Mrs Alcott?"

The two heads nodded curt agreement.

"And this is your house?"

Two more nods.

"And, Mr Alcott, you have no doubt that the dead man is your business partner, Mr Cruikshank?"

Alcott's head, rising tortoise-like from the top of the Teapot, twitched from side to side. "No doubt at all."

"He had been wearing the clown costume all evening?"

"Yes. It's one of our most popular lines. As partners, we always try to demonstrate both the traditional and the new. Mr Cruikshank was wearing one of Festifunn's oldest designs, while I—" Unconsciously, he smoothed down the Teapot frame with his spout. "—chose one of the most recent." He gestured proudly to the Pillar-box. "My wife's is also a new design."

Some response seemed to be required. The Inspector murmured, "Very nice too", which he hoped was appropriate.

"And your guests?"

"They're all dressed in our lines too."

"Yes. That wasn't actually what I was going to ask. I wished to enquire about your guest list. Are all the people here personal friends?"

"Not so much friends as professional associates," replied the Teapot tartly.

"So they would all have known Mr Cruikshank?"

"Oh, certainly. Mr Cruikshank always made a point of getting to know our staff and clients personally." The Teapot's tone implied disapproval of this familiarity.

"So I would be correct in assuming that this Fancy Dress Party is a business function?"

The Teapot was vehement in its agreement with this statement. The party was very definitely part of Festifunn's promotional campaign, and as such (though this was implied rather than stated) tax-deductible.

"You don't think we do this for fun, do you?" asked the crumpled Pillar-box.

"No, of course we don't." The Teapot assumed an accent of self-denying righteousness. "It's just an opportunity to demonstrate the full range of our stock to potential customers. And also it's a kind of thank-you to the staff. Something that I wouldn't do voluntarily, I hasten to add, but something they demand these days as a right. And one daren't cross them. Even the novelty industry," he concluded darkly, "is not immune to the destructive influence of the trade unions."

"But presumably everyone has a good time?"

Mr Alcott winced at the Inspector's suggestion. "The Fancy Dress Party was not originally my idea," he said in further self-justification.

"Mr Cruikshank's," Walsh deduced smoothly.

"Yes."

"Then why is it held in your house?"

"Have you recently examined the cost of hiring outside premises?"

"I meant why not in Mr Cruikshank's house?"

The Pillar-box tutted at the idea. "Mr Cruikshank's house would be totally unsuitable for a function of this nature. It's a terrible mess, full of odd machinery and designs he's working on . . . most unsalubrious. I'm afraid his style of living, too, is—was—most irregular. He drank, you know."

The Inspector let that go for the moment. "Mr Alcott, would you say Mr Cruickshank had any enemies?"

"Well . . ."

"I mean, did he tend to annoy people?"

"Certainly."

"In what way?"

"Well, I have no wish to speak ill of the dead . . ."

"But?"

"But Mr Cruikshank was . . ." The Teapot formed the words with distaste. ". . . a practical joker."

"Ah." The Inspector smiled. "Good thing to be in your line of business."

"By no means," the Teapot contradicted. "Most unsuitable."

Again Walsh didn't pursue it. Time enough for that. "Right now, I would like from you a list of your guests before I start interviewing them." He took a notebook from his pocket, then turned round to the desk and picked up a pencil that lay beside an old-fashioned biscuit-barrel.

"Well, there's Mr Brickett, our Sales Manager . . ."

Inspector Walsh bent to write the name down. The pencil squashed softly against the paper. It was made of rubber.

"I'm sorry. That's one of our BJ153s. Joke Pencil—Many Minutes of Mirth."

"Ah."

At that moment the uniformed constable arrived with the tea-tray. The three helped themselves and then, when the Inspector again looked round for something to write with, the Teapot said, "There's a ball-point pen just the other side of the biscuit-barrel."

"Thank you." The Inspector picked it up to continue his list.

"Sugar?" the Pillar-box offered, adding righteously, "We don't."

"Well, I do." He took two lumps, put them in the tea, and reached for a spoon. When he looked back, the lumps of sugar were floating in the top of his cup.

"I'm sorry, Inspector," said the Teapot. "You've got some of our GW34s. Silly Sugar—Your Friends Will Be Tickled To Death."

The young man looked sheepish. Since he was dressed as a sheep, this wasn't difficult.

"Might I ask, Mr O'Brien . . ." Despite the request for permission, Inspector Walsh was clearly going to ask anyway. ". . . why you went out to the greenhouse at the time that you discovered the body?"

"Well, I . . . er . . . well, um . . ." the young man bleated.

"I think you'd do better to tell me," Walsh advised portentously.

"Yes. Well, the fact was, I was . . . um, there was a young lady involved."

"You mean a young lady was with you when you found Mr Cruikshank?"

"No. No, no, she was still in the house, but I was . . . er . . . sort of scouting out the . . . er . . . lie of the land. Do I make myself clear?"

"No."

"Oh. Am I going to have to spell it out?"

"Yes."

"Well, you see, this young lady and I are . . . er . . . rather good friends. I'm at Festifunn in Indoor Firework Testing and she's in Fancy Dress Design, so we see quite a lot of each other and . . . er . . . you know how it is . . ."

The Inspector nodded indulgently, awaiting further information.

"Unfortunately, her father doesn't approve of our . . . er, er . . . friendship. He thinks, as a profession, Indoor Fireworks is too . . . er . . . volatile. And my landlady's a bit old-fashioned, so we can only really meet at work, or in secret . . ."

"Yes?"

"Which, I mean, is okay. It works all right, but it sometimes leads to complications. Like tonight."

"What happened tonight?"

"Well, um . . ." Insofar as it is possible for a sheep to blush, the Sheep blushed. "You see, it comes down to . . . sex."

"It often does," Walsh observed sagely.

"Yes. Well, um . . . do I really have to tell you this?"

"Yes."

"Right. Well, normally we . . . um . . . go into my car for . . . um . . ."

"I understand."

"Thank you. But you see, this is where feminine vanity raises problems. At least it did tonight. You see, my friend, as any woman would, was anxious to look her best for the party and, since she works in Fancy Dress Design, nothing would stop her from coming in her latest creation. No woman could resist such an opportunity to show off her skills."

"No," Walsh agreed with a worldly shake of his head. "And may I ask what your friend is dressed as?"

"An Orange," the Sheep replied miserably.

"Ah."

"And I've only got a Mini."

"I begin to understand why you were checking out the greenhouse, Mr O'Brien."

The Sheep looked, if it were possible, even more sheepish.

"And what happened to the trifle?"

"The top flipped off, there was a loud squeak, and I saw the mouse in the bottom of the dish."

"Would that be a real mouse?" Inspector Walsh asked cautiously.

Joan of Arc was so surprised at the question that she removed the cigarette which drooped from her generously lipsticked mouth. "No, a rubber one. It's just the basic BT3, Squeaking Mouse, incorporated into the HM200, Tricky Trifle."

"Oh, I see. And Mr Cruikshank offered it to you?"

"Yes. I shouldn't have fallen for it. Good Lord, I handle half a dozen HM200s a day in the shop. But it was a party, you know, I wasn't concentrating—perhaps even a bit tiddly." She simpered. "Honestly, me—a couple of Babychams and I'm anybody's."

She moved her body in a manner calculated to display her bosom (a wasted effort for someone dressed in complete armour).

"I see," said Inspector Walsh again, more to change the subject than for any other reason. "Why I'm asking about the incident, Mrs Dancer, is because we believe you may have been the last person—except, of course, for his murderer—to see Mr Cruikshank alive."

"Oh, fancy that."

"And handing you the Tricky Trifle may have been his last action before his death."

"Good Lord." Joan of Arc paused, then set her painted face in an expression of piety, as if prepared to hear voices. "Oh well, I'm glad I fell for it then. It's how he'd have wanted to go."

"I'm sorry?"

She elaborated. "He loved his jokes, Mr Cruikshank did. He designed almost all the novelties at Festifunn. Always working on something new. His latest idea was a customized Jack-in-a-Box. Really novel. Clown pops out when the box opens and a personal recorded message starts up. You know, you get different ones—jolly for kids' parties, fruity for stag nights, and so on.

"Full of ideas, Mr Cruikshank always was. Really loved jokes. So, you see, I'm glad about the Tricky Trifle. Because if he had to die, he'd have been really chuffed to die after catching someone out with one of his own novelties."

The Inspector was tempted to ask how anyone could be "chuffed" while being suffocated by a custard pie, but contented himself with another "I see." (In his early days as a detective, Walsh had worried about how often he said "I see" during interrogations, but long since he had come to accept it as just an occupational hazard.) "And before this evening, Mrs Dancer, when did you last see Mr Cruikshank?"

"Well, funnily enough, I saw him this afternoon."

"Ah."

"Yes, he came into the shop."

"Was that unusual?"

"Not unusual for him to come in, no—he liked to keep in touch with what was happening in the business—but unusual for him to come in two days running."

"I see. What did he come in for?"

"Oh, a chat. See how the stock was going. He was particularly worried about the Noses. Always get a run on Noses this time of year. We're very low on Red Drunken and Warty Witch's—and completely out of Long Rubbery."

"Oh dear," the Inspector commiserated. "And this afternoon,

when Mr Cruikshank came into the shop, did you notice anything unusual about him?"

"No." Joan of Arc stubbed her cigarette out on her cuirass as she reconsidered this answer. But she didn't change her mind. "No. Well, he had a knife through his head, but—"

"I beg your pardon?"

"Knife-Through-Head—JL417. As opposed to Tomahawk-Through-Head—JL418—and Nail-Through-Head—JL419."

"Uhuh." Curiosity overcame Inspector Walsh's customary reserve. "Which one of those is the most popular?"

"Oh, 417," Joan of Arc replied without hesitation. "Sell a few Nails, but very little call for Tomahawks these days. It's because they're not making so many Westerns—all these space films instead. Mr Cruikshank was trying to come up with a Laser-Beam-Through-Head, but it's not as easy as it sounds."

"No, I suppose not." Walsh digested this gobbet of marketing information before continuing. "And did Mr Cruikshank often come into the shop with a knife through his head?"

"Yes. Well, that or some other novelty. Boil-On-Face, Vampire Teeth, Safety-Pin-Through-Nose, that sort of thing. Lived for his work, Mr Cruikshank."

"And he didn't say anything strange that afternoon?"

"No." She pondered. "Well, yes, I suppose he did, in a way."

"Ah."

"He said he'd come to say goodbye."

"Goodbye?"

"Yes, he said someone was out to kill him, and he didn't think he'd live more than twenty-four hours."

Walsh sat bolt-upright. "What! Did he say who was out to kill him?"

"Oh yes." Joan of Arc reached casually into her habergeon and brought out a packet of Players Number Six. She put one in her mouth, reached past the biscuit-barrel and picked up a box of matches. She opened it and a green snake jumped out. "BK351," she said dismissively.

"Mrs Dancer, who? *Who* did he say was out to kill him?"

"Oh, Mr Alcott."

"But that's terribly important. Why on earth didn't you mention it before?"

"Oh, I thought it was just another of Mr Cruikshank's jokes."

"So what did you do when he told you?"

"Oh, I just offered him some Squirting Chocolate and went back to stock-taking the Severed Fingers."

"You have to understand that I'm a professional accountant . . ." The Baby self-importantly hitched up his nappy and adjusted the dummy-string around his neck. ". . . and I am bound by a code of discretion in relation to the affairs of my clients."

"This *is* a police investigation, Mr McCabe . . ."

"I am aware of that, Inspector Walsh."

". . . into the most serious crime one human being can commit against another."

"Yes."

"So I suggest you save time and answer all my questions as fully as possible."

"Oh, very well." With bad grace, the Baby threw his rattle on to the desk and sat down.

"I'm going to ask you a direct question, Mr McCabe, and I require you to give me a direct answer."

The Baby's bald head wrinkled with disapproval at this proposal. But he said nothing, just stared pointedly upwards at the ornate ceiling-rose over the desk.

"Right, Mr McCabe, was there any cause for dissension between the two partners in Festifunn?"

"Well . . . As you have probably gathered, Inspector, Mr Alcott and Mr Cruikshank were men of very different personalities . . ."

"I had gathered that, yes."

"And so, inevitably, they did not always see eye to eye on the daily minutiae of the business."

"There were arguments?"

"Yes, there were."

"Threats?"

"Occasionally."

"What form did the threats take?"

"Well, they—" The Baby stopped short and coloured. The flush spread from his head to just above the navel. "Inspector, are you suggesting that *Mr Alcott* . . ."

"We have to consider every possibility, Mr McCabe. In our experience, people are most commonly murdered by their loved ones. Since, in this case, Mr Cruikshank had no immediate family, we are forced to consider those who worked closely with him."

"If you're making accusations against Mr Alcott, I don't think I can answer any further questions without a solicitor present."

The Baby sat back complacently after this repetition of something he'd heard on television. Then Inspector Walsh spoiled it by asking, "Whose solicitor?"

"I beg your pardon?"

"Whose? Yours? Mr Alcott's?"

"Oh. Um . . ."

"Anyway, I'm not making accusations at the moment, so just answer the questions!"

The Baby was suitably cowed.

"Right, was there any recent cause for more serious disagreement between the two partners of Festifunn?"

"Well . . ."

"Answer!"

"Yes, right, fine." The words came out quickly. "There has recently been an offer to take over the firm. An offer from the Jollijests Corporation."

"And the partners disagreed about the advisability of accepting the offer?"

"Precisely. Mr Alcott recognized it for the good business proposition it was. Mr Cruikshank opposed it on the somewhat whimsical grounds that he didn't want Festifunn's output limited to the manufacture of party hats and squeakers."

"Sounds a reasonable objection."

The Baby gave a patronizing smile. "When you've been in the novelty business as long as I have, Inspector, you will understand that it is not an area where sentiment should be allowed to overrule common sense."

"I see. So the argument about the proposed take-over was quite violent?"

"Certainly. At the last board meeting, Mr Cruikshank's behaviour was most unseemly. He used language that was distinctly unparliamentary." Then, after a pause, "He drank, you know."

"Yes, I did know. But he wouldn't accept the deal?"

"Under no circumstances. In fact he said, if it were to take place, it would be *over his dead body*."

The words were out before the Baby realized their significance and coloured again.

At first, Walsh restricted himself to another "I see." Then, piecing his question together slowly, he asked, "So, from the point of view of Mr Alcott's plans for the future of Festifunn, Mr Cruikshank's death couldn't have come at a more convenient time?"

Mr McCabe rose with all the dignity that a fifty-year-old accountant in a nappy can muster. "I don't see that I have to answer any further questions, Inspector. You can't make me. I suggest that you carry on the rest of your investigation without my assistance."

"Fair enough." Walsh didn't bother to argue. "Thank you, anyway, for all the invaluable help you've already given me."

The Baby, moving away, turned his head to flash a venomous look at his interrogator.

"Hey, watch out! That Yorkshire terrier's misbehaved." The Inspector pointed to where the Baby's knobbly-veined foot was about to land. Neatly on the carpet, like a pointed cottage loaf, lay the brown, glistening lump of a dog's mess.

The Baby sneered openly. "When you've been in the novelty business as long as I have, Inspector, you will learn to recognize the product. That, if I'm not very much mistaken, is an AR88—Naughty Puppy—All Plastic, Made In Taiwan." He bent down to pick it up. "Oh."

He was very much mistaken.

Sergeant Trooper broke into Mr Brickett, the Sales Manager's, disquisition on the boom in Revolving Bow-ties in the Tyneside area. "I put it down to unemployment," he was saying. "People got time on their hands, that's when they need a laugh and we—"

"Sorry to butt in, sir, but it's important. Got the preliminary medical report, Inspector." The Sergeant handed over a buff envelope.

"Oh, thank you. Mr Brickett, if you'd mind just stepping outside, and we'll continue when . . ."

"Fine, fine." Mr Brickett, who was dressed as the Tin Man from *The Wizard of Oz*, obligingly squeaked his way out of the door.

"This is very interesting," commented Inspector Walsh, as he scanned the report.

"Yes. Looks like he would have died of the overdose of sleeping pills without the custard pie. Mogadon, they reckon."

The Inspector looked sternly at his underling. "You aren't meant to read this."

"No, well, I—" Trooper tried to get off the hook by changing the subject. "I've checked. Mrs Alcott uses Mogadon. What's more, there are twenty-five tablets missing from her supply. She knows, because she started a new bottle last night."

"Hmm. That's very good, Trooper, but it doesn't change the fact that you shouldn't have looked at—"

"And, on top of that, the boys were looking round Mr Alcott's workshop and, shoved under a couple of old sacks, they found— this."

On the word, the Sergeant dramatically produced an old paint-pot lid, to which clung the powdery traces of a thick pinkish substance.

"Polyfilla, sir," he announced with a dramatic efficiency which he then weakened by lapsing into another of his jokes. "What they stuff dead parrots with."

Receiving not the slightest encouragement to further humour, he hurried on. "And exactly, according to the forensic boys, what the custard pie was made of."

"Hmm. Prospect doesn't look too promising for Mr Alcott, does it, Trooper?"

"No, sir. Interesting thing is, though, this bit of the report suggests he needn't have gone to all that trouble."

Inspector Walsh didn't even bother to remonstrate as he followed his Sergeant's stubby finger to the relevant paragraph.

"My investigation," the Inspector began, "is now nearly complete, and I have gathered you all here because I wish to piece together the murder, and some of you may be able to confirm as facts details which at the moment are mere supposition."

He paused impressively, and looked around the crowded study. Towering over the assembly were the built-up shoulders of Charles I, whose head dangled nonchalantly from its owner's fingers. The Teapot, which had resumed its lid, sat primly behind its desk, with the Pillar-box, equally prim, at its side. A Salt Cellar and a Pepper Mill leant sleepily against each other. A Nun had her hand inside Julius Caesar's toga. A large cigar protruded from the Gorilla's bared teeth. A Rolling Pin, whose year at secretarial college hadn't prepared her for the effects of gin on an empty stomach, swayed gently. The Front Half of the Pantomime Horse had collapsed in a heap on the floor, while the Back Half had its arm lasciviously round The-Princess-Of-Wales-On-Her-Wedding-Day. Hereward the Wake snored contentedly in the corner, and Attila the Hun ate a jelly with a plastic spoon.

There was little movement, except from the Orange, which kept slipping off the Sheep's knee, and from the Baby, who kept sniffing his hands apprehensively.

"Right, now," the Inspector continued, "what has happened here this evening has been a crime of vicious premeditation. There is one person in this room who has always borne a grudge against the deceased, Mr Cruikshank, and seen him as an obstacle to the advance of his own career.

"That person planned this crime with great—but, alas, insufficient—care. That person appropriated some of Mrs Alcott's sleeping pills and, probably by crushing them into his drinks, forced Mr Cruikshank to take a fatal overdose.

"Then, not content to let the old man slip quietly away to oblivion, that person made assurance doubly sure by mixing a cruel custard pie of Polyfilla—and with that he asphyxiated his already incapable victim."

The Inspector allowed another impressive pause. This time there was no movement. The Orange defied gravity on the Sheep's knee. The Baby ceased momentarily to worry about the smell of his hands. Even the Rolling Pin stopped swaying.

"There is only one person in this room who had the motivation and the opportunity to commit this despicable crime. And that person is . . ."

Long experience of denouements had taught him how to extend this pause almost interminably.

It had also taught him how suddenly to swing round, point his finger at the Teapot and boom in the voice of the Avenging Angel, "Mr Alcott!"

All colour drained from the face framed by pot and lid. The pale mouth twitched, unable to form sounds. You could have heard a pin drop. The Rolling Pin, deserted by all faculties but a sense of timing, dropped.

"What? It's not true!" the Teapot finally managed to gasp.

"But it is, Mr Alcott," Inspector Walsh continued implacably. "All the evidence points to you. There is no question about it."

"No!"

"Yes. And the sad irony of the whole crime, Mr Alcott, is that it was unnecessary. Our medical report reveals that Mr Cruikshank was suffering from terminal cancer. Had you only waited a couple of months, nature would have removed the obstacle to your plans."

"What?" the Teapot hissed.

"I am afraid I am obliged to put you under arrest, Mr Alcott. And I would advise you not to make any trouble."

"No!" the Teapot screamed. "You will not arrest me!" And its handle shot out to a desk drawer, only to reappear holding a small, black automatic.

Inspector Walsh checked his advance for a second, but then continued forward. "You're being very foolish, Mr Alcott. Threatening a police officer is a very serious—"

"Stop or I'll shoot!"

"*Shooting* a police officer is an even more serious—"

"I'll fire!"

The room was silent. Except that she hadn't recovered from the last time, you could have heard a Pin drop again.

And still the Inspector advanced on the Teapot behind the desk.

"I will fire! One—two—three. Right, you've asked for it!"

The entire room winced as the Teapot pulled the trigger.

There was a click and a flash of movement at the end of the gun.

When they opened their eyes, they all saw the little banner hanging from the barrel. BANG! it said in red letters.

The Orange began to giggle. Others would have followed her example but for the sudden movement behind the desk. The Teapot's spout had reached into the other drawer and emerged with a gleaming knife appended.

"Out of my way, Inspector!"

Walsh stood his ground. The Teapot came lunging at him, knife upraised.

Suddenly, Joan of Arc interposed her body between the Inspector and certain death. The knife plunged up to its hilt into her chest.

The room winced again, waiting for the spurt of blood and her collapse.

But neither came. Joan of Arc pulled the knife from the Teapot's nerveless spout. "NH257," she said contemptuously. "Retractable-Blade-Dagger. Recognize it anywhere."

This second failure (and the accompanying laugh) was too much for the Teapot. Clasping its handle to its lid, it collapsed backwards into the chair behind the desk. Then it slumped forward and, with cries of "Damn! Damn! Damn!" began to beat clenched handle and spout against the desk-top.

It must have been this which animated the biscuit-barrel. With a shrieking whistle, the lid flew off and a model clown on a long spring leapt into the air.

Then, over the screams and giggles, a disembodied voice sounded. It was an old voice, a tired voice, but a voice warmed by a sense of mischief.

"Hello, everyone," it said, and the reaction showed that everyone recognized it. "If all's gone according to plan, Rodney Alcott should by now have been arrested for my murder. And I will have pulled off the greatest practical joke of my career.

"The fact is, I'm afraid, that Rodney didn't kill me. I, Hamish Cruikshank, killed myself. I heard from my doctor last week that my body is riddled with cancer. I had at best three months to live and, rather than waste away, I decided it was better to choose my own manner of departure. About which you all, I'm sure, will now know. I have prepared the custard pie, will shortly take the overdose of Mogadon and, as I feel drowsiness creep over me, will bury my face in the soft blanket of Polyfilla. Oh, Mr Cruikshank, I heard you all saying—plastered again.

"But, by my death, I will take my revenge on Rodney Alcott for what I have always regarded as his unpardonable crime. No, not his meanness. Nor his selfishness. What I refer to is his total lack of sense of humour, his inability ever to laugh at any joke—whether mine or someone else's—and the fact that he has never in his life provided anyone with that most precious of worldly commodities—laughter.

"Well, it may have taken my death to do it, but let me tell you—Rodney Alcott's going to give you a good laugh now!"

The recorded voice stopped with a click. Whether it was that or some other invention of the old man's fertile mind that triggered the device, Hamish Cruickshank's timing, to the end, remained perfect.

The ceiling-rose above the swivel chair opened, and a deluge of bilious yellow custard descended on the Teapot below.

And the staff and clients of Festifunn laughed and laughed and laughed. And Inspector Walsh and Sergeant Trooper couldn't help joining in.

"And you're not even going to charge him with threatening behaviour?" asked the Sergeant.

"No. He's paid his dues. Gone to bed now with one of the Pillar-box's remaining Mogadon. No, case is finished now. Just have another cup of tea, and we'll be on our way. Mrs Dancer, do you think tea's possible?"

Joan of Arc, who had lingered after the others had left, smiled a motherly acquiescence. "Don't see why not."

"All I want to do is put my feet up for ten minutes."

The Inspector sank heavily into an armchair. As he did so, a loud flubbering fart broke the silence of the room.

At the door, Joan of Arc, without even turning round, said, "KT47. Whoopee Cushion. Hours of Fun. Your Friends Will Roar."

PRIVATE AREAS

FAITH IS OFTEN the willing acceptance of what is demonstrably untrue, and the basis of marriage is faith. Once that faith breaks down, the marriage may break down too, and end in spite, despair, hatred or, as in the case of Henry and Vera Laker, murder.

Marriage, like other disputes, is a continual process of demarcation. Two people living together have to define their own boundaries, territorial, moral and emotional, and this takes a long time. What is more, the boundaries keep changing. However organized the couple are in dividing their lives during the early days of marriage, changing circumstances—the arrival of children, financial successes and failures, or just the inevitable advances of age—call for constant redefinition.

When Henry and Vera Laker married, in 1947, the boundaries had been comparatively easy to draw. He was thirty, and she ten years younger. He had seen active service during the War, while she had been at school for most of its duration, away from the dangers of bombs, with nothing but half-heard radio bulletins, unread newspapers, and the ever-present fact of rationing to remind her that it was on.

Age, then, and greater experience of the world, meant that Henry was the dominant partner. Society approved of this, for, though the War had brought many new freedoms to women, the institution of marriage was a conservative bastion and slow to change its traditional image. As all the clichés demanded, the man wore the trousers, his home was his castle, and he was the breadwinner.

All of these were true in the Lakers' household. Henry commuted every day to the City, where he won the family's bread. He worked in an insurance company for a salary undisclosed to his wife. At the beginning of every month he handed over her housekeeping, in cash—she did not have a bank account. In the first year of their marriage, she more than once found she had run out of money by the end of the month—particularly if it had the full complement of 31 days—and had to ask her husband for a supplement. On these occasions he scolded her, with the result that she learned to manage better. Within a couple of years she was even contriving to save a little each month.

When she did the shopping, she paid in cash. She had no credit accounts, and bills that came through the post were opened by, and paid by, her husband.

In the early years they did not have alcohol in the house and went out rarely. Vera had never been to a pub in her life. She would have demurred at the idea if Henry had suggested taking her into one (which he never did); and the thought of her going alone was as alien—and indeed on about the same level—as the thought of her soliciting on a street corner.

Once a year, just before Christmas, Henry took Vera to the annual firm's dinner-and-dance, a function of excruciating politeness, during which the wives sat stiffly in dresses that showed their shoulders, until spoken to by the firm's boss, to whom, for months afterwards, they were convinced they had said the wrong thing. Vera spent a long time thinking about what to wear for this occasion, which was completely wasted effort, because for the first five years of their marriage, she wore the same dress each year, with different "accessories". ("Accessories" were then an essential part of the female wardrobe.)

Each year, Henry wore his father's dinner suit, which very nearly fitted him.

At the firm's dinner-and-dance—and indeed on other social occasions, when there were any—Henry led the conversation. He did not expect Vera to initiate a subject when in company. He would probably have been very offended if she had done, but Vera knew her place, and his good humour was not tested in that way.

The same distribution of responsibility carried over into the Lakers' sex life. Their intercourse, whose frequency did not differ much from the national average, occurred always on Henry's instigation. It was predictable and short, but Vera, knowing her duties, never opposed his demands or considered the possibility of variation. Contraception, in rubber form, was Henry's responsibility. Like his salary cheque and the household bills, it was unseen.

Their home was as rigidly demarcated as if it had been fenced into units. The only area over which Vera had uncontested hegemony was the kitchen, though when the children arrived, she was allowed the same control of the nursery. In the rest of the house, she had cleaning, sweeping, and dusting rights; decoration and structural repairs were Henry's province.

Substantial jobs in the garden were also his, digging, mowing the lawn, clearing leaves. Vera was delegated to weeding and the tending of flowers, which was held to be an appropriately feminine pastime.

The same went for the tending of children. And having them. Interest in such distasteful processes was not thought proper to a man and so, while Vera screamed and sweated her way through three labours under the unforgiving eyes of spinster midwives, Henry went to work as normal and spent his evenings in the pub, an atypical indulgence which the exceptional circumstances justified.

When the children had arrived, they very definitely remained Vera's responsibility. Their feeding, their cleaning, even their illnesses, were not subjects Henry wished to know about. If they screamed during the night and woke him, he would turn over with a bad-tempered remark about her lack of control, and leave Vera to get up and quiet them. If she failed to do this promptly, he would be even more annoyed.

He could no more have changed a nappy than she could have paid a bill.

This then was their life in the early years of marriage. Both knew the boundaries; both respected them. Neither would have contemplated the idea of having an affair, even if the opportunity had arisen. Which it didn't.

And, if asked, both would have said they were happy. They were married, and the life they lived was what marriage was. Anything outside their boundaries was probably dangerous, and certainly irresponsible.

They both knew human life was an imperfect system, and

both thought they were getting as much out of it as most other people.

And when life's deficiencies became too apparent, they both had escape routes to take their minds off the inadequacy of their existence.

Their palliatives were predictable, each supplying to the imagination what, for each, the real relationship lacked.

For Vera, it was romantic fiction, which she read voraciously through all sorts of domestic crises. The books calmed her, taking her back to the days of her extremely innocent early adolescence, when a legitimate girlish pastime was "waiting for Mr Right", living in expectation of the arrival of a *deus ex machina*, upright, honest and strikingly handsome, who would come into her life and change it, without effort, to a continuing dream of unbroken fulfilment.

Marriage to Henry had not altered these interior fantasies. His less-than-godlike appearance, his less-than-godlike generosity in flower-giving and other romantic gestures, the messy little reality of sex—none of these had impinged on Vera's dream world. She still waited for Mr Right.

The fact that she had achieved the peak of her adolescent aspirations, and found a real man to marry her, was irrelevant. The Mr Rights who lived in her mind, undergoing constant minor alterations according to what she was reading at the time, had nothing to do with Henry. She was not even disappointed that Henry was not like them. She had never expected him to be; indeed, if he had borne any similarity to them at all, she probably would have been disappointed, deprived of a certain richness in her fantasy life. She wished to guard her dreams intact.

These dreams were not erotic. Possibly Vera was not very highly-sexed. Her upbringing would definitely have discouraged any such tendency, and Henry's perfunctory attitude to sex was not calculated to stir latent passions.

No, the Mr Rights in her mind did not rip off her clothes and leap on her. They were very decorous, and rarely seen without the full uniform of evening dress. They were surrounded by roses.

They wore them in their button-holes, sent her huge bunches of them, and presented her with individual blooms at every meeting. They were usually seen across dinner tables, or on balconies against summer evening skies. They were tall and strong, their only weakness manifested in a certain mistiness in the eyes when they looked at her. They understood her, all of her.

And they did their job well. They kept her calm, they kept her off smoking, drinking and tranquillizers. They satisfied needs in her, whose existence her husband did not even suspect.

Henry also had needs unsatisfied, but his were different. His mind, like hers, was peopled by figures who had taken up residence in early adolescence and continued their occupation, with only cosmetic changes, through his messy wartime sexual encounters and the regularities of marriage. His squatters were female and as physical as Vera's were spiritual. In place of evening dress, they usually wore nothing. Any garments they did have were distinctly impermanent—blouses to be ripped open in a spatter of buttons, brassières with capitulating clasps, skirts that flew up at will, suspenders that unpopped at a finger's pressure, and briefs that melted away before his probing hands.

They were born, not of books, but of pictures. Postcards, on the whole. Grubby black and white scenes of ineptly posed women, faces leering with blank allure, bodies splayed out for the unknown viewer. Sometimes there were men, too, humourlessly thrusting away at them. Their plots were no less predictable than those of Vera's books, and the relief they supplied was just as effective, and just as harmless.

Henry kept his growing collection of pictures in the room designated his "study", in a locked filing cabinet. Its drawer was labelled "Accounts", a sufficient deterrent to Vera's curiosity, which was anyway not strong.

In the evenings, after supper, he would frequently go upstairs to "go through his accounts". On these occasions he would lock the study door, a needless precaution, because, if Vera did want to make contact, she would just shout to him up the stairs.

What he did with the contents of his "Accounts" drawer was his own affair. It caused no noticeable harm to his character or his marriage, and indeed may have helped to alleviate the pressures caused by their collision.

So both Henry and Vera had areas in their minds of privacy which could not be invaded, and from which they drew strength.

Henry had one other private area which could have been invaded by Vera at will, but one of the earliest ground-rules of their marriage forbade such intrusion, and Vera felt little urge to break the terms of the treaty.

His other secret was his diary. Every evening when he went to bed he would fill in the allotted space, and replace the book by the bedside, where it would remain all day. While he was at the office, Vera would clean around it, occasionally picking it up to dust its cover; never would she contemplate opening it. The notion did not occur to her that the diary might contain anything to surprise or alarm; she thought her husband's life as predictable as her own.

This lack of curiosity was completely justified. The nightly entries were no more than a catalogue of trains caught and clients met. Whole weeks would pass with the days' records indistinguishable. Every word was humdrum fact; there was no chronicle of emotions, no expression of aspirations, no comment on international or domestic events. Why he kept the diary at all was a mystery, probably even to himself. It was a habit he had got into while in the Forces, maybe in an attempt to differentiate, or at least to count, the soldier's identical days.

And when Henry Laker developed a habit, it stayed with him. So the diary stayed by the marriage bed, unread by Vera. It was, perhaps, a symbol of trust in a marriage otherwise devoid of symbols.

And so their lives continued. There were material changes. The children grew up. There was a bit more money around, and slowly Henry overcame his instinctive parsimony to the extent of keeping a bottle of sherry in the cupboard and taking the family on an annual holiday to the sea. They moved twice, each time to a slightly larger house.

And in each move, the filing cabinet moved to a new "study", its drawers firmly locked. As time went by, the "Accounts" section spread, first to two, then three, and finally all four drawers, reflecting the enrichment of Henry's fantasy life.

But this expansion of source material made only small changes to the voracious women who peopled his imagination. True, they came out of the shadows of monochrome into full colour, and their posing shook off all trace of inhibition, but the images in Henry's mind while he "went through his accounts" remained those of his adolescence, with the slightest of variations.

Vera's Mr Rights didn't alter much either. Their dinner jackets changed in cut, they even occasionally appeared on beaches in neatly-pressed leisurewear, their faces were moulded by the plastic surgery of imagination into the outlines of television stars, but their impeccable manners and—more important—their respect for, and understanding of, Vera remained exactly as when they had first visited her in her teens.

So, while marriage kept their bodies claustrophobically together, Henry and Vera Laker's minds drifted further and further apart.

But, even so, there need never have been a crisis, a moment when the clash of their fantasies detonated the explosion that led to murder. Plenty of marriages survive till death with the partners' private fantasies intact, secret hatreds, lusts and disappointments dying, unvoiced, with their owners.

And it could have happened with the Lakers.

But it didn't.

Partly, it was external pressures. The world they found themselves in in the late seventies was very different from the one they had married into in 1947. Sex was no longer a subject for secret mutterings, quiet talks and ambiguous allusions; it now screamed out from every hoarding, every cinema, even the hitherto decorous television screen.

Their children, in spite of an upbringing which had combined conventional morality with shamefaced obscurantism on the subject, had a completely different attitude to sex. For them it was another consumer product, something like the alcohol, records and clothes they so lavishly bought, something to be enjoyed. Any other view of it provoked derisive laughter and talk of "hang-ups".

The fact that their children were so patently—indeed blatantly—promiscuous made it hard for Henry and Vera not to feel their own attitudes were being challenged.

It was not a good time of life for either of them, anyway. Henry was nearly sixty, but the lusts of the body showed no signs of diminishing. On the contrary, they seemed stronger and less amenable to control. The provocation of a cinema poster or the unbrassièred relaxation of one of his sons' girlfriends could stir him in seconds to paroxysms which were but ill satisfied by "going through his accounts".

And now that naked girls lounged on every hoarding, the efficacy of his drawersful of pictures seemed impaired. Part of their potency for him had always been their secrecy. They were objects not readily available. They were his. Private. But now everyone could get them. He found more explicit material than his own collection under his fifteen-year-old son's bed. His imaginative life was diminished, sullied.

And, inevitably, as age encroached on his horizon, and the new world blared its message of instant fulfilment, he began to have doubts, to fear that perhaps he had not led his life as effectively as he could. Perhaps all the time he had spent "going through his accounts" had been a poor substitute for reality. As everything he read now screamed at him, the world was full of real flesh-and-blood women, hungry for men's attention.

Had he deluded himself all these years?

Had he missed out?

Vera's confusions resolved themselves into the same question. She found the physical changes of her late forties difficult to cope with; the long knowledge of their inevitability did not make the reality any easier. The body which she had managed so long without thinking about it suddenly became capable of cruel surprises.

And the mind which she had always subdued also threatened to become uncontrollable. She realized the precarious nature of the mental balance she had achieved in her adult life. Her old resource, the conjuration of a smiling Mr Right, was no longer adequate. Instead, her mind filled, unbidden, with images of different men, crude physical figures whose animal quality both appalled and intrigued her.

For the first time in her life, Vera Laker felt lust.

It wasn't focused; it had nothing to do with her continuing occasional couplings with Henry; it was just a fierce restlessness, stirred embarrassingly by the sight of a youth on a bicycle or the flash of a torso in a television commercial.

And this new imperative cast doubts on all her previous life.

Had she repressed her true nature all those years?

Had she missed out?

And yet it need not have led to murder. Plenty of couples suffer comparable pressures and regain individual equanimity and a mutual relationship. It was inevitably a time of stress: they could no longer ignore the fact that they were getting old; the children had left home and removed Vera's *raison d'être*; retirement loomed for Henry like a great void.

But they would have coped, had a bad couple of years, and then come through.

If it hadn't been for the diary.

It started as an accident, an accident that could have happened at any time during their marriage, but in fact came about after thirty years.

Vera was dusting the bedroom. She did this with the same ferocious doubt that now attended all her actions. Should she be doing it? In a world where strident women proclaimed their rights on television, wasn't she making herself a laughing-stock? Was she any better than a slave, a passive instrument of masculine will?

These self-lacerating thoughts, together with the pills her doctor (inevitably male) had patronizingly prescribed, made her clumsy, and, as her duster flicked savagely at the bedside table, it dislodged Henry's diary, which fell on to the carpet.

Open.

The entry was for about a month before.

"May 10th. Up 7.30. Office 9.15. 10.00 Meeting with Carson, Brown and Fuller. Lesley's farewell drinks in the Feathers at lunchtime. 3.00 Policy. Planning Group Meeting. Home 6.30. Watched some television. To bed 10.30."

It was not, to put it mildly, exciting. If that represented the worst secret that the forbidden room of this particular Bluebeard's castle contained, then his wife had little to fear. No grounds for anxiety. Even the one unknown name, Lesley, even if it were female and not a surname, belonged to someone who had clearly left the firm. To harbour suspicions about her would be obviously inappropriate.

And yet the name stuck in Vera's mind.

Along with the fiercely physical men who had gatecrashed her demure fantasies, had come women too. Not women to whom she felt attracted, but shadowy, silhouetted women, seen always in the distance with a man.

The man was Henry.

Again, the new public frankness was partly to blame. When every television play was about men having affairs, when women in newspapers and novels constantly denounced masculine deceit, it was natural for her to start wondering about Henry. He had always seemed so distant from her, so contained, so unromantic. Previously, she had just thought that that was his nature, but increasingly she began to wonder if he was like that because all his affections were directed to another woman. She knew nothing of his life from the moment he left the house in the morning to the moment of his return at six-thirty. She met his colleagues at the firm's annual dinner-and-dance, and other rare social occasions, but they talked about nothing except work. Anyway, they were hardly likely to volunteer information about an office romance of Henry's. Men conspired together in their deceit of women; every modern novel told her that.

So it was quite possible that Henry was conducting an affair with someone in the office.

More than possible, it was likely.

Had probably been going on for years.

Round the office everyone knew; and she, Henry's wife, stuck at home, the only one in ignorance, was a long-standing office joke. Sly, disparaging remarks were made about her every time Henry went off with . . .

Went off with who?

Now that she had read the diary, she could supply the name.

Lesley.

She didn't check back through the entries for further references. The one insight had been sufficient. Henry, for years, had been having an affair with Lesley.

This knowledge polarized her feelings for her husband. What had previously been acceptance and apathy was now stripped down to bare hatred. She found herself staring with fascinated loathing at the breadth of his neck as he, unthanking, ate the meals she prepared. As he dressed, unaware of her, in the mornings, she gazed at the porcine grossness of his bristly body.

To think that he had deceived her for so many years, had accepted all her care and work, while his mind was with Lesley. While he was thinking of being in bed with Lesley. And, no doubt, when he was actually in her bed, Lesley and Henry would laugh at the expense of Vera, poor, stupid, unknowing Vera.

It was only a matter of time before she mentioned Lesley's name. Something so constantly in her mind had eventually to be voiced.

It happened when Henry came home an hour late one evening, at seven-thirty rather than six-thirty. This was almost unprecedented in the long history of their marriage. He was hardly ever late without prior warning.

During that last hour's waiting, the day's hatred grew to an intensity that frightened Vera. Now there could be no doubt. Now he was blatantly staying out with his mistress.

His signature tune of key in the lock and slamming door announced his arrival. Vera was almost surprised; in her mind he was never going to come back. He had moved in with Lesley, might return for some clothes but basically had recognized the end of the marriage.

He stumped into the kitchen, where she stood, frozen, by the cooker.

"Delayed for an hour outside Clapham Junction," he snorted. "Some bloody fool had thrown himself on the line."

Vera laughed harshly. "Oh, you weren't with Lesley?" she found herself saying.

Henry looked up blankly. "Lesley?"

"Yes, Lesley. You know—Lesley!"

He still looked uncomprehending.

"The Lesley," she spelled out, "who used to work in your office, and who had a farewell drinks party on May the tenth."

Henry's face clouded with anger.

"Have you been reading my diary?"

The revelation of Vera's betrayal of trust had a profound effect on Henry. The long-established ground-rule of their marriage had been broken; now his wife might be capable of any perfidy. He felt absolved of all responsibility for her. He had looked after her for thirty years, and this was how she had thanked him.

But there was more to it than that. The moment had shaken him profoundly, and the strength of his perturbation was so great because she had mentioned Lesley. Not only mentioned her, but implied that Lesley was the sort of girl with whom he might have an affair.

Vera had in fact confirmed Henry's growing conviction, that he was the sort of man who should be having an affair with a young girl.

Because Lesley had affected him greatly during the short time she had worked in his office. It was guilt at his secret concupiscence that had prevented him from mentioning the farewell party to Vera, afraid lest some embarrassing blush might betray his thoughts.

Lesley had been eighteen, revelling in the new knowledge of the effect her body had on older men. She had dressed in the abandoned way all young girls now affected, fully aware of the magnetic contours of her free-hanging breasts and tight buttocks. Henry had not been the only man in the office driven almost apoplectic by her presence.

She had stayed briefly with the firm, quickly bored by insurance and anxious to flaunt her secretarial and other skills in the more glamorous worlds of advertising or television.

Henry had lusted after her fiercely whenever he saw her, though she did not replace the long-lease residents of his imagination. It was still the wild women of his adolescence with whom he "went through his accounts".

But Vera's betrayal changed that. Her belief that he could be having an affair reinforced his own. Henry's imaginings, like Vera's, now focused on the individual reality of Lesley.

It was a week before he did anything about it, a week of sliding concentration at the office and loaded silences at home.

Then, suddenly, he saw a way of reconciling the confusions in his mind, of mixing the now-inadequate charms of his old fantasies with the flesh-and-blood of Lesley.

It was through that organ of now-invaded privacy, his diary.

The idea came to him in a moment. When, after Vera's resentful supper, he had gone upstairs to "go through his accounts", he took the diary with him.

The filing cabinet drawers remained locked. He opened the diary, and started. He was surprised how easy it was, how natural. For the first time, his diary became a record, not of facts, but of thoughts. Two private areas merged.

"8 July. Up 7.30. Office 9.15. 11.00 Actuarial Review. Canteen lunch. Met Lesley there. She said she was desperate for me, and suggested I went back to her flat. We got a cab, and with great difficulty managed to keep our clothes on until we got to the flat. We were hardly inside the door before she was down on her knees, ripping open my fly and . . ."

He wrote on in the same vein for an hour. All the fantasies he had shared with the shadow-women of his teens were shared on the page with Lesley. He wrote on and on, spilling over the allocated space for the 8th of July, on and on. It was in the middle of August when he stopped.

He felt better than he had for years. Through the diary he had reconciled the demands of fantasy and reality; he felt an integrated personality.

And, also, he was taking a justified revenge on Vera. If she was going to read his diary, then he'd damned well give her something worth reading.

Surprisingly, it was a week before she opened the book again.

Every night for that week Henry retired upstairs after supper, and wrote with a demented concentration many a professional novelist would have envied. He reduced the size of his handwriting, fitting two lines where one was ruled, but by 14 July, he was mid-way through December and contemplating buying another diary.

It was, as it happened, on 14 July that Vera opened the book.

Again, really, it was an accident, the diary again displaced by reckless dusting. This time it fell open at the middle of September, the pages curling with the intense pressure of the pen that had covered them.

And this time Vera read everything.

At six-thirty she was waiting behind the front door for Henry's return. She carried a meat tenderizer.

It was when Henry turned to close the door that she hit him first. Then, as he fell, she just went on hitting him. When she stopped, exhausted, his head might have been a lump of meat.

Vera directed the police investigators to the diary, by way of explanation of her actions. That led them to interview Lesley at her latest job in an advertising agency.

She remembered Mr Laker's name from her time with the insurance company, but she couldn't remember which one he was or what he looked like. To her, they had all been just old men.

THE THIRTEENTH KILLER

THE WOMAN WALKED into St Mary's churchyard at a quarter past one in the morning on 13 February, and felt the crackle of money in her coat pocket. It was reassuring, but not reassuring enough. Not enough money, in fact. One five-pound note and four ones. The second man had said he only had four, and, since the job was done and he had threatened to throw her out of the car, she had been in no position to argue.

Just two punters—not a lot for a cold night's work. Two depressed kerb-crawlers, desperate for their perfunctory relief. She knew she had been working a bad pitch, but the other girls had been around for a long time and had territorial rights. Most of them had protectors to enforce those rights, too. Couldn't expect it to be easy starting up in a new town.

And she'd had to leave London. The size of the rents had driven her out of Soho, and none of the club-owners were going to offer her anything now her looks had gone. It was ironic to think that only eight years before she'd been Big Tony's girl and queened it at the Salamander Club. But cancer had wasted Big Tony away to nothing, the Salamander had been sold up and reopened as a specialist cinema club, and now she was just a tired old whore trying to make another start.

She'd chosen the town deliberately because of the Thirteenth Killer. Since he'd started his reign of terror, it was said that the girls were keeping off the streets. Meant there might be a chance for someone who was brave enough, or desperate enough, to move in and clean up. She was certainly desperate enough; she tried not to think about the need for bravery.

But nine pounds for a night's work was hardly cleaning up. The rent on her room was 23 a week. And it wasn't even a room she could work from; it was a good couple of miles from the best pickings. Besides, the landlord lived on the premises, and she'd soon be out on her ear if she started bringing men back. She'd tried to get a place in Nelson Avenue, the so-called "Red Light Area", but once again she had been up against a lot of girls with traditional rights. It meant her only chance was working the streets, working in cars, with all the attendant risks.

But she didn't let it depress her. Depression required the exercise of imagination, and that was something she had deliberately curbed all her life. She knew she would survive, and things might get better. That thought wasn't born of optimism—optimism again was a function of imagination—but it was a logical assessment of her chances.

Because now she had another source of income. A chance encounter had opened up new possibilities. Her hard face wrinkled into a smile as her worn-down heels clacked across the path between the tombstones.

She was so engrossed in her thoughts that she didn't see the tall figure detach himself from the yew tree's shadow. Nor did she hear his swift approach across the deadening grass beside the path.

The harsh smile was still on her lips as the brand-new bicycle chain was whipped over her head and snatched tight round her neck. Only a clicking noise came from her mouth as the hands in their blue rubber gloves pulled the chain tighter and tighter.

When she slumped, the tall figure, still maintaining the tension on her neck but keeping at arm's length, started to drag her body across the grass to the yew tree. Here he stopped and continued to pull on the chain with all his strength for a full three minutes.

Then he let the body drop to the ground. She lay dead on her side. He rolled her over on to her back, then the blue rubber fingers deftly straightened the legs and crossed the arms on her chest.

They reached into the pocket of his dark blue jacket and withdrew a polythene bag. From this they extracted a slip of blue paper. It was two inches long and one inch wide, and had been cut with kitchen scissors from a sheet of Basildon Bond Azure notepaper. In the middle of it were three words, typed in capitals by an IBM electric typewriter fitted with a Bookface Academic golf-ball.

The words were "THE THIRTEENTH KILLER".

The woman gaped horribly. Pushing down the swollen tongue with one blue rubber finger, he inserted the slip of paper into her mouth.

He looked round to see that there was no one in sight, checked that he had omitted nothing from the ritual with the corpse, then, keeping in the shadows of the wall, moved silently out of the churchyard.

The body would be discovered in the morning. And, when the police had examined it, there would be no doubt that the Thirteenth Killer had struck again.

At one twenty-five on the morning of 13 February, on the other side of St Mary's churchyard wall, Constable Norton spoke into his walkie-talkie. "Sergeant, just reporting that I've found the front door open at Wainwright's, the newsagents in Lechlade Road. I'm going in to investigate."

The tiny speaker crackled back at him. "Do you want me to get one of the squad cars round?"

"No, don't bother. Mr Wainwright's an absent-minded old sod at the best of times, and when he's been drinking . . . He's forgotten to lock up more than once before now. I'll go in and check. If I don't call again in fifteen minutes, then send a car round."

"Okay. As you know, we want all cars on the alert tonight for . . ."

"Yes, I know, it's the thirteenth. Cheerio, Sarge." The whole Police Force knew it was the 13th, the whole town knew, gradually the whole country was getting to know the date's significance.

The other murders had taken place on the 13th, the first two only a month apart, and then the third after a three-month gap. It had taken three for the pattern to become clear, three before the police got a special "Thirteenth Squad" organized to investigate, three before the press caught on and some reporter managed to extract the name, "The Thirteenth Killer", to swell his headlines.

Since then, nothing. Nine months had passed and vigilance naturally relaxed. The whores were slowly coming out on the streets again. It was Constable Norton's belief that the Thirteenth

Killer wouldn't strike again. The increased police effort, the publicity, it had all scared him off.

For nine months every cop in the town had been on the alert, his head ringing with "privileged information". That's what the Superintendent they put in charge of the Thirteenth Squad had called it—privileged information. They all knew about the stranglings with a bicycle chain, the laying-out of the bodies, the macabre message in the mouth on Basildon Bond Azure notepaper, typed by a Bookface Academic golf-ball. They even knew about the blue rubber gloves, which had left traces on the chains.

And they all knew they must never give away any of this privileged information. Not to their wives, not to their lovers, not to their priests, to no one. There was always the danger of some nut trying a carbon copy murder.

Constable Norton didn't expect a carbon copy murder by a nut, any more than he expected another authentic attack. In his view, the case was over, stale and over.

And, increasingly, the rest of the Force was coming round to his opinion. Oh, some of the young ones—like that Constable Tate— they still thought there'd be another. Tate obviously thought he was going to solve the case single-handed, kept volunteering for nights down round Nelson Avenue, even snooping there when he was off-duty. He saw himself as the great hero who was going to nail the bastard. He was young and ambitious.

Norton remembered when he had been like that, when he'd joined the Force and for his first few years in London. Seemed a long time ago. Anyway, he'd had to leave London. And he was better off here. Nice quiet manor most of the time, even a good chance of promotion. Married a few years back, two kids. Not as much money as back in the London days, but safer.

It took him five minutes to reach Wainwright's, the newsagents.

The door was locked, but he had a key that fitted. As he raised it to the lock, he noticed he was still wearing the blue rubber gloves.

They were safely in his trouser pocket when he knocked on Mr Wainwright's bedroom door. The old man took a bit of rousing from his alcohol- and pill-induced slumbers. He opened the door, half-heartedly clutching a poker, still too bleary even to be frightened.

"Don't worry, Mr Wainwright, it's only me, Constable Norton."

The old man grunted, uncomprehending.

"You left your front door unlocked again, you naughty boy."

"Oh. I thought I'd . . ."

"Well, you hadn't. Less of the bottle and a bit more concentration, me old lad, or you'll have all the villains in the area helping themselves to your takings."

"Yes, I . . ." The old man's head was aching. "What time is it?"

Norton flashed a look at his watch, deducted nine minutes, and said, "One twenty-six."

"Ah. I . . . should I come down and . . . ?"

"No, no, I'll slip the latch, don't worry. You just get back to bed. But don't let it happen again, eh?"

"No, I . . . er . . ." But, given permission to go back to bed, the old man was already on his way. As he slumped under the covers, he mumbled a "Thank you", and immediately started breathing deeply. Norton waited a couple of minutes until the breathing had swelled to snores, and then went back down to the shop.

That's the advantage of being a good cop, he thought wryly—knowing all the people on your manor, knowing who drinks too much, who's on sleeping pills, who's likely to be a bit vague about time.

He slipped the latch on the door and checked it was firmly locked, then looked at his watch. Twelve minutes since his last call to the station.

"Sergeant, Constable Norton. All okay at Wainwright's. As I thought, old fool had been hitting the bottle and forgot to lock up. So I gave him a telling-off and he's gone back to bed."

"Okay, Norton. Thanks for calling in. And don't forget, it's the thirteenth. Keep a look-out for . . ."

"Yes, Sarge, of course, Sarge." A brief pause. "You know, I don't think it's going to happen again."

"Don't tell anyone on the Thirteenth Squad, Norton, but, actually, neither do I."

As he paced his beat, Constable Norton went through what he had to do. The main thing was to keep calm, and he didn't think that'd be a problem. He'd been calm enough when he'd pocketed the Bookface Academic golf-ball from that insurance office where there'd been a break-in. He'd been calm enough when he sent his son out to buy a new bicycle chain; and calm enough when he'd said he'd broken it and sent the boy out for another. He'd been calm when he'd asked his wife to buy some rubber gloves for cleaning the car.

Come to that, he'd been calm enough while he killed the woman.

And he knew he'd had to do that. He'd been over the problem many times in the last three weeks, and he couldn't see any other way round it.

He'd thought, when he got transferred from the Metropolitan, he was okay. The bribery enquiries were getting close, but not close enough. He reckoned he got out just in time.

He'd been lucky, too. The only person who could really point the finger at him was Big Tony, and Big Tony had died of cancer just at the most convenient moment. So Norton had started in the new town with a clean slate, and seemed to be making a success of it.

Or rather, was making a success of it until he picked up the woman for soliciting. Her recognition of him had been instantaneous, and she'd come up with far too much detail of meetings at the Salamander Club, dates, times, the sums of money involved. What he'd expected to be a quick trip down to the station to charge her had ended with him pleading and agreeing to a hundred-pound pay-off the next night.

There had been another pay-off each week since then. Three hundred quid. That was a lot on his pay. The wife hadn't yet realized what was happening to their savings; when she did, he'd have to invent some story about losing it on the horses.

But it couldn't go on like that. The woman was likely to get more greedy rather than less. She was used to a lot of money from her days with Big Tony, and the idea of screwing it out of a cop was one that would appeal to her.

It was after the first pay-off that he had thought of the Thirteenth Killer idea, and the more he thought about the idea, the better it seemed.

The woman was, after all, an ideal victim. Shiftless, unattached, a prostitute like the others. A second-class citizen, the sort whom most of the population righteously reckoned invited danger by her choice of work. No one would mourn her and, so long as the details of the murder were right, no one would be suspected, except for the Thirteenth Killer. The press would have a field day, the whores would go back off the streets for a few weeks, and one more unsolved murder would join a sequence that Norton reckoned had already stopped.

So he just had to keep calm, and it'd be all right. Sure, he'd be questioned, because the murder had taken place on his patch, but he knew who'd do the questioning and he knew they'd be sympathetic. The Thirteenth Killer had made a point of doing the other women in well-patrolled areas, but no one in the Force wanted to draw attention to this. The police were already looking silly enough, as the deaths accumulated.

No, it'd be all right.

He didn't think the body would be found till daylight. A lot of commuters went through St Mary's churchyard on their way to the station. Norton went off duty at six, so he didn't reckon he'd be called to the scene of the crime.

The only important thing he had to do was to get rid of the blue rubber gloves. And that had to be managed with care. He knew enough about the workings of the forensic boys—once again his "privileged information" was helping—to realize the traces he might have left on the gloves, prints, minute hairs, a whole collection of microscopic clues that could link him to the murder.

He also knew, from his own tedious experience, the detail of the police searches that would follow the discovery of the woman's body. To dispose of the gloves anywhere on his beat would be too risky.

But he had planned for that, too. He felt a glow of satisfaction as he contemplated the extent of his planning.

The gloves had to be burnt. Burnt with intense heat until they congealed, melted, and were consumed.

And they were going to be burnt in the one place where police investigators would never look for them.

He continued evenly pacing his beat.

It wasn't yet light at six-fifteen as he approached the back entrance of the police station. The welcome blast of heat from the antiquated radiators greeted him as he walked inside.

He smiled at the irony. The heating system at the Station had long been scheduled for modernization, but the work kept being delayed. And as long as it was delayed, the old coal-fired boiler remained roaring away in the basement. Right next to the constables' locker room.

All he had to do was go downstairs and slip the gloves under the lid of the boiler. There'd be nobody around. The other constables would have nipped into the locker room sharp at six and already be on their way home or warming up with cups of tea in the canteen.

As he walked along towards the basement stairs, a WPC came rushing along the corridor. "Sensible lad, Norton," she said, "coming in the back way."

"What do you mean?"

"Can't get through the reporters at the front."

"Eh?"

"Haven't you heard? The Thirteenth Killer's struck again!"

And she hurried on.

He assessed how hard the news had hit him. So . . . someone had found the woman's body earlier than he had expected. So . . . his interrogation would come that much earlier.

But it didn't worry him. He still felt calm. He could cope.

Just get rid of the gloves, and he could cope.

He had started down the stairs when Constable Tate came bursting out of the Operations Room. The youth was transformed. He walked ten feet tall and positively glowed with triumph. "Norton," he shouted, "have you heard?"

The urge to get down to the boiler was strong, but Norton curbed it. Act naturally. Act naturally, and everything will be all right.

He managed a wry grin. "Yes, Tate, I've heard. The Thirteenth Killer has struck again. I take it all back. You were right and I was wrong."

"Thank you. Very decent of you to say so."

"So now all that remains is for us to find the bastard."

"But we have!"

"What?"

"Or rather *I* have."

"You . . . ?"

"I was patrolling Nelson Avenue at half-past twelve and I actually saw the attack. Had to chase the bastard for miles, but I got him! Caught him absolutely red—no, get it right—caught him *blue*-handed! Isn't it great news? He's in the . . . Here, are you all right?"

Norton was not all right. The shock hit him like a punch in the stomach and he vomited instantly.

"Good God, you poor soul. Have you got a handkerchief? Let me mop you up."

"No, I . . ."

But Norton was too weak to stop Constable Tate from reaching into the trouser pocket. He just swayed feebly against the wall as the young man drew out the rolled pair of blue rubber gloves.

It was at that moment that everyone came rushing out of the Operations Room with news of another sensation.

A woman's body had been found in St Mary's churchyard.

DON'T KNOW MUCH ABOUT ART

I HAVE BEEN described as not very bright. Partly, I reckon, it's my size. People who look like me have appeared as dumb villains in too many movies and television series. And if you've had a background as a professional wrestler, you find the general public doesn't have too many expectations of you as an intellect.

Also, I have to face it, there have been one or two unfortunate incidents in my past. Jobs that didn't turn out exactly like they was planned. Like when I was in the getaway car outside that bank and I drove off with the wrong passengers. Or when I got muddled after that bullion robbery and delivered it all back to the security firm. Or when I wrote my home address on that ransom demand. Okay, silly mistakes, sort of thing anyone could do in the heat of the moment, but I'm afraid it's the kind of thing that sticks in people's minds and I have got a bit of a reputation in the business as a dumbo.

Result of it all is, most of the jobs I get tend to be—to put it mildly—intellectually undemanding. In fact, the approach of most of the geysers who hire me seems to be, "We couldn't find a blunt instrument, so you'll have to do."

Now, of course, my own view of my mental capacity doesn't exactly coincide with that, but a chap has to live, and a recession isn't the time you can afford to be choosy. I mean, you read all this about rising crime figures, but you mustn't get the impression from that that villains are doing well. No, we feel the pinch like anyone else. For a start, there's a lot more blokes trying to muscle in. Side-effect of unemployment, of course, and most of them are really amateurs, but they do queer the pitch for us professionals. They undercut our rates and do bring into the business a kind of dishonesty that I'm sure wasn't there when I started. The cake isn't that much bigger than it ever was, and there's a hell of a lot more blokes trying to get slices.

Result is, I take anything I'm offered . . . driving, bouncing, frightening, looming (often booked for looming I am, on account of my size). No, I'll do anything. Short of contract killing. Goes against my principles, that and mugging old ladies. As I say, it's no time to be choosy. When this country's got more than three million unemployed, you just got to put off your long-term ambitions, forget temporarily about career structure, and be grateful you got a job of any sort.

So when I was offered the Harbinger Hall job, never crossed my mind to turn it down. Apart from anything else, it sounded easy and the pay was bloody good. Five grand for a bit of petty larceny . . . well, that can't be bad, can it? Sure, there was always the risk of getting nicked, but didn't look like there'd be any rough stuff. Mind you, never be quite sure in stately homes. Tend to be lots of spears and shotguns and that stuck on the walls, so there's always the danger that someone might have a fit of temperament and cop hold of one of those.

Still, five grand for a weekend's work in a slow autumn was good money.

The initial contact come through Wally Clinton, which I must say surprised me. It was Wally I was driving to Heathrow after that jeweller's job the time I run out of petrol, so I didn't think I was exactly his Flavour of the Month. Still, shows how you can misjudge people. Here he was letting bygones be bygones and even putting a nice bit of work my way. Take back all that I said about him at the Black Dog last New Year's Eve.

Anyway, so Wally gets in touch, asks if I'm in the market and when I says yes, tells me to go and meet this bloke, "Mr Loxton" in this sauna club off St Martin's Lane.

Strange sauna club it was. Not a girl in sight. I think it actually must've been for geysers who wanted to have saunas. All neat and tidy, no little massage cubicles with plastic curtains, no funny smell, no nasty bits of screwed-up tissue on the floor. Most peculiar.

Bloke on the door was expecting me. Give me a big white towel and showed me into a changing room that was all very swish with pine and clean tiles. He told me to take my clothes off, put on the towel and go into the sauna. Mr Loxton would join me shortly.

Don't mind telling you, I felt a bit of a grapefruit sitting on this wooden shelf with nothing on but this towel. When I first went in I sat on the top shelf, but blimey it was hot. Soon realized it got cooler the lower you went, so I went to the bottom one. Still uncomfortably hot, mind. Geyser my size really sweats when he sweats.

I tried to work out why Mr Loxton had chosen this place for the meet. I mean, a sauna's good if you're worried the opposition might've got shooters. Isn't anywhere you can put one when you've got your clothes off. Nowhere comfortable, anyway. But this wasn't that kind of encounter.

On the other hand, it wasn't bad if you didn't want to be identified. The lights in the sauna was low and it was a bit steamy. Also, people don't look the same when they're starkers. Oh, I know they do lots of corpse identification from secret birthmarks and moles on the body and that, but the average bloke without clothes on looks very different. For a start, next time you see him, chances are he'll be dressed, and you'd be surprised how many clues you get to what a person's like from what they wear. I reckoned Mr Loxton was meeting there to maintain the old incog.

I felt even more sure of that when he come in. He had a big towel round him under his armpits like me, but he also got a small one draped over his head like a boxer. He didn't turn his face towards me, but immediately went over to a wooden bucket in the corner, picked out a ladleful of water and poured it over this pile of stones. Well, that really got the steam going, and when he did turn towards me, he wasn't no more than a blur.

"You are Billy Gorse."

I admitted it. Wasn't spoken like a question, anyway, more a statement.

"Thank you for coming. Wally Clinton recommended you for a job that needs doing."

He might have hid his face with all the towels and the steam, but he had a voice that was really distinctive. Private school, you know, and a bit prissy. I'm good with voices. Knew I'd recognize his if I ever heard it again.

I stayed stumm, waiting for the details, and he went on. "What I want you to do, Gorse, is to steal a painting."

"Blimey," I said, "I don't know much about art."

"You don't need to."

"But surely . . . paintings . . . I mean specialist work, isn't it? Not like walking in and nicking someone's video. If a painting's any good, it's got security systems all round it. And then finding a fence who'll handle them sort of goods—"

"All that side is taken care of. All I said I wanted you to do was to steal a painting."

"You mean I'd be, like, part of a gang?"

"There's no need for you to know anything about anyone else involved. All you have to do is to follow instructions without question."

"I can do that."

"Good. Wally said you could. You do the job on the last weekend of October."

"Where?"

"Have you heard of Harbinger Hall?"

I shook my head.

"Then I suppose you haven't heard of the Harbinger Madonna either."

"Who's she?"

"'She' is the painting you are going to steal."

"Oh. Well, like I said, I don't know much about art."

"No." His voice sounded sort of pleased about that. Smug.

He asked me where he could send my instructions. I nearly give him my home address, but something told me hold my horses, so I give him the name of Red Rita's gaff. She often holds mail for me, on account of services rendered what I needn't go into here.

Then Mr Loxton reached into his towel and pulled out a polythene bag. Thought of everything, he did. Didn't want the notes to get damp.

"Five hundred in there. Two thousand when you get your instructions. Second half on completion of the job." He rose through the steam. "Stay here another ten minutes. If you appear in the changing room before I've left the building, the contract's cancelled." He reached for the door handle.

"Oh, Mr Loxton . . ."

His reaction was that half-second slow, which confirmed that he wasn't using his real name. No great surprise. Very few of the geysers I deal with do. Not for me, that. Always stick to "Billy Gorse". Only time I tried anything different, I forgot who I was half-way through the job.

"What did you want, Mr Gorse?"

I'd got what I wanted, but I said, "Oh, just to say thank you for the job, Mr Loxton."

He done a sort of snort and walked out the sauna.

Long ten minutes it was in that heat. When I come out I was sweating like a Greek cheese.

Instructions come the following week as per. I went down Red Rita's for reasons that aren't any of your business and after a bit, she give me this thick brown envelope. Just my name on it. No stamps, nothing like that. Just come through her letter-box. She didn't see who dropped it.

I didn't open it till I got back to my place next morning. First I counted the money. Fifties, forty of them all present and correct. Then there was this postcard of some bird in blue with this nipper on her knee. That was presumably the picture I was going to nick. I didn't take much notice of it, but unfolded the typewritten sheet of instructions.

No mention of my name and they wasn't signed either. Plain paper, no other clues to where it might've come from. It was all typed in capital letters, which I must say got my goat a bit. Reckon Wally Clinton'd been casting aspersions on my literacy, the cheeky devil. Anyway, what I had to do was spelled out very clear.

FIRST—FILL IN THE ENCLOSED BOOKING FORM, BOOKING YOURSELF INTO THE "STATELY HOME WEEKEND" AT HARBINGER HALL FOR 29 AND 30 OCTOBER. SEND THE FULL PAYMENT BY MONEY ORDER. (ALL YOUR EXPENSES WILL BE REPAID.)

SECOND—THIS FRIDAY, 21 OCTOBER, TRAVEL DOWN TO HARBINGER HALL AND TAKE THE CONDUCTED TOUR OF THE

BUILDING (THESE RUN EVERY HOUR ON THE HOUR BETWEEN
10 A.M. AND 4 P.M.). WHEN YOU REACH THE GREAT HALL,
LOOK CAREFULLY AT THE PAINTING OF THE MADONNA, NOTING
THE VISIBLE SECURITY ARRANGEMENTS AROUND IT.

WHEN THE TOUR REACHES THE END OF THE LONG GALLERY
UPSTAIRS, LINGER BEHIND THE GROUP. AS THE REST OF THEM
GO INTO THE BLUE BEDROOM, OPEN THE DOOR LABELLED
"PRIVATE" AT THE END OF THE GALLERY. YOU WILL FIND
YOURSELF AT THE TOP OF A SMALL STAIRCASE. GO DOWN THIS
QUICKLY AND YOU WILL FIND YOURSELF IN A SMALL LOBBY.
ON THE WALL OPPOSITE THE FOOT OF THE STAIRS YOU WILL
SEE THE BOXES CONTROLLING THE BUILDING'S ALARM SYSTEM.
THESE ARE OPERATED BY A KEY, BUT YOU WILL SEE THE WIRES
WHICH COME OUT OF THE TOP OF THE BOXES. WHEN YOU
ACTUALLY COME TO STEAL THE MADONNA, YOU WILL CUT
THROUGH THESE WIRES. HAVING SEEN THEIR POSITION,
RETURN AS QUICKLY AS POSSIBLE UP THE STAIRS AND REJOIN
YOUR GROUP. COMPLETE THE REST OF THE TOUR AND RETURN
HOME WITHOUT FURTHER INVESTIGATION.

FURTHER INSTRUCTIONS WILL FOLLOW NEXT WEEK.
MEMORIZE THE DETAILS IN THESE SHEETS AND THEN BURN
THEM.

I done like I was told and before the Friday I got a confirmation of
my booking on this "Stately Home Weekend". I read the brochure
on that and I must say it didn't really sound my scene. Tours of the
grounds, lectures on the history of the place, full medieval banquet
on the Saturday night, farewell tea with Lord Harbinger on the
Sunday. I mean, my idea of a fun weekend is going down Southend
with a few mates and putting back a few beers. Still, I'd put up with
a lot for five grand.

So, the Friday I do as I'm told. Get the train out to Limmerton, and
from there they've got this courtesy bus takes you out to Harbinger
Hall.

Not a bad little gaff old Lord Harbinger's got, I'll say that for
him. Don't know any more about architecture than I do about art,

but I can tell it's old. Don't build places like that nowadays, not with blooming great pillars in front of the door and all them windows and twiddly bits on the roof.

Nice position and all. It's high, like on top of this hill, looking out over all the rest of the countryside. That's how you first see it in the bus from the station. As you get nearer, you lose sight for a bit, because it's a really steep hill with trees. So you sort of zigzag up this drive, which is really a bit hairy and makes you glad the old bus's got decent brakes. And then suddenly you come out the top and suddenly you're right in front of the house and it's blooming big. And there's car parks off to the right and left, but the bus drops you pretty well by the front door.

I looked around as I got out. You know, some of these stately homes've got sort of zoos and funfairs and that, you know, a bit of entertainment. And, since I had to spend a whole weekend there, I thought it'd be nice to know there'd be something interesting to do. But no such luck. Place hadn't been developed like that. Maybe the grounds wasn't big enough.

In fact, not only hadn't the place been developed, it looked a bit tatty. I mean that sort of place isn't my style. Blimey, if I owned it, I'd knock it down and put up a nice executive Regency-style townhouse with double garage and Italian suite bathroom. But even I could tell this one needed a few grand spending on it.

And if my busload was anything to go by, the few grand wasn't going to come very quickly from tourists. Okay, end of the season and that, but there wasn't many of us. Had to wait around till a few more come from the car parks before they'd start our guided tour, and then it was only about a dozen of us. Well, at a couple of sovs a head, takes you a long time to make money that way.

The guide that took us round had done the trip a few thousand times and obviously hadn't enjoyed it much even the first time. The spiel come out like a recording, jokes and all. Didn't look a happy man.

And what he said was dead boring. I never got on with history at school, couldn't see the percentage in it, so all his cobblers about what Duke built which bit and when didn't do a lot for me. And to think that I'd got a whole weekend of lectures on it coming up. I began to think I was going to earn my five grand.

Anyway, eventually we get to the Great Hall, and I see this picture all the fuss is about. Didn't go for it much on the postcard; the real thing's just the same, only bigger. Not big, though, compared to some of the numbers they got on the walls. I don't know, two foot by eighteen inches maybe. Don't know why they wanted to nick this one. Some of them was ten times the size, must've been worth a lot more. Still, not my decision. And a good thing, come to think of it, that they didn't want me to walk out with one of the twenty-foot numbers under my arm.

So the picture's just this Mum and her sprog. Frame was nice, mind. All gold and wiggly, like my brother-in-law's got round the cocktail bar in his lounge. And at the bottom of the frame there's this little brass plate nailed on. It says:

MADONNA AND CHILD
Giacomo Palladino
Florentine
(1473–1539)

Never heard of the git myself.

Anyway, I'd memorized my instructions like a good boy, so I have a good butcher's at the pic. Can't see a lot in the way of security. I mean, there's a sort of purple rope strung between uprights to keep the punters six feet away from the wall, but that isn't going to stop anyone. Of course, there might be some photo-electric beam or some rocker device what sounds the alarm if you actually touch the thing. I step over the rope to take a closer look.

"Art-lover, are we, sir?" asks this sarcastic voice behind me.

I turn round and see this bloke in uniform. Not the guide, he's up the other end blathering about some king or other. No, this geyser's just some sort of security guard I noticed hanging around when we arrived.

"No," I says, with what people have described as my winning smile. "Don't know a blind thing about art."

"Then why are you studying the Madonna so closely?"

I'm about to say that I'm just interested in what security arrangements she got, and then I twig that this might not be so clever, so I do this big shrug and step back over the rope and join up with the other punters. I glance back as we're leaving the hall and this guard's giving me a really beady look.

Upstairs I follow the instructions without sweat. Dawdle doing the old untied shoe-lace routine while the rest troop in to hear the history of the Blue Bedroom, quick look round to see I'm on my own in the gallery, then through the old "Private" door and down the stairs.

It's just like they said it would be. These big metal-covered boxes opposite me with coloured lights and chrome keyholes on them. And at the top the wires. Not that thick. Quick snip with the old metal-cutters. No prob.

I think for a minute. I know some of these systems got a sort of fail-safe so's they sound off if anyone tampers with the wiring. For a moment I wonder if someone's trying to set me up. Certainly are one or two geysers what I have sort of inadvertently offended in the course of my varied career, but this'd be a bloody elaborate way of getting their own back. Anyway, there's the two and a half grand I already got. Nobody's going to spend that kind of bread just to fix me. I hurry back upstairs again.

I've just closed the door when I see the security guard coming in the other end of the Long Gallery. Don't know whether he saw me or not, but he still looks beady. "Looking for something, sir?" he calls out, sarcastic again.

"Little boys' room," I say, and nip along to the Blue Bedroom.

Next package arrives the Wednesday, three days before I'm due on my Stately Home Weekend. I'm actually round at Red Rita's when we hear it plop through the letter-box, but needless to say by the time I open the front door to see who brought it, there's nobody in sight.

Since the whole thing's getting a bit close and Red Rita's tied up with someone else, I open the package there. There's money in it, which I wasn't expecting this time. It's in fives and ones and a bit of change and covers my expenses so far. What I paid to book the weekend, return fare London to Limmerton, even the two quid for my guided tour. Someone's done their research. Makes me feel good. Nice to know you're dealing with geysers who knows what's what. There's a lot of berks in this business.

As well as the money there's a car key. Just one, on a little ring attached to a plain yellow plastic tag. And of course there's the instructions. Block capitals again, which miffs me a bit. Again, they're so clear an idiot could understand them. I wonder if someone's trying to tell me something.

ON THE MORNING OF SATURDAY 29 OCTOBER AT 9 A.M., GO TO THE UNDERGROUND CAR PARK IN CAVENDISH SQUARE. THERE, IN BAY NUMBER 86, YOU WILL FIND A RED PEUGEOT WHICH YOU CAN OPEN AND START WITH THE ENCLOSED KEY. ON THE BACK SEAT WILL BE A LARGE SUITCASE, TO WHICH YOU WILL TRANSFER YOUR CLOTHES, ETC. FOR THE WEEKEND. *DO NOT REMOVE ANYTHING FROM THE SUITCASE.*

IN THE GLOVE COMPARTMENT OF THE CAR YOU WILL FIND MONEY TO PAY THE PARKING CHARGE. DRIVE DIRECTLY TO HARBINGER HALL. GIVEN NORMAL TRAFFIC CONDITIONS, YOU SHOULD ARRIVE THERE AT ABOUT HALF-PAST TWELVE, JUST IN TIME FOR THE BUFFET LUNCH WHICH OPENS THE STATELY HOME WEEKEND.

DURING THE WEEKEND TAKE PART IN ALL THE ACTIVITIES OFFERED AND GENERALLY BEHAVE AS NATURALLY AS POSSIBLE. ABOVE ALL, DO NOT DRAW ATTENTION TO YOURSELF.

THE MOMENT FOR THE THEFT OF THE MADONNA WILL COME LATE ON THE SUNDAY AFTERNOON WHEN THE TOUR GUESTS ARE ABOUT TO LEAVE. AT THE END OF THESE OCCASIONS THE TRADITION HAS DEVELOPED OF LORD HARBINGER, HIS FAMILY AND STAFF LINING UP IN THE FRONT HALL TO SAY GOODBYE TO THEIR GUESTS. THE PREMISES WILL BE CLEARED OF DAY VISITORS BY FOUR O'CLOCK ON THIS, THE LAST DAY OF THE SEASON. THERE WILL BE NO STAFF GUARDING THE MADONNA.

FOLLOW THESE INSTRUCTIONS EXACTLY. AFTER TEA WITH LORD HARBINGER, THE STATELY HOME WEEKEND GUESTS ARE GIVEN HALF AN HOUR TO PACK AND ASKED TO APPEAR IN THE FRONT

HALL AT SIX TO SAY THEIR GOODBYES AND GET THE COACH TO THE STATION OR GO TO THEIR OWN CARS. DO ANY PACKING YOU HAVE TO AND GO DOWN TO THE FRONT HALL AT TEN TO SIX, *LEAVING YOUR SUITCASE IN YOUR BEDROOM.* WHEN MOST OF THE OTHER GUESTS ARE DOWNSTAIRS, MAKE A SHOW OF REMEMBERING YOUR SUITCASE AND HURRY BACK TO YOUR BEDROOM TO GET IT. *THE NEXT BIT HAS TO BE DONE QUICKLY.* GO FROM THE PRIVATE APARTMENTS TO THE LONG GALLERY AND DOWN THE STAIRCASE TO THE ALARM BOXES. CUT THROUGH THE WIRES AT THE TOP OF THE BOXES. THERE IS A DOOR TO THE RIGHT OF THESE WHICH LEADS DIRECTLY INTO THE GREAT HALL. GO THROUGH, GO STRAIGHT TO THE MADONNA AND REPLACE THE ORIGINAL PAINTING WITH THE COPY IN YOUR SUITCASE. IT WILL JUST BE A MATTER OF UNHOOKING THE PICTURE AT THE BACK. WITH THE ALARMS NEUTRALIZED, THERE ARE NO OTHER RESTRAINING DEVICES.

PUT THE ORIGINAL PAINTING IN YOUR SUITCASE AND RETURN UPSTAIRS THE WAY YOU CAME. GO BACK TO YOUR ROOM AND THEN GO DOWN THE MAIN STAIRCASE TO THE FRONT HALL. THE WHOLE OPERATION SHOULD TAKE YOU LESS THAN FIVE MINUTES AND WILL NOT BE NOTICED IN THE CONFUSION OF THE GUESTS' GOODBYES. JOIN IN WITH THESE AND BEHAVE PERFECTLY NATURALLY. ALLOW ONE OF THE STAFF TO TAKE YOUR SUITCASE OUT TO YOUR CAR, AND ASK HIM TO PUT IT ON THE BACK SEAT.

DRIVE STRAIGHT BACK TO LONDON. RETURN THE CAR TO THE CAVENDISH SQUARE GARAGE, PARKING IT IN BAY 86 OR AS NEAR TO THAT AS YOU CAN GET. REMOVE YOUR OWN BELONGINGS FROM THE SUITCASE, BUT LEAVE THE CASE ITSELF AND THE PAINTING, ALONG WITH THE CAR KEY AND PARKING TICKET INSIDE. THEN LOCK THE CAR BY PRESSING DOWN THE LOCKING BUTTON INSIDE AND CLOSING THE DOOR WITH THE HANDLE HELD OUT.

WHEN YOU RETURN TO THE ADDRESS USED BEFORE, YOU WILL FIND THE SECOND TWO AND A HALF THOUSAND POUNDS WAITING FOR YOU.

AS BEFORE, MEMORIZE THESE INSTRUCTIONS *AND BURN THEM.*

ow I got my principles, but crime is my business and it's a sort of
atural reaction for me to have a look at any plan what comes up
id see if there's anything in it for me. You know, anything extra,
ver and above the basic fee.

And, having read my instructions, I couldn't help noticing that,
ssuming all went well with the actual nicking, from the moment I
ft Harbinger Hall on the Sunday night I was going to be in
mporary possession of an extremely valuable painting.

Now I been in my line of work long enough to know that nasty
ings can happen to villains carrying off the goods. You hear cases
f them being hi-jacked by other gangs, mugged, somehow getting
st on the way to their handover, all that. And though I didn't
incy any of those happening to me, I wasn't so down on the idea of
iem *appearing* to happen to me. I mean, if I'm found on the
oadside with the side of my motor bashed in, a bump on my head
id the suitcase gone, the bosses won't be able to *prove* I knew the
oke who done it.

Don't get me wrong. I wasn't planning anything particular, just
ort of going through the possibilities in my mind. Like I said, I
on't know anything about art, but I do know that you need
xtremely specialized help if you're trying to unload a well-known
tolen painting.

One of the advantages of Red Rita's line of work is that she does
et to meet a big variety of people and when I mentioned, casual
ke, that I wanted a bit of background on the art scene, it turned
ut she did just happen to know this geyser who was a dealer in the
ess public transactions of international art-collectors. And he was
nother of the many who owed her a favour and yes, she'd be quite
appy to fix up a meet. For me, darling, anything.

suppose I shouldn't have been surprised, if I'd thought about it. I
iean, bent bookies are still bookies, bent solicitors do their stuff in
olicitors' offices, but I really hadn't expected a bent art dealer to
vork out of a posh little gallery off Bond Street. Still, that was the
ddress Red Rita give me, and when I got there it seemed that Mr
Depaldo was expecting me. The sniffy tart at the desk said she
vould just check he was free and left me looking at a series of pics of

what seemed to be a nasty accident in the kitchens of a Chines
restaurant. I don't know how people buy that stuff. I mean, if yo
can't tell what it's meant to be, how do you know you're not bein
taken for a ride? Don't get me wrong, I'm not against all art. M
brother-in-law's got this collection of sunsets painted on blac
velvet and with those, well, you can *see* they're good. But a lot (
this modern stuff . . . forget it.

So I'm shown up to Mr Depaldo's poncy little office, and he's
real smoothie. Striped shirt, bow tie, you know the number. If
didn't know about his connection with Red Rita. I'd have put hir
down as a wooftah.

But her hold is clearly strong. Plain from the start he don't war
to see me, but Rita's threatened to blow the lid on something if h
won't. So he just about managed to be polite.

I ask him if it's possible to sell a stolen picture and he says
through a lot of unnecessary grammar, that it is.

Then I mention the Harbinger Madonna, and he sort of perks u
like a conman spotting a mark. And I ask him how much h
reckons it's worth.

"Well, it's hard to tell. Prices at auction are so unpredictable.
mean, there aren't many Palladinos around, certainly no others c
that quality. The last one to come on the market was a Sain
Sebastian back in sixty-eight. Went to eight hundred."

Didn't seem that much to me. I mean, paying me five grand an
only getting eight hundred for the goods, well, that's no way to rur
a whelk-stall.

Old Depaldo must've twigged what I was thinking, because h
says, rather vinegary, "Eight hundred *thousand*, of course. But tha
was fifteen years ago. And an inferior work. If the Madonna cam
to auction now, she must go to at least two."

"Two?" I queried, not wanting to be caught out again.

"Million."

"That's at auction?"

"Yes, Of course, a . . . private deal wouldn't realize nearly a
much."

"Like what?"

You know, all fences give you the same pause before they com p with a figure. Doesn't matter if you're talking a colour telly, a orryload of booze or a "Last Supper", they all hesitate before they heat you. "Maybe one. Say seven hundred and fifty to be safe."

Even if he'd been telling the truth, it sounded like a lot of money. Made my five grand for actually taking the risk and doing the job ook a bit pathetic.

"And if it did . . . become available, you could handle it?"

He nodded, looking sort of eager. Obviously he knew there was a ot more in it for him than he let on. "There are only two people in London who could make the arrangements, and I'm one of them."

"But I'm the first one who's talked to you about it?"

"Yes."

So perhaps my bosses had got a deal set up with the other geyser. What's your commission rate, by the way?"

"Sixty per cent," he says, cool as an ice-cream down the neck. You see, in these matters the risk must be judged in relation to ow much one has to lose."

Meaning he'd got his poncy gallery and his sniffy tart downstairs nd his international reputation; and I was just a cheap heavy. I let t pass. Reckoned I could work out some fine tuning on the figures ater if it became necessary.

"Any idea," he asks, really keen now, "when this exceptional roperty might come on the market?"

"No," I tell him. "Only asking for information, aren't I?"

He looks a bit miffed.

"But if it ever was to come up," I go on, "you'd be interested in andling it?"

"Oh yes," he says.

I haven't made any plans yet, mind. But it is nice to have things orted out in case you need them.

Saturday morning I do like a good boy should. Get to Cavendish Square car park on the nose of nine, find the car in Bay 86. Red Peugeot, like they said. Ordinary saloon, not one of the hatchback obs. The key opens the door and fits the ignition. I try it on the oot, which seems to be locked, but it doesn't fit. Needs a different key. Never mind.

On the back seat there's this suitcase as per. One of those that sor
of opens up like a big wallet with a zip three-quarters of the wa
round. Then inside there's straps to hold your clothes in. One side
strapped in, is this hard rectangular package wrapped in cloth. Go
to be the copy of the painting, but I don't think it's the moment t
have a dekko. I take my gear out of the polythene carrier I got it i
and strap the lot in the other side. Just clothes, shaving tackle. An
a pair of metal-cutters. Oh, and a thing called a priest. Little stic
with a weighted tip. Fishermen use them to finish off fish. Mine'
clobbered a few slimy customers in its time, and all. Wouldn't eve
carry a shooter, but the priest's handy.

Car starts first turn of the key, so I reckon it had only been lef
there that morning. In the glove compartment there's the parkin
ticket. Clocked in 8:12. Pity I hadn't thought to arrive earlier. B
nice to know who I was dealing with, apart from the steamy "M
Loxton".

There was the right money in the glove compartment for th
parking. Seemed a bit steep for such a short stay, and I mentioned
this to the bloke at the barrier.

"Rates just gone up, mate. Here's the new tariff." And he giv
me a printed sheet with my receipt.

I shoved it in my pocket. I should worry. Wasn't my money I wa
spending.

I never really thought it would be, but the Stately Home Weekend
was way off my scene. I mean, we was treated all right, you know
all the staff deferential and that, trying to give you the feeling o
being privileged, but you got the feeling they didn't really mean it
like they was sniggering behind their hands all the time.

Okay, some things we was allowed to do that the ordinary
day-trippers wasn't. We could leave our cars directly in front of the
house, we could go through most of the doors marked "Private",
we was actually allowed to *sit* on the chairs. But all the time they
was pretending to treat us like regular house party guests, the staff
seemed to be just watching out for us to make fools of ourselves. I
mean, like turning up in the wrong clothes or not picking the right
knives and forks at meals, they really seemed to be on the lookout

for that sort of thing. And I'm afraid for me it was particularly difficult. Social graces didn't figure large in the Borstal educational curriculum.

Mind you, the other punters seemed to lap it up. I saw they was getting the old sneers from the staff just as much as I was, but they didn't seem to notice. They really thought they was being treated just like house guests, like they was there by personal invite of Lord Harbinger and not paying through the nose for the privilege of lounging around his gaff and seeing him for a rationed hour and a half of tea and farewells on the Sunday afternoon.

Also, let's face it, they wasn't really my sort of people. I daresay I got a lot of flaws in my character, but one thing nobody's ever called me is a snob. And that's what this lot was, every one of them.

A lot of them was Americans and in fact they was generally less offensive than the English ones. I mean, their grasp on culture was so sketchy that all they seemed to do was keep saying how old everything was. Apparently Harbinger Hall had been featured in some naff television series that they'd seen over there and they spent a lot of time walking round the place acting out their favourite bits and taking photos of each other in various settings. Funny lot, the Yanks, I always thought that.

Still, they was at least friendly. The English punters reckoned as soon as they saw me that I wasn't "their sort of person". Dead right they was too. I wouldn't want to be some nasty little factory owner who, just because he's made a bit of bread, reckons he can go around buying breeding. I may not have a lot in the way of social gloss, but at least it's all mine.

Anyway, the English ones certainly disapproved of me. I'd catch them talking behind their hands about me when I come in the room. "Sticks out like a sore thumb," I heard one cheeky little pickle-manufacturer say. "You'd think they'd vet the applications of people who come on these weekends."

Under other circumstances I'd have pushed the little git's false teeth out the other end, but I remembered that I wasn't meant to be drawing attention to myself so I laid off him.

You'll have got the impression by now that the company wasn't that great, and let me tell you the entertainment, so-called, was even worse. Dear oh dear. I already told you my views on history, and I really thought that old git of a guide had said everything there was to say and a bit more about Harbinger Hall when I done my day-trip. Don't you believe it. For the Stately Home Weekend they got in blooming Professors of History to take us through the lot, Duke by Duke. Then another berk come and took us through the family portraits and, as if that weren't enough, some snooty old blue-rinse give us a lecture on eighteenth-century house-keeping. Tell you, I done some boring jobs in my time, but I'd rather spend a solid week watching for some fence to come out of his front door than ever sit through that lot again.

The Medieval Banquet wasn't no better. My idea of a good Saturday night is going out for a few beers and, if you're feeling a bit exotic, ending up at the Chinkie or the Indian; not sitting in front of seventeen knives and forks while gits march up and down holding up stuffed pigs and peacocks. As a general rule, I don't mind music, either—good sing-song round the Joanna or a nice tape of James Last, Abba, that sort of number; but please God may I never again be put in a position where I have to act natural while listening to a bunch of birds singing madrigals to a lute.

But I stuck at it, like a right little swot. Fixed my mind steadily on the old five grand. Or maybe on a bit more than that.

Being the size I am, I got a pretty well-developed appetite, and all them lectures and that had sharpened it a bit, so, even though they wasn't serving anything I fancied, I had a good go at all this stuffed pig and peacock and fruit tarts and what-have-you. Even forced myself to drink some of the mead, which is not an experience I'd recommend to anyone with taste buds.

Anyway, result of all this is, I wake up in bed round one in the morning with this dreadful heartburn. Well, it's more than heartburn, really. It's that round the chest, but it seems to be moving down the body and turning into something less tasteful. Not to put too fine a point on it, I have to get to the bog in a hurry.

Well, they're real mean with the wattage on the landings and, sense of direction never having been my special subject, I go through all kinds of corridors and staircases before I find what I'm looking for.

And, dear oh dear, when I get there, what a spectacle it is. Blooming great dark wood seat like something out of an old rowing boat, and the pan's got all these pink and blue roses all over it. Out the back there's this sort of plunger like it was going to detonate a bomb. You'd really think in a place like Harbinger Hall they'd get decent facilities. I mean, more like the sort of thing my brother-in-law's got—low-level avocado with matching sink and gold-plated dolphin flush-handle.

Still, I'm in no condition to bother about Lord Harbinger's lack of design sense. It's lock the door, down with the pyjama trousers and settle in for a long session.

Embarrassing though it is to confess, I'm afraid I must've dozed off. Mead must've got to me. Because next thing I know I'm hearing voices. I don't mean "hearing voices" like loonies hear; I mean there's a couple of geysers nattering outside the bog door. So I holds my breath (amongst other things) and listens.

Well, first thing is, I recognize one of the voices. Told you I was good on them, didn't I? Yes, you guessed. Mr Loxton from the sauna, wasn't it?

"I saw our contact this afternoon," he's saying. "All set up for tomorrow evening. It'll be a quick handover."

"That's not what I'm worried about. It's the bit before."

"It'll be fine. I've talked to the staff and it sounds as if the other guests are certainly going to remember him."

"But if he's as dumb as he appears, are you sure he's capable of actually doing what he's meant to?"

"It's not difficult. If he does blow it, we just call the police and have him arrested."

"Not keen on that," the other says sharply. His voice was older, real upper-crusty, sounded like a Cabinet Minister being interviewed, know what I mean. "Police might want to investigate a bit too deeply. No, we've got to hope the whole affair goes through as planned."

"I'm sure it will." Mr Loxton sounds all soothing and . . . what's the word? You know, like a head waiter who thinks he's going to get a big tip.

"Yes. And you're sure he's not suspicious?"

"No chance. Picked with great care. He's as thick as two short planks."

"Good. Goodnight."

The older voice was moving away. I unlocked the door dead quiet and risked a quick flash through the crack. One who's just spoken's out of sight, but I see the other just as he's said "Goodnight". Mr Loxton's voice. Mean-looking bastard he is when you blow the steam away. But important thing is, he's wearing the striped trousers and that of one of the Harbinger Hall staff. As I suspected, I am part of an inside job.

That's not all I've learnt, though. Maybe it's the reference to "two short planks", which I've heard more than once in my passage through life, but I feel sure Loxton and his chum was talking about me.

I've forgotten my gutrot by the time I get back into bed. Can't be distracted by things like that—need all my mind for thinking.

I can't work out what's happening yet, but I know it's something I don't like. I been set up a few times in my career, and there's a feeling you get when it happens. You don't know the details, but you know something's not kosher. Like when your bird's having it off with someone else.

I go through the whole thing to myself, listening out for the bits that don't ring true. I try to remember if there was any little bits struck me as odd at the time. And I come up with a few.

First, there's the fact that Wally Clinton put up my name. Now, like I explained, he had no reason to sugar-daddy on me. I nearly shopped him once and he had to give a very big birthday present to the boys in blue to get off the hook. Wasn't my fault, but Wally was never bothered by details like that.

My first thought is Wally is just out to get his own back, get me nicked when I cut through the alarm cables, but somehow that don't match the wallpaper. It's too complicated. He don't need to bring in Loxton and all this set-up. And two and a half grand's a month's takings to a smalltimer like Clinton. He's not going to throw it away on me.

"Picked with great care," Loxton said. What's that mean? I begin to wonder. Think about my reputation in the business, where, as I happened to mention, I am reckoned a complete dumbo who'll do whatever he's told without question.

That's it, of course. Loxton wanted someone guaranteed thick as a bunch of duvets; and Wally Clinton recommended me.

Hurtful though this conclusion is, I don't dwell on it. If that is the case, other things follow. Yes, I am being set up, but set up for something bigger than revenge for Wally. I try to think what else in the deal needs a deodorant.

I remember that right from the start I'd been impressed by the efficiency of the villains I was dealing with. Attention to detail. They'd given me instructions you couldn't go wrong with. They'd paid back my exact expenses. They'd even left the right money for the parking in Cavendish Square.

That thought stopped me. Cavendish Square Garage was where the car was meant to go back to. I was to drive there from Harbinger Hall. On my little lonesome. They'd set the whole thing up real tight until I left the Hall and then I could do what I liked. I know they thought I was thick, but surely even someone thick was going to realize that there was other things they could do with a couple of millionsworth of canvas than leave it in a garage. Considering the care they'd taken with everything else, they really hadn't thought that bit through. Why?

Something else suddenly barged into my mind. I went across to where my bomber jacket was hanging and felt in the pocket. The new price-list the bloke at the garage had given me.

There it was. Give me a nasty turn when I saw it.

"THE GARAGE IS CLOSED ALL DAY SUNDAYS."

They hadn't bothered to think through the details of the hand-over once I'd stolen the painting, because they knew I wasn't going to get that far.

Then I remembered the other thing that didn't fit in. The locked boot of the Peugeot.

Picking locks isn't my Number One talent, but I got a decent set of skeletons and I get by. Could've done the Peugeot boot quicker with a jemmy, but I didn't want no one to see I been snooping. So I was patient and after about ten minutes had it open.

And what a treasure trove my little pencil torch lit up inside. Complete Do-It-Yourself burglar kit. Sets of chisels, jemmies, wire-snips, pliers, big crowbar, the lot. Stethoscope, too, presumable for the old listening-to-the-tumblers routine when opening safes. Not that many villains do that nowadays.

Don't use dynamite much either. Not in sticks. Plastic explosive's much easier to handle. Less likely to have accidents. Still, whoever had stocked out that car boot reckoned I might need dynamite for the odd safe-job.

They also reckoned I was going to need something else. The rectangular outline of the suitcase was familiar, and that of the cloth-wrapped object inside even more so. I felt the knobbly ridges of the frame as I undid it.

It was a painting, of course. Same size as the Madonna. Old, like the Madonna. But it wasn't the Madonna. Difficult to see what it was, actually. Or what it had been. The paint was all flaked and stained. Could have been anything. Can't imagine anyone would have given two quid for that one, let alone two million.

But the odd thing about it was that screwed to the frame at the bottom there was this brass plate, which said,

> MADONNA AND CHILD
> Giacomo Palladino
> Florentine
> (1473–1539)

Someone was certainly setting me up, but I couldn't right then work out what for.

The Sunday was as boring as the Saturday. Some gamekeeper git give us a long lecture on grouse-shooting; there was a berk who went on about coats of arms; the "Traditional Sunday Lunch" was full of gristle. And whoever done the gravy ought to be copped under the Trades Descriptions Act. I mean, if the upper classes have been fed gravy like that since the Norman Conquest, no wonder they're a load of wimps.

The afternoon was, in the words of the old brochure, "less structured". That meant, thank God, they couldn't think of anything else to bore us silly with. Guests were encouraged to wander round the grounds until the great moment of tea with Lord Harbinger.

I didn't bother to go out. I just lay on my bed and thought. I was piecing things together. Though nasty things have been said about it, there is nothing wrong with my intellect. It just works slowly. Give it time and it'll get there.

Trouble is, thinking takes it out of me, and I must've dozed off. When I come to, it was quarter to five and the old Royal Command tea had started at four-thirty. I got up in a hurry. Half of me was working out what was up, but the other half was still following instructions. I had to behave naturally, go through the weekend without drawing attention to myself.

As I hurried across the landing, I looked out through the big front window. I could see the red Peugeot parked right outside.

And I could see Mr Loxton closing the boot and moving away from it. Thought I'd be safely inside having my tea, didn't you, Mr Loxton?

The tea give me the last important fact. As soon as I was introduced to Lord Harbinger, it all come together.

"Good afternoon," he said with a reasonable stab at enthusiasm. "Delighted to welcome you to Harbinger Hall."

It was the voice, wasn't it? The bloke Loxton had been speaking to the night before. I realized just how inside an inside job it was.

And I realized other things that give me a nasty trickly feeling in my belly.

Half-past five the tea broke up. Lord Harbinger switched off like a lightbulb and, in spite of the Americans who would have liked to go on mingling with the aristocracy forever, everyone was hustled out of the drawing-room to go and get packed. I went up to my bedroom like the rest.

Wasn't a lot to pack, was there? But for the first time I took a butcher's at the package in my suitcase. After what I seen in the car boot the night before, could have been anything.

But no. It was a copy of the Madonna. Bloody good, too. I couldn't have told it apart from the real thing. But then I don't know much about art, do I?

Ten to six, following my instructions to the letter, down I go to the hall, leaving my suitcase in the bedroom. There's already a few of the punters milling around and piles of cases. Casual like, I take a glance at these and see, as I expected, that there's one there just like the one I left in the bedroom. Expensive for them on suitcases, this job. Mind you, if it all worked, they'd be able to afford it.

I hear Loxton's voice suddenly, whispering to Lord Harbinger. "I'll get away as quickly as I can afterwards."

"Fine," says the noble peer.

Just before six, most of the punters have arrived and the Harbinger Hall staff are all starting to make a farewell line like something out of a television serial. The Americans think this is wonderful and start cooing.

"Oh, blimey," I say loudly. "Forget my own head next!" Then, for the benefit of the people who've turned round to look at me, I add, "Only forgotten my blooming case, haven't I?"

They turn away with expressions of distaste, and I beetle upstairs. Do it by the book. To my bedroom, pick up the suitcase, to the Long Gallery, down the "Private" staircase. Out with the old metal-cutters, reach for the cables at the top of the alarm boxes, snip, snip. I'm tense then, but there's no noise.

Into the Great Hall, put the suitcase on the table. Unzip it all the way round, take the copy of the Madonna out of its cloth wrappings, and do what I have to do.

Slam the case shut, back up the stairs, Long Gallery, bedroom, back down the main staircase towards the hall, stop on the stairs, panting a bit. Whole operation—three and a half minutes.

Now you've probably gathered that I have got this unfortunate reputation for bogging things up. Just when the job's nearly done, something always seems to go wrong. Bad luck I call it, but it's happened so often that some people have less charitable descriptions.

So, anyway, there I am standing on the stairs in front of all these people and I reach up to wipe my brow and—you'll never believe it—I haven't had time to zip up my suitcase again and I'm still holding the handle and it falls open. My aftershave and what-have-you clatters down the stairs with my pyjamas, and there, still strapped in the suitcase for all to see, is the Harbinger Madonna.

"My God!" says Lord Harbinger.

I say a rude word.

Various servants come forward and grab me. Others are sent off to the Great Hall to see the damage. Loxton's the first one back. He looks dead peeved.

"My Lord. The alarm wires have been cut. He's replaced the Madonna with a copy!"

"What!" Lord Harbinger blusters.

"Shall I call the police, my Lord?" asks another servant.

"Um . . ."

"All right." I shrug. "It's a fair cop. Story of my life. Every job I seem to screw up. And this one I really thought I'd worked out to the last detail."

"Shall I call the police, my Lord?" the servant asks again.

"Um . . ."

"You better," I say. "I really have got caught with the goods this time. I'm afraid the police are going to want a really thorough investigation into this."

"Ye-es." His Lordship sounds uncertain. "Under normal circumstances of course I'd call the police straight away. But this is rather . . . um . . . awkward."

"Why?" I ask. "I'm not pretending I haven't done it."

"No, but, er . . . er . . ." Then finally he gets on the right track. "But you are a guest in my house. It is not part of the code of the Harbingers to call the police to their guests, however they may have offended against the laws of hospitality."

"Oh," I say.

"Gee," says one of the Americans. "Isn't this just *wonderful*?"

Harbinger's getting into his stride by now. He does a big point to the door like out of some picture and he says, "Leave my house!"

I go down the rest of the stairs. "Better not take this, had I, I suppose?" I hold up the Madonna.

"No."

I hand it over, sort of reluctant. "You better keep the copy. I got no use for it now. And I suppose the police will want to look at that. Might be able to trace back who ordered it."

"Yes," says his Lordship abruptly. "Or rather no. You take that back with you."

"But—"

"No. If the police could trace you through the copy, I would be offending the rules of hospitality just as much as if I had you arrested. You take the copy with you."

"But I don't want it."

"*You will take it, sir!*" he bellows.

"Oh, all right," I say grudgingly.

"Oh, heck. This is just so *British*," says one of the Americans. Made her weekend, it had.

They give me the picture from the Great Hall, I put it in my suitcase, and I'm escorted out by Loxton. The punters and staff draw apart like I'm trying to sell them insurance.

Outside, Loxton says, "God, I knew you were thick and incompetent, but it never occurred to me that you'd be *that* thick and incompetent."

I hang my head in shame.

"Now get in your car and go!"

"Oh, it's not my car," I say. "It's stolen. Way my luck's going, I'll probably get stopped by the cops on the way home. I'll go on the coach to the station."

Loxton doesn't look happy.

Takes a bit of time to get all the punters on to the bus. Loxton stands there fidgeting while further farewells are said. I sit right at the back with my suitcase. Everyone else sits right up the front. I'm in disgrace.

The bus starts off down the steep zigzag drive towards Limmerton. I look back to see Loxton rush towards the Peugeot, parked right in front of Harbinger Hall. I look at my watch. Quarter to seven. All that delayed us quite a bit.

I see Loxton leap into the car. Without bothering to close the door, he starts it and slams her into reverse. He screeches backwards over the gravel.

But it's too late. The Hall's saved, but he isn't.

The back of the Peugeot erupts into a balloon of orange flame. From inside the bus the sound is muffled. A few of the punters turn curiously, but just at that moment we swing round one of the hair-pins and there's nothing to see.

I piece it together again in the train. They've left me in a compartment on my own. I'm still like some kind of leper. They all feel better having had their guesses at the sort of person I was confirmed.

Lord Harbinger had money problems. Cost a lot to keep the Hall going, and the trippers weren't coming enough. Stately Home Weekends might bring in a few bob, but they took such a lot of staff, there wasn't much percentage in it.

But he had got the Madonna. Couldn't just sell it, wouldn't look good, public admission of failure. Besides, either he or Loxton had worked out a scheme that'd make more than just selling it. They'd have it stolen, get the insurance *and* sell it. But they need a real mug to do the actual thieving.

Enter Yours Truly.

I had to raise suspicions when I came for my day-trip, then stick out like a sore thumb on the Stately Home Weekend. When I'd actually done the theft, switched the real Madonna for the copy, Loxton would have offered to take my bag to my car. He would have switched my suitcase for the empty one and put the Madonna in another car, in which he would later drive it up to London to do his deal with Mr Depaldo's rival.

I would have driven off in the Peugeot, maybe full of plans to doublecross my paymasters and do a little deal of my own. They weren't worried what I had in mind, because they knew that half an hour away from Harbinger Hall, the dynamite in the back of the car would explode. When the police came to check the wreckage, I would be identified as the geyser who'd been behaving oddly all weekend, the one who'd obviously cut the alarm cables and switched the paintings. My profession was obvious. There was my record if they ever put a name to me. And if not, there were all the tools of my trade in the boot of the car.

Together with the dynamite, whose careless stowing caused my unfortunate demise.

And some burnt-out splinters of wood and shreds of canvas, which had once been a painting. A very old painting, tests would reveal. And the engraved brass plate which was likely to survive the blast would identify it as Giacomo Palladino's masterpiece, "Madonna and Child". Another great art work would be tragically lost to the nation.

Had to admire it. Was a good plan.

They only got one thing wrong. Like a few others before them, they made the mistake of thinking Billy Gorse was as thick as he looked.

I felt good and relaxed. Pity the train hadn't got a buffet. I could have really done with a few beers.

Go to Red Rita's later, I thought. Yeah, be nice. Be nice to go away with her, and all. Been looking a bit peaky lately. She could do with a change. South America, maybe?

I got my suitcase down from the rack and opened it.

Found it grew on me, that Madonna.

And I was very glad I hadn't changed the two pictures round in the Great Hall.

I may not know much about art, but I'm beginning to realize what it's worth.

"Oh, Miss Black," Jeremy Garson's voice crackled authoritatively over the intercom, "could you come through for a moment, please?"

Isabel, who knew Jeremy well, recognized when he was trying to impress. As soon as she had seen the elegant red-haired woman, whose appointment had been registered in the diary as "11 o'clock—Mrs Karlstetter", she had known it would only be a matter of time before he started showing off. And then his secretary would be paraded in the office, another accessory, another labour-saving device to go with the desk-top calculator, the miniature memo-recorder, the telephone amplifier and the imposing, but unused, telex-machine.

Jeremy was leaning back in his swivel-chair when she went in, his poise undermined by a little glint of insecurity in his eyes. At times he looked absurdly like his father, for whom Isabel had worked until John Garson's premature death, but the old man's eyes had never betrayed that fear.

"Yes, Mr Garson?" She knew the rules. No Christian names when he was trying to impress. No lapse into assertions of her own personality. Just the image of efficiency, shorthand pad and freshly sharpened HB pencil at the ready.

Jeremy smiled proprietorially. "Mrs Karlstetter, you met Miss Black briefly. She's an absolute treasure. Runs the whole office for me."

He chuckled, to point up the humorous exaggeration of this last remark. "Miss Black, Mrs Karlstetter has not come to us to arrange the fitting of a burglar alarm."

"Ah."

"She has not come to take advantage of the advertised services of Garson Security. She is aware of the . . . other side of our business."

He vouchsafed Mrs Karlstetter a brilliant smile. "It's quite all right. Miss Black knows all about the detective agency operation.

She's done all the paperwork for it since my father first . . . branched out in that direction. So we can speak freely."

Mrs Karlstetter nodded, acknowledging Isabel as she might a new wall-unit pointed out for her commendation.

"Miss Black, if you could note down what Mrs Karlstetter says . . ."

Isabel sat on the least eminent chair and translated the red-haired girl's words into neat squiggles of shorthand.

"Basically, I think my husband is trying to kill me."

Mrs Karlstetter left an appropriate pause for awestruck reaction.

"The fact is, I have always been a very light sleeper—no, worse than that, I have always slept very badly, almost always had a couple of hours awake in the middle of the night . . ."

"I'm not a doctor," said Jeremy with his disarming smile.

"I know. And if I wanted a doctor's help, I would have gone to one years ago. But I don't believe in drugs. I think many of them haven't been properly tested out, you know, for all their side-effects."

"So you've just lived with your insomnia?"

"Yes. One gets used to it. I've just assumed that it's going to be with me for the rest of my life."

"Uhuh."

"But for the last four months I've suddenly started sleeping very deeply."

"Well, surely that's good news."

"It would be, if I thought the sleep was natural."

"You think you're being drugged?"

"Yes."

"By your husband?"

"There's no one else it could be. There's only the two of us in the house."

"How do you think he does it?"

"He gets a bedtime drink for me every night. Hot milk. I think he puts something in that."

"Have you tried not drinking it?"

"No. I don't want him to realize I'm suspicious, in case that makes him try something more drastic. But he's been away on usiness a bit recently, and those nights I've prepared the drink myself . . ."

"And?"

"And I've slept as badly as ever."

"Hmm. You haven't confronted him with it?"

"I'm afraid to."

"And you haven't thought of going to the police?"

"What would I say? I can't risk them blundering in. If I'm going to do anything about it, I've got to be discreet."

"Which is why you've come to me?"

"Yes. I heard from a friend of mine, Mrs Littlejohn, that you sorted out a problem about her solicitor defrauding her . . ."

Jeremy Garson nodded complacently. "So what do you want me to do?"

"I want you to prove that I'm not imagining all this. My husband's working late tonight—won't be back before eleven—and I'm out playing bridge. I want you to search the house for some evidence, find the drug or whatever it is . . . before it's too late. I'm sure he's increasing the dose. I have great difficulty waking up in the mornings, and I get these terrible headaches. I'm sure he's killing me . . . slowly but surely killing me."

"Can you think of any motive?"

"None at all. I want you to find that out too."

"Hmm. How do I get into the house?"

"I'll leave the kitchen fanlight open. You can reach the catch of the large window through that."

"Breaking and entering . . ." Jeremy mused.

"Yes. Will you do it for me? Please."

Isabel looked up from her shorthand pad to see her boss's reaction. A break-in was unnecessarily dramatic. And risky. There were simpler ways of searching the house.

Jeremy Garson gave his most debonair smile. "Yes, I'll do it, Mrs Karlstetter. Just relax, and leave it all to me."

Isabel held the torch, while Jeremy fiddled with the set of keys Clipper Jenkins had made for him between prison sentences. "I still think it's some kind of set-up," she repeated doggedly.

"No, Isabel. I'm a good judge of people and I'd stake my reputation as an investigator that Mrs Karlstetter is absolutely genuine."

He tried another key in the lock of the drawer. The leather-topped desk, like everything else in the large suburban house, was discreetly expensive. Whatever problems the Karlstetters had, lack of money was not among them.

The edge of Isabel's torchbeam caught a photograph on the desk. The Karlstetters' wedding. Married within the last ten years, from the style of clothes. Mr Karlstetter a good twenty years older than his wife. Second marriage perhaps?

This key worked. Carefully Jeremy turned it and reached to slide the drawer. "Oh, gloves," he said, and punctiliously put on a rubber pair, oblivious of the neat set of fingerprints he had already laid on the desk-top.

The drawer was full of papers and envelopes, amongst which he rummaged carelessly before his hand closed round something in the furthest corner.

"Ahah." He turned triumphantly to face Isabel, who caught the full blast of the alcohol on his breath. He had had a long lunch at "The Black Fox" with a man "who was going to sign a very big contract for a complete security system for his factory" (though no contract seemed to have emerged from the encounter), and then a couple of stiffening whiskies before the break-in at the Karlstetters.

In his hand was a squat bottle about six inches high. Isabel directed the torch on to the label.

"Phenergan," she read.

"Would that put someone to sleep?"

"Oh yes. Very popular with mothers of small children—especially when they're teething."

"So, if someone were to build up the dose slowly . . ."

"I think it'd be hard work to kill someone. It's just an anti-histamine."

"Well, perhaps Mr Karlstetter is softening his wife up on this and then going to move on to something stronger."

"Perhaps," said Isabel sceptically.

"Anyway, we've proved there's something fishy going on. Why would a man keep this hidden away in a locked drawer if he wasn't using it for nefarious purposes?"

Isabel shrugged. "Could be a lot of reasons. Hay fever . . ."

"No, I'm sure we've got the proof Mrs Karlstetter asked for. Come on, let's go."

"I think we ought to look upstairs first."

"Why?"

"Might be something else relevant."

There was. In the drawer of Mrs Karlstetter's bedside table was a small bottle of pills. Again the label identified the contents.

"Valium," Isabel announced flatly. "Mrs Karlstetter takes valium."

"So? So do a lot of housewives."

"She told you she never touched drugs. Because of the side-effects."

The outline of Jeremy's shoulders shrugged. "So she lied to us. So she's inconsistent. So what?"

"So it just makes me more suspicious. These and her 'unwilling sleep'."

"Another of your father's quotations?"

"Yes. 'Mortality weighs heavily on me like unwilling sleep.' Keats. 'Sonnet on Seeing the Elgin Marbles'."

There was a tremble in her voice. It was over two years since her father's death, but a sudden reminder of him could still stab her like a physical pain.

Jeremy responded to her moment of weakness, but, as ever, his response was inappropriate. She felt his arms round her and smelt his whisky breath murmuring "Isabel" in her ear.

She was not shocked. She had been found suddenly attractive at the end of too many parties to be shocked. Besides, it was not the first time Jeremy had touched her. But the last had been twenty years before, when he had been about to go up to university, when she had been about to move from the suburbs to London to work, when their lives had seemed likely to turn out very differently.

"Isabel," he continued, his voice muffled in her hair, "let's go somewhere together. Go out to dinner. Not tonight. Thursday. Go out to dinner on Thursday."

"What about Felicia?" she asked, hoping his wife's name would bring him to his senses. And yet, to her annoyance, not hoping it whole-heartedly.

"Felicia and the kids'll be away. Going to London for a couple of days. Come on, Isabel. Dinner on Thursday—what do you say?"

As the word left her lips, she cursed her stupidity in saying "Yes".

Jeremy was in the office before her the next morning. Most unusual. He looked full of himself.

"I've rung Mrs Karlstetter."

"Oh yes?"

"Yes. And I told her about the Phenergan. She was very pleased."

"And?"

"And she wants us to compile a dossier proving her husband's guilt, so that she can take it to the police."

"I see. And you said we'd do it?"

"She is paying us, Isabel."

"Yes, of course."

Jeremy rose from his swivel-chair and wandered over to the window. "I've got a few ideas of what to do next, but I haven't yet decided which should come first . . ."

"I would have thought the first priority was to find out a bit more about Mr Karlstetter."

He turned to face her. "Yes, that's what I reckoned."

"So I should think the best thing would be to ring Mrs Karlstetter again to find out where her husband works—oh, and get the number of his car."

Jeremy Garson smiled. "That's what I thought, Isabel."

"Oh, good morning. Is that Mr Karlstetter's office?"

"Yes." The secretarial voice at the other end of the phone sounded young, but confident.

"Is he there?"

"No, I'm afraid he's in a meeting."

"Oh, well perhaps I should try later."

"Can I help?"

"Perhaps you could. I'm ringing from Scotland Yard," Isabel ~~s~~ied.

"Oh."

"There's no need to be alarmed. This is only a routine check. ~~T~~he fact is that a Ford Granada similar to Mr Karlstetter's was ~~s~~tolen last night and used in a raid on a jeweller's shop. According ~~t~~o Mrs Karlstetter, her husband was working late last night, so ~~p~~resumably his car was in the office car park. I just wanted to ~~c~~onfirm that with him."

"Ah." The secretarial voice sounded uncertain. "Um, yes. Well, ~~i~~n fact, his car wasn't here all yesterday evening."

"Oh."

"No. Um, there was rather a rush job on yesterday, and he . . . ~~e~~r . . . wanted me to stay late for some dictation, but I had to get ~~b~~ack to my flat for . . . er . . . because I was expecting a phone-call ~~f~~rom Australia, so we . . . er, worked at my flat."

"And where is your flat?"

"Notting Hill."

"Ah."

"Shall I get Mr Karlstetter to phone you when he's finished his ~~m~~eeting, because I'm sure he wouldn't want anyone to think—"

"No, no need to worry. The raid on the jeweller's was in ~~P~~laistow. Miles from Notting Hill. No, you've answered my query. Thank you very much. Now I've just got to work through about a ~~h~~undred more Granada owners."

Isabel Black put down the phone with some satisfaction. Maybe ~~t~~he case was going to be easier than she'd feared.

"Jeremy," she said, when she went into his office, "mind if I go ~~u~~p to Town? It's something on the Karlstetter thing."

"No, fine. I'd come myself, but I've got this lunch at Umberto's ~~w~~ith a racehorse trainer who's interested in a surveillance system . . ."

"Of course."

Mr Karlstetter worked for an oil company, whose central office was in a large block near Victoria Station. Which was ideal for Isabel's purposes.

She parked her car on a meter round the back of the building, opposite a row of rubbish bins awaiting collection. A moment's casual sifting produced what she wanted. A brown A4 envelope for internal mail. Most of the boxes on the front had names filled in, but, as is always the case in big organizations, the envelope had been thrown away before they'd all been used. Isabel wrote "Mr Karlstetter" in the next vacant box, put her outdoor coat in the car, and went round to the front of the building.

In the foyer, in front of the lifts, were a cluster of armchairs and low tables. She lifted a magazine off one of them. *Oil News*. That'd do. She put it into the envelope and, ignoring the sign which said "All Security Passes Must Be Shown", walked up to the Commissionaire behind the Reception desk.

"Mr Karlstetter?" she asked, holding the envelope up in front of him.

"Seventh Floor. 7106," said the Commissionaire helpfully.

Mr Karlstetter's secretary was, as anticipated, a pretty little thing. Early twenties, with a good figure and a knowing eye.

Isabel had studied the other names on the internal envelope. "From Mr Rogers," she said, naming the last one as she handed it over.

"Oh." The secretary looked at her curiously. "Why didn't Linda bring it?"

Isabel made a rueful face. "They can't think of things for me to do. I'm being retrained. Transfer from Manchester."

Mr Karlstetter's secretary nodded without interest.

Isabel left it at that and went out of the room. Leave the more intimate bit for the Ladies.

There was only one on that floor, so she reckoned it was a safe bet, though it might mean a bit of waiting.

She bolted herself into one of the cubicles, propped her handbag mirror against the wall, so that it gave her a view through the gap under the door, and waited.

It was after twelve, so there was quite a lot of pre-lunch coming and going. At quarter to one her quarry arrived. Isabel waited till she heard the cubicle locked behind Mr Karlstetter's secretary, then flushed her lavatory and emerged. She put her handbag on the shelf beneath the mirror, and started to apply a neutral-coloured lipstick. (Under normal circumstances she didn't wear make-up, but she had come prepared.)

The other lavatory flushed, and Mr Karlstetter's secretary came out. She smiled vague recognition at Isabel, washed her hands, and began to repair her more elaborate make-up. She took out a soft brush to highlight the cheekbones.

"Ooh, that's good, isn't it?" Isabel commented in her dowdiest voice.

"Hmm."

"Really doing yourself up."

"Oh, nothing special."

"Mr Karlstetter taking you out for lunch then?"

The brush froze in mid-air, and the secretary turned from the mirror to blaze at Isabel, "What do you mean?"

"Oh, sorry I spoke. Thought it was common knowledge, about you and him."

"What?"

"I've only been here a few days, but everyone seems to know."

"Oh." The girl looked dejected, and very young. "It's meant to be a secret."

"Oh. Sorry. Difficult to keep secrets in an organization like this."

"Yes. These last four months haven't been easy. I'll be glad when we don't have to keep it a secret any more."

"Oh, when's that?" asked Isabel ingenuously.

"When we're married," Mr Karlstetter's secretary replied defiantly.

Which perhaps provided a motive for Mr Karlstetter to want to get his wife out of the way.

An affair between a boss and his secretary. The oldest, shoddiest cliché in the book. Suddenly Isabel had to ring Jeremy to cancel their stupid dinner date for the following evening. Strangle it at birth. Stop it before anything started.

There was no reply when she rang at two. She kept trying, from various call-boxes on Victoria Station. At ten to four he was finally back from lunch.

And a good lunch too, if the fuzziness of his voice was anything to go by.

But when she heard him, something inside her, something that infuriated her, wouldn't let her say what she'd intended.

"Look, I want to try to follow Mr Karlstetter tonight. Mrs Karlstetter said he was working late at the office again . . ."

"That's right."

"But he's told his secretary—who, incidentally, was what he was working late on last night—"

"Oh, really?"

"Yes. He's told her he's spending the evening at home."

"Ah."

"So I'm going to try to find out what he's up to."

"Good. I'd come up and help you, Isabel, but I think Felicia and the kids are kind of expecting me to . . ."

"Of course, Jeremy."

Maybe Mr Karlstetter did actually work late that evening. Isabel, from her car parked opposite, saw his secretary leave the building on the dot of five-thirty, but it was over two hours later, just when she was starting to think she'd missed him, that Mr Karlstetter himself appeared. She recognized him easily from the photograph she'd seen at his home. A man fighting ungracefully against encroaching age.

Fortunately, there was not much traffic at that time of night and Isabel was able to follow discreetly without losing him. He made straight for Victoria Station. Oh no, had he changed his mind? Was he actually going home to his wife after all?

But he'd only gone to the station to pick up a taxi from the rank in front. Isabel discovered how much easier it was to do the "Follow that taxi" routine in her own car than in another taxi.

He stopped outside Jules Bar in Jermyn Street and, when he had paid off the driver, went inside. Isabel parked a couple of streets away and followed him in.

The bar was full, but she managed to find a couple of seats at one of the tables. She ordered two drinks from the waitress, aware that a girl waiting angrily for a man who's late looks less conspicuous than one drinking on her own.

Then she looked round for Mr Karlstetter. He was over in the corner with his arm round a girl. She was also thirty years younger than him, but she wasn't his secretary. The couple talked intimately, while Isabel maintained a masquerade of alternately looking at her watch and, with venom, at the untouched gin and tonic opposite her.

After about half an hour, Mr Karlstetter and the girl left. With a final gesture of annoyance, Isabel stumped out after them.

Fortunately they had difficulty in getting a taxi, so she had time to get her car and be ready for them.

This time the journey took them South of the river. This girl's flat was in York Mansions, Prince of Wales Drive.

Isabel waited outside. At half-past ten Mr Karlstetter emerged, looking pleased with himself.

It took him a long time to find a cab, and Isabel kept having to resist the temptation to offer him a lift.

But eventually he got a taxi back over the river and disappeared into Victoria Station. Back home to his wife, presumably, after another hard evening at the office.

Isabel thought about it. A man who wants to marry a younger girl might possibly contemplate murdering his wife to get her out of the way. But a man who is two-timing the younger girl and only using the idea of marriage to keep her on the boil surely wouldn't bother to go to such lengths. In complicated deceptions the existence of a wife is always a useful long-stop, the ultimate excuse when things get difficult.

As she drove back into the suburbs, a thought struck her. If he'd used his car for his philandering on Tuesday night, why would a man suddenly turn to taxis for the same purpose on a Wednesday?

Then she realized—and laughed out loud at the realization—that he'd only do it if Scotland Yard had been making enquiries about his car's movements.

". . . so I'm absolutely convinced, Jeremy, that she's set the whole thing up herself. She knows what he's up to, and she wants to get her revenge. She doesn't really think he'll get arrested for trying to kill her; she just wants to scare the living daylights out of him."

"Are you sure, Isabel?"

"Positive. That's how that sort of woman works."

"What do you mean—that sort of woman? She's very attractive."

"That's neither here nor there. I'm certain that's what's happened. She's just drawing attention to herself and trying to get revenge."

"Hmm."

"You challenge her with it, Jeremy. I bet she'll confess. Her 'unwilling sleep' is completely self-induced. When did you say she was coming in?"

"Six o'clock this evening."

Mrs Karlstetter arrived looking very elegant and confident. She was in Jeremy's office a long time before the intercom buzzed. Isabel stayed waiting at her desk outside. There might be something that needed tying up. Also, however much she tried to push it from her mind, she couldn't forget the plan that Jeremy had suggested for Thursday evening.

"Oh, Miss Black," the intercom asked peremptorily, "could you bring in some Kleenex, please?"

When Isabel went in, Jeremy was saying, "I'm sorry, Virginia, but you couldn't have hoped to deceive me. When I am engaged to investigate something, I'm afraid I always find out the truth—oh, thank you, Miss Black."

Isabel handed over a couple of Kleenex to the weeping Mrs Karlstetter.

"If you could just hang on for a little longer, Miss Black. We're nearly through."

"Of course, Mr Garson."

Half an hour later, the intercom buzzed again. "Oh, Miss Black, could you get on to Tiberio's Restaurant, please, and book me a table for two for eight o'clock tonight. One of the ones in the alcoves."

To her annoyance, Isabel's voice trembled as she fulfilled this commission. So he hadn't forgotten.

At half-past seven, the intercom buzzed again. "Oh, Miss Black, do you think you could just type up Mrs Karlstetter's invoice. I'd like her to have it before we go out to dinner."

"Yes, of course, Mr Garson."

"Thank you. You're a treasure." Even over the crackles of the intercom, his voice sounded warm. "So if you could just leave the invoice on the typewriter, that'll be all. See you in the morning."

Isabel typed up the invoice, hitting the keys with something approaching savagery.

THE HAUNTED ACTRESS

MARIANA LYTHGOE TOOK the centre of the stage as if by right. It was a matter of habit and instinct, helped by the natural deference of those around her. But the dominance of her presence was never resented; force of personality demanded a tribute that was willingly given. Nor was that force of personality noticeably diminished by the actress's seventy years. Though the famous brown eyes were foxed with grey, they retained their magnetism.

The stage whose centre she so naturally took was, on this occasion, a small one. It was a low wooden table, surrounded by a cluster of plastic-upholstered armchairs, in BBC Radio's Ariel Bar.

The audience was also small, but more theatrically discriminating than many she had faced in her long career on the stage. Every member was, to a greater or lesser extent, "in the business". They had all just completed recording a radio play, for which the producer, Mark Lear, had lured Mariana Lythgoe from her much-publicized retirement.

It was a tribute, Charles Paris thought wryly, to her enduring magnetism that Mark was now listening to her with such concentration. During the two days of the recording the producer had been patently earmarking a young, purple-haired actress for his attentions, and the fact that he was deferring the inevitable post-production chat-up for Mariana said a lot for the old lady's power.

"But, of course, no one remembers me now," she was saying with self-depreciating charm.

"Absolute balderdash," Mark Lear protested. "The less work you do, the more you seem to be in the public eye."

She laughed in fond disagreement.

"No, really, Mariana. You should have heard the reaction I got from people who heard you were going to do this play for me. And then there's been all this recent publicity about your autobiography."

"A nine-days' wonder," she said dismissively. "Publishers spend their lives creating nine-day wonders. A month hence everyone will have forgotten about the book."

"Don't you believe it," Mark persisted. "Then there's this new production of *Roses In Winter* at the Haymarket. There hasn't been a single review of it which hasn't mentioned you."

"Oh . . ." The vowel was long with denial, but still asked for more.

"That's the way to get reviews," the producer continued, "—without even being in the show. Get all the critics saying, 'It's hard to forget Mariana Lythgoe's creation of the part of Clara in Boy Trubshawe's original production.' You ever had any notices like that, Charles?"

Charles Paris grimaced. "No. I've had one or two that wished I hadn't been in shows I was in, but none that actually praised me *in absentia*."

Mark laughed. "Well, I'm afraid the poor kid who's playing Clara in this production hasn't got a chance. What's her name?"

"Sandy Drake," Mariana supplied. "I haven't seen it, but I gather she's awfully good," she added loyally.

"The only good things I've read about her have been in comparisons with you," said Mark. Charles couldn't decide whether the producer was being more than usually sycophantic or whether this was just the effect Mariana Lythgoe had on people. From his own reactions to her, he inclined to the second opinion.

"No, but really," Mark continued, "she's only getting your reflected glory. Same with that nephew of yours."

"Oh, now, darling, I won't have you saying that. Dick's sorting out a wonderful career for himself, without any help from me."

"Hmm. Well, I read an article on him in the *Standard*, and the whole piece seemed to be about you. You needed to be a trained detective to find the one reference to Dick."

"Ah." Mariana let out a long sigh. "Wouldn't it sometimes be nice to have a trained detective on hand."

Mark pointed to Charles. "Well, there's the one you want, Mariana."

Charles Paris felt the faded brown eyes burning into him. "Are you a trained detective?"

"Far from trained," he hastened to assure her. "A dabbler. Strictly amateur. Weekends . . . oh, and of course during those brief, brief patches of 'resting'."

This understatement of their endemic unemployment brought its predictable laughter from the other actors present, which Charles hoped was sufficient to shift the subject of conversation.

"Right," he said, standing up. "Who wants another drink?"

But, as he took the orders, and as he made his way to the bar, he could still feel the old actress's eyes on him.

"And you really think someone's out to get you?"

"Yes," Mariana Lythgoe replied firmly.

Charles looked out of the tall windows over Regent's Park. Her flat was on the top of one of the beautiful wedding-cake blocks north of the Marylebone Road. At one time its interior had been expensively decorated, but little had been spent on its upkeep since. The furnishings had a wistful air of dated elegance, like an old stage set that has done duty in a tour of many theatres.

"And when you say 'get you', what do you mean?"

"I'm not sure." She sat regally in an upright armchair, a cut-glass goblet of gin and tonic in her freckled hand. From her bearing, she could have been on stage as Cleopatra. She spoke slowly as she defined her thoughts. "I think I mean 'to frighten me'. I think someone is trying to harass me with a view to frightening me."

"I wouldn't think you frighten easily."

She inclined her head at the compliment. "No, I don't. As a rule. I am not frightened by anything rational, anything that I can make sense of. But anyone can be frightened by a sudden shock."

Charles nodded. "Why should anyone want to frighten you, though? What might there be in it for them?"

"I don't know. It's because the whole thing's irrational that it actually *is* frightening."

Charles was silent for a moment, thinking. Then he spoke. "But there must be a reason. Unless we're dealing with someone who's mentally unbalanced, the person who is persecuting you must be doing it for a reason. That reason might be to punish you for some imagined wrong. . . . Know anyone you've offended recently?"

The splendid head was shaken slowly from side to side. "No. There's no one I've offended wittingly."

"Or they could be trying to frighten you to stop you investigating something they want kept quiet. Anything you can think of that might . . . ?"

Again the head was shaken slowly but positively.

"Or to back up a blackmail threat, to show that the people you're dealing with mean business. But that, of course, presupposes that you have had a blackmail threat. . . ."

She shook her head for the third time. "There has been no mention of blackmail. The letters contained nothing that could be construed in that way."

"What letters are these?"

"Oh, I'm *sorry*. I haven't shown them to you. It's the letters that really got me worried. The phone-calls were ambiguous, but the letters . . ."

As the old lady eased herself out of the armchair and moved across to a writing desk, Charles queried her mention of telephone calls.

"Oh, nothing was said, Charles. Just the telephone ringing and no one at the other end when I answered it."

"Heavy breathing?"

"Perhaps. I didn't notice it. They could have been that sort of call, of course. I gather any lady listed in the telephone directory is likely to get a few of those."

"I'm surprised you're in the directory."

Mariana smiled knowingly. "My dear, when I was *famous*, of course I kept my name out of the book. But now . . ." She shrugged. "Now my name doesn't mean a thing, so the danger of *nuisance* from my admirers is considerably lessened."

She produced three letters, held together by a paper clip, from the writing desk, and handed them over to Charles.

Their threats were not specific, but disturbing. Unsettling for an old lady. "WE'RE OUT TO GET YOU, MARIANA" was the basic message. As she had said, there was nothing that could be interpreted as blackmail.

"When did these come? Presumably not all together?"

"No. Over the last three weeks. The first one was here when I got back."

"Got back?" Charles echoed.

"Oh yes, darling. I was doing a little . . . now what did the sweet girl at the publishers call it? . . . *promotional tour*, that's right. Being driven round the country and talking to all these very young people in radio stations. Very strange. Of course, one was used to press interviews about plays, but at least then you were going to the places to *perform*."

"A book is a kind of performance."

"Is it?" She looked at him with vague earnestness, not untinged with humour. "A very self-indulgent performance in the case of my book. Just an old lady maundering on about herself. I can't imagine why anyone's going to be interested in that."

Charles was now getting used to her method, and could recognize that this, though cast with the usual charm, was angling for contradiction and compliment. He withheld both, but Mariana did not appear discomfited. Instead, she looked at him with a new irony, possibly a new respect.

"How did these letters arrive?" he asked.

"Pushed through the letter-box."

"No stamps?"

"No."

"So someone came through the main entrance of the block and up the stairs to deliver them."

"Yes. Lots of people come and go here. The security is very slack."

"No doorman?"

"Not as such. The caretaker lives in the basement of the adjacent block, but he never seems to be there. Has another job, many of the residents believe. What do they call it . . . moonshining?"

"Moonlighting."

She inclined her head wryly in acknowledgement of her error.

"Why haven't you been to the police about the letters?" asked Charles suddenly.

"The police." She articulated the word pensively, as if it were a new idea. "I'm sure the police have quite enough to think about without being worried by old ladies."

"I wouldn't say—"

"Besides . . ." Her timing of the word stopped him neatly.

"Besides what, Mariana?"

"Well . . . one wouldn't want the police involved if it turned out that the person doing this was . . ." Her voice went suddenly quiet. ". . . someone one knew."

"Does that mean you *do* have an idea of who might be responsible?"

"No. No. Of course not."

Charles let it go at that. For the time being. "You say the block's not very secure. What about the flat itself?"

"There are two locks on the front door. It would be hard for anyone to get past those." After a pause, she added, "So long as I remember to lock them."

"And do you?"

"Usually. But old ladies get absent-minded."

Charles smiled. There was a teasing quality, almost a flirtatiousness, about the way she kept harping on her age.

"However," Mariana continued, "the kitchen door is less secure."

"Kitchen door?"

She led him across to the small room which had been planned and decorated in the days before the concept of kitchen units and toning work surfaces. A glass-topped door opened on to the top landing of a zigzag fire escape. It was secured by one fairly primitive lock.

"Wouldn't hurt to get another lock on this. A few bolts, too. The glass is a hazard."

"But it does make the kitchen light."

Charles nodded. "You could get it replaced with reinforced glass. At the moment it's an invitation to anyone who wants to walk in."

"Yes." For the first time in the evening, Mariana looked frail. "Yes, I suppose I had better get it done. Though it seems rather a lot of trouble to protect an old lady who'll be dead soon in the natural course of events."

Charles put a hand on the angularity of her shoulder. "Don't you believe it. You've got another twenty years in you."

"Oh, I hope not. Sometimes I think it'd be rather a relief if whoever-it-is came and got me quickly."

"'Got you'—we're back to that. Do you think they really mean violence against you? Do you think they're really out to kill you?"

Mariana Lythgoe gave a thin smile. "They wouldn't need much violence."

"What do you mean?"

"I have a serious heart condition. All it's going to need to kill me is a sudden shock."

The pounding on the door first merged with, then detached itself from Charles's dream. He fumbled for the light-switch, screwed up his eyes and looked at his watch. Quarter to three.

He opened the door of his bedsitter and was confronted by an aggrieved Swedish girl in a brushed nylon nightdress. The rest of the rooms in the house were occupied by Swedish girls, all, like this one, built on the lines of night-club bouncers. In their dealings with Charles, they all always wore aggrieved expressions, though on this occasion the annoyance had some justification.

"It is for you the telephone," the girl snorted, and stumped upstairs, her footsteps heavy with offence.

He took up the receiver that dangled from the landing payphone. "Yes?"

"It's Mariana." The famous voice was breathless, almost gasping. "Something's happened."

"I feel terrible," she said, handing him a cup of coffee, "disturbing you in the middle of the night. I'm sorry, I over-reacted. It was just such a shock."

"Don't worry about it." Charles felt better now. The taxi ride had shaken the sleep out of him. "Your reaction was quite reasonable. It must have been horrible for you."

"It was. But I feel better now. I'm sorry."

"You didn't think of ringing the police?"

"Over something like this? They'd have thought I was mad."

"I don't know. There's the trespass element, anyway. Whoever planted that thing broke into your flat to do so. Any sign of forcible entry?"

"No." She looked sheepish. "Mind you . . ."

"What?"

"I was out most of today and I'm afraid when I came back . . . I found I'd left the kitchen door unlocked."

She looked pathetically at him, fearing his reprimand, so Charles just said, "Never mind. Let's just have another look in the wardrobe."

Mariana stayed in the sitting-room as he went into the bedroom. He turned off the bedside light and moved towards the wardrobe, just as she must have done a few hours previously.

She had woken, she said, at half-past two, woken with that raw knowledge that there was no chance of sleep for another couple of hours. She had read for a little, then decided to get up and make a cup of tea. It was early November, chilly when the block's central heating was off, and she had gone to the wardrobe to fetch a cardigan. She had turned off the bedside light to save going back across the room, got up and walked across to the wardrobe. Then she had opened the door and seen it.

It was a luminous skeleton, about two foot high, and it had been suspended from a hanger in front of the clothes. To eyes that expected it, the cardboard outline looked faintly ridiculous. To an old lady taken completely by surprise, it must have been horrifying.

Charles detached the figure. Its limbs were joined with paper clips. It had been manufactured by Hallmark in the United States. It looked brand-new.

There was something familiar about the ornament. Charles had seen things like it somewhere before.

He concentrated and the memory came back to him. Yes,

Hallowe'en. A couple of years previously he had gone to a Hallowe'en party given by some expatriate American friends, and they had garlanded their house with cut-outs of pumpkins, witches and skeletons.

Maybe there was an American connection with Mariana Lythgoe's persecutor.

Mariana was so ready to give him a copy of her autobiography that Charles felt remiss in not having asked for it earlier. She brushed aside his request for a loan, insisting that he should have a copy of his own and inscribing it to him with fulsome, but apparently genuine, affection.

The next day, rising late after making up the night's deficit of sleep, Charles started to read the book. It was a day for reading, cold, dull November, as usual no work to go to. He sat till the pubs opened at five-thirty, in his armchair, feeding coins into the meter for his gas-fire and reliving Mariana Lythgoe's extraordinary life in the theatre.

The story was extraordinary not for any particularly bizarre incidents, but for the sheer breadth of experience it demonstrated. She had known and worked with every major theatrical figure of the twentieth century. Charles knew she was famous, but the variety of justifications of her fame amazed him.

But the book was not just a catalogue of dropped names. Her personality came across in every line; the story was written just as she spoke, and a reader who had never met, seen or even heard of Mariana Lythgoe could not have failed to be charmed by it.

From the point of view of the current investigation, the book offered very little. Even allowing for the fact that the writer was giving her own version of events, Mariana did not seem to be the sort of person who made enemies. She had worked with some notorious ogres of the theatre, but seemed with all of them to have maintained extremely sunny relationships. Professional revenge was an unlikely motive for the persecution.

The only name of which Charles made a mental note was Boy Trubshawe, the director of the original production of *Roses In Winter*. Mariana indulged in no criticism of his professional work, but did detail some of the practical jokes for which he was famous, and in her description of these (some of which sounded rather heartless), her writing almost took on a note of censure. That, coupled with the nature of the attack that had been made, raised in Charles the mildest of suspicions of Boy Trubshawe.

But there was nothing which impugned the director's professional reputation. Of *Roses In Winter*, Mariana wrote, *"Given such a wonderful script and such a wonderful cast, there was no doubt that Boy Trubshawe was about to have his first major success. Which he duly did."*

It was of course possible that the director did not share this assessment of his contribution to the triumph of *Roses In Winter*. The theatre is a profession which attracts outsize egos, and Boy Trubshawe might have found Mariana's reference to him too dismissive.

To follow up this thought, Charles went the next day to the London Library, a haven of Victorian quiet in St James's Square, and climbed up to the Biography section. He wasn't exactly sure what he was looking for, but as soon as he saw a book entitled *Boy—The Star-maker*, he knew that he had found it.

It was a show-business autobiography of the late thirties, and it showed all the vices of the genre. Here the names dropped with the subtlety of a pile-driver, an additional dullness given by the unfamiliarity of many of them, vogue names of show-business parvenus who didn't last the distance.

But Boy Trubshawe was not content only to drop names; he also felt it a duty to chronicle his own part in developing the careers of the famous. There was no humour in the "Star-maker" of the title; Boy Trubshawe appeared genuinely to believe that all of those he mentioned owed their eminence exclusively to his favour.

There was a whole chapter on Mariana Lythgoe. The director described how he had spotted her talent, how he had nurtured it, how he had sat back to watch it flower. Ostentatiously, he did not ask for praise, but the reader was left in no doubt that Mariana Lythgoe "owed it all to him".

The account, at least in its emphasis, did not tally with her own. Charles Paris decided that Boy Trubshawe deserved a visit.

"I am a trifle *jette laggé*," announced the director, over-emphasizing the unattractive franglais coining. "Just back from the States. New York. Staying with a *chum*."

He then went on to name one of the British actors who had made a recent conquest of Broadway. Habits of name-dropping died hard. What was more, the tone implied that Boy's relationship with the actor was *very*, *very* close. Meeting the octogenarian director in the flesh did nothing to dispel the impression his autobiography had made on Charles. Boy Trubshawe was a particularly unpleasant example of the bitchy theatrical queen. He knew everyone, but could allow no one to be mentioned without some snide aside.

The neat little Chelsea flat, all velvet chairs and fine porcelain, fitted its owner's appearance. He wore a blue blazer, grey flannels, cream silk shirt with, at the neck, a roguishly-knotted Indian print scarf.

Charles didn't feel he was going to enjoy the ensuing interview, so reckoned there was nothing to be gained by subtlety. "I've come to talk about Mariana."

"Dear Mariana," Boy Trubshawe cooed. "The *grande dame* of the English stage." Then, inevitably, he added the diminishing qualification. "In ambition, if not in deed. How sad for the poor darling that the Queen never has coughed anything up for her in the Birthday Honours. Dear Mariana *thinks* of herself as a Dame—how sad that she's been passed over."

Charles pressed on. "You know that Mariana's just written an autobiography?"

"Well, I had heard, yes. Writing books now—what will the little minx think of next?"

"Have you read the book?"

Boy Trubshawe widened his eyes coquettishly. "Now *why* should I do a thing like that? I mean, I'm delighted for Mariana that she's managed to persuade some publisher that she's *marketable*. Good for her, splendid effort . . . but what possible interest could her little book have for me?"

"You worked together a lot. I thought it might have a bit of nostalgic appeal."

"Now, my dear, just because Mariana lives in the past, there's no need to suppose that I do too. *I* know exactly what I did for Mariana's career—I don't need books to tell me that."

"What did you do for her then?"

"Simply shaped her whole life. She had nothing before she met me. Oh, talent, yes . . . a *modicum* of talent. It was I who taught her how to *husband* that modicum. And she followed my advice so well that people even started to believe that she was *rather good*."

He smiled ingratiatingly, apparently expecting some reaction of amusement. Presumably, in his usual circle, his sallies of bitchery were greeted with gales of laughter. But Charles knew too many people in the theatre whose malice passed as wit, and determinedly withheld even a sycophantic smile.

"Were you in New York for Hallowe'en?" he asked abruptly.

Boy Trubshawe was thrown by the change of tack. "Well, yes. Yes, I was," he stuttered.

"Shops full of seasonal decorations?"

"Yes."

"Pumpkins . . . witches . . . ?"

"Yes." He still looked bewildered.

"Skeletons . . . ?"

The old man's face coloured with petulance. "What is this? What are you talking about?"

"Someone," said Charles fiercely, "is making Mariana's life misery. And I'm trying to find out who it is."

"But surely you don't suspect . . ." The blotched but manicured hands flopped on to Boy's chest in a gesture of identification. ". . . *moi?*"

If Charles could be said to have a usual method of investigation, it would have to be described as "tentative" or "indirect", but on this occasion he broke away from type. Boy Trubshawe was annoying him, and Charles saw no reason to hide the fact.

"You have a reputation as a somewhat insensitive practical joker, Mr Trubshawe. I want to know if you've been practising this habit on Mariana recently?"

The eyes widened in mock-innocence. "And why should I do that?"

"Because in her book she didn't accord you the kind of praise and thanks which you seem to feel to be your due."

"No, she certainly didn't!" the old man snapped, making a nonsense of his earlier denial of having read Mariana's book. Then he let out an unattractive little snigger. "So someone's been playing nasty tricks on Mariana?"

"Yes. Someone broke into her flat sometime the day before yesterday and planted a particularly nasty—"

Charles was stopped by Boy's limply upraised hand. "Don't look at me, chum. Can't say I'm sorry to hear about the old duck's discomfiture . . . but I only got back from the States in the wee small hours yesterday."

And the director smiled smugly.

"I didn't take to Boy, certainly. He's a nasty bit of work."

"Oh, I wouldn't say that, Charles."

"Come on, Mariana. He is. Bitchy and horrible. You don't owe him any loyalty."

"Well . . ." She looked pained at the idea of having to think ill of anyone.

"*But* he has got an alibi. Well, I haven't checked it, but if he says he came back on a certain flight . . ."

"Oh yes, you have to believe him."

"So we're back to trying to think of someone else with a grudge against you. Having read your book—which, incidentally, I enjoyed very much—" Mariana coloured daintily at the compliment "—I can't imagine there's anyone else you've offended."

"I hope not."

Charles rubbed his chin reflectively. It was the morning after his encounter with Boy Trubshawe. A watery November sun trickled into the room where they drank coffee.

"So we have to think of people who might have some other motive . . . Hmm. What about this girl in the revival of *Roses In Winter*?"

"Sandy Drake?"

"That's the one. Must be pretty galling for her to have these constant, unflattering comparisons with you."

"Do you really think . . . ?"

Charles shrugged. "Possible. I mean, if she were unbalanced or . . . I haven't met her. Have you?"

Mariana shook her head.

"Well, I could ask around. I'm sure I've got friends who've worked with her at some point."

"Doesn't really sound very likely that . . ."

"No. Well, look, let's think of the obvious motive. Inheritance. Who's your heir?"

"Oh, surely that couldn't be . . . I mean, I haven't got any money. Nothing to leave."

"Do you own this flat?"

"Yes, but . . ."

"At today's prices that's worth having. Then there'll be royalties from the book and a few other things. You'd be surprised how much you're worth, Mariana."

The old lady gave a little dismissive smile. "Would you like some more coffee, Charles?"

"You haven't told me."

"What?" She turned an expression of self-conscious innocence on him.

"Who inherits."

"Oh, well, I'm sure there wouldn't be any reason to—"

"Who?"

"My nephew. Dick." She followed this admission up quickly. "But I'm sure he'd never—"

"Do you see a lot of him?"

"No. Not a great deal. But when we do meet, he's always perfectly friendly."

"Is he well off?"

"Well, he's . . . You know, it's difficult when you're making your way in the theatre. At first there are a few years when . . . I'm sure he's doing fine now."

"Perhaps I ought to go and have a word with him."

"Oh, no, Charles, no." She sounded horrified. "No, there's no need for that. It would be terribly embarrassing."

"Perhaps so. I just feel I should be doing something for you.

Some sort of investigation. There are so few leads to follow up and Dick at least has a kind of motive to get rid of you."

"It's all right, Charles. Don't feel you have to do anything."

"But if I don't, all we can do is sit and wait for something else to happen."

"Then perhaps that's what we'd better do." She flashed her famous smile at him. "And let's look on the bright side. It's quite possible that nothing else *will* happen."

The subject was left and they chatted for another hour about Mariana's book and some of the productions in which she had starred. Charles, even after more than thirty not very successful years in the theatre, remained incorrigibly stage-struck and enjoyed the conversation. But at twelve, in spite of Mariana's offer of lunch, he felt he should go.

"I'll see you downstairs."

"Oh, don't worry."

"I have to go down just to see if there's any post. Not that there ever is much except bills these days. Most of the people who might have written to me are long dead."

"Maybe today," said Charles jovially, "will be your lucky day. Maybe today you will receive something totally unexpected."

He was right. She did.

Fortunately she opened the package down in the hall while he was still there.

The note read: "WON'T BE LONG NOW, MARIANA."

With it was an audio cassette.

"You will not escape my vengeance. I have sworn to destroy you and that oath will be fulfilled. You may try to escape, but all attempts will be in vain. As surely as if by a court of law, your death sentence has been pronounced."

A click sounded on the tape, then a slight hiss as it ran on. Charles left it for a few moments before switching off.

It was a male voice, fairly young, full, well-articulated, slightly theatrical perhaps.

He looked across at the old actress's haunted face.

"Do you recognize it, Mariana?"

"No," she whispered, with an appalled shake of her head. "No, I don't."

Charles knew she was lying, but no amount of persuasion could elicit the truth from her.

He rang the BBC from the payphone at the bedsitter and asked for Mark Lear's office.

"Charles. How are you? Hey, you remember that actress who was in the play we did with Mariana Lythgoe—the one with purple hair? Well, let me tell you she is the most amazing—"

"Mark, listen. I want you to identify a voice for me."

"What?"

"You know the radio scene. I've got a recording of a voice that sounds to me like someone who's done a lot of radio. I'm going to play it on the cassette down the phone and I want you to tell me if you recognize it."

"What is this?"

"Just listen, Mark. Please."

Charles held the portable cassette to the receiver and pressed the start button.

"*You will not escape my vengeance. I have sworn—*"

"Of course I recognize it."

Charles stopped the machine.

"Who?"

"I should recognize it. I only produced him in—"

"WHO?"

"Dick Lythgoe. As I say, I was the producer on—"

But Charles wasn't in the mood for showbiz recollections.

"Thank you, Mark."

Charles got the name of Dick Lythgoe's agent through the actor's directory, *Spotlight*. As he was doing so, he looked at the actor's photograph. There was a family resemblance to Mariana, but in her nephew the sharp outlines of her famous face were blurred, the eyes were set more closely together and the mouth showed a slight droop of petulance.

The agent told Charles that his client was not currently working, thinking at that stage the inquiry came from a potential employer. But when Charles said it was a personal matter and asked for Dick Lythgoe's address, he got no further information. Though it was annoying, Charles couldn't object to this. He hoped his own agent would show similar discretion in the same circumstances (though he didn't feel total confidence that his would).

However, a few calls to friends in the business soon elicited an address for Dick Lythgoe in Kilburn, which was within walking distance of Charles's bedsitter.

It was a house divided into flats. Blue paint had flaked off the frontage, leaving a mottled effect. There was a tangle of wires and doorbells by the front door, but none of the stained cards offered the name "Lythgoe". Charles stepped back and looked through the rusted railings to the separate basement entrance. He walked down the worn steps, picking his way over polythene bags of rubbish which had been dumped there.

Dick Lythgoe's surroundings suggested that he could certainly use an inheritance.

The fourth ring at the doorbell brought him to the door. His face looked crumpled, as if he had just woken up. It also showed that Dick Lythgoe's *Spotlight* photograph had been taken some years before. And those years had not been kind to its subject. His hairline had retreated, leaving only a couple of ineffectual tufts on top, and the skin around the eyes had pouched up. Dick Lythgoe was no longer going to impress Casting Directors as a Juvenile Lead.

"What do you want?" he asked truculently.

"I want to talk about Mariana."

A spasm of anger twisted the face. "Oh God, story of my bloody life! It's all anyone ever wants to talk about. My bloody aunt. I should have changed my name before I went into the bloody theatre!"

"Then why didn't you?" asked Charles.

The lower lip trembled, then decided not to answer. The silence was quite as expressive as words. Dick Lythgoe had clung to his famous name for shrewd business reasons; without it he might have had even less success.

"Anyway, what do you want? Are you another bloody journalist? Because let me tell you before you start, I don't talk about my dear auntie for free. If you want more heart-warming insights into the private life of the First Lady of Yesterday's Theatre, you're going to have to find fifty quid. At least."

"I'm not a journalist," said Charles. "I am just a friend of your aunt's."

Dick Lythgoe looked him up and down with an insolent smile. "Have to admire the old girl's resilience, don't you?"

Charles ignored the innuendo. Like Boy Trubshawe, the actor was making him uncharacteristically angry. "Someone is conducting a campaign of persecution against Mariana and I'm going to find out who it is."

"Campaign of persecution?"

"Yes. And I have some pretty strong evidence of who's doing it. I think you'd better let me come inside."

Dick Lythgoe gaped at this sudden assertiveness, but drew aside to admit the older man.

The flat inside was a tip. Dirty plates, glasses and encrusted coffee-cups perched on every available surface. There was a smell of damp from the house, compounded by a human staleness. Charles wanted to throw open every window in the place.

"Sorry about the mess," Dick Lythgoe mumbled. "My girlfriend walked out a few weeks back." He slumped on top of a pile of grubby shirts draped over an armchair. "Now what is this?"

"Your aunt has received a series of threatening phone-calls and anonymous letters. An unpleasant practical joke has been played on her. Today she received this tape."

Charles had the portable recorder set up in readiness and pressed the start button.

Dick Lythgoe sat in silence while the message ran through.

"Now," demanded Charles as it ended, "do you deny that that is your voice?"

"No," the actor replied, again with his insolent smile. "I don't deny it."

Charles poured another slug of Bell's whisky into Mark Lear's glass and, topping up his own, went across to sit on his bed. "And there's no doubt that's where the speech came from?"

"None at all. As Dick said, it was part of a *Saturday Night Theatre* he recorded for me last year. I was about to tell you that when you rang off this morning."

"Oh, damn. When was the play broadcast?"

"January of this year."

"So somebody must have got hold of the tape and—"

"They wouldn't need to do that. Just record it off air."

"Yes. If they did, it implies a degree of long-distance planning."

"Mm. And, I would have thought, rules Dick out of your suspicions."

"I suppose so."

"Come on, he's not going to send a threat like that that's so easily identifiable. It took you less than a day to find out where it came from."

Charles nodded ruefully. "Mind you, he wasn't to know Mariana had talked to anyone about what was happening. He may have thought that she would keep it to herself, then listen to the tape when it arrived and drop dead of a heart-attack on the spot . . . ?"

Mark Lear gave his friend a pitying look. "And then the body is discovered with the tape still in the tape recorder just beside it. No criminal would leave such a huge signpost pointing straight at him, would he?"

"No. So I'm really back to Square One. Trouble with this case is a dearth of suspects."

"Who else have you got?"

"No one, really. Well, I had one other, but he's ruled out by sheer logistics."

"Who was he?"

"Boy Trubshawe."

"Oh, him. Malicious old queen, isn't he?"

"You can say that again. Do you know him well?"

The producer shook his head. "No, met him for the first time this week. Sort of cocktail party at Lucinda's. He'd just come in from a trip to the States, which he was very full of."

"Yes, I know."

"Not a single reputation on Broadway was unsullied by the end of the evening."

"That's my Boy," said Charles wryly. "When was this?"

"What, Lucinda's party?"

"Uhuh."

"Monday night."

"Can't have been."

"What do you mean?"

"Monday night Boy was still in New York. I know that. I saw him Wednesday and he said he'd come back in the small hours of Tuesday morning."

Mark Lear shook his head. "Charles, I know I drink too much in the BBC Club, but I can tell the days apart. I have good reason to remember Monday night. After Lucinda's I had dinner with that actress with the purple hair and let me tell you—"

Charles cut short this sexual reminiscence. "Good God! You swear that Boy Trubshawe was here on the Monday?"

"Of course I do. What the hell should I—"

"So he lied to me! And he could easily have—"

The phone rang from the landing. Charles was silent.

"Aren't you going to answer it?"

"No. It'll be for one of the Swedish girls."

But apparently none of the Swedish girls was in. The phone rang on.

Charles picked up the receiver.

"It's Mariana."

"What's up? Has something happened?"

"Charles, I'm worried."

"Why?"

"I thought I could hear some noise from the fire escape. Outside the kitchen."

"What sort of noise?"

"Well, as if someone . . . I don't know . . . as if someone—"

There was a sudden sound of breaking glass from Mariana's end of the phone. She let out a little whimper. There was a heavy thud.

Then silence.

The caretaker was roused from his basement in the adjacent block and, responding to the urgency of Charles's demands, hurried up the stairs and unlocked the door to Mariana's flat.

She lay by the door between the sitting-room and the kitchen. The phone, receiver off, was on the floor at the full extent of its cable. When she rang Charles, she must have been trying to see what was happening in the kitchen. The glass of the door to the fire escape was shattered.

Mariana herself was moaning softly. As Charles gently raised her body to cradle it, she put her hand to her forehead where a marked swelling showed already.

"She all right?"

Charles looked up into the anxious face of the elderly caretaker. "I think so. Better get a doctor. Do you know who her doctor is?"

The old man shook his head.

Mariana's eyelids opened and the pupils swam into focus. "Charles," she whispered gratefully.

"Mariana, who is your doctor?"

She spoke slowly, as if drunk. "Oh, he doesn't make house calls. If I'm ill, I have to go there."

"I think he'll come this time. What's his name?"

She told him. "But it's not necessary. I'm all right."

Charles told the caretaker to ring the doctor, as he picked Mariana up gently and moved towards the bedroom.

"Shall I ring the police as well, guv?"

Charles looked off into the kitchen. "No, hold fire on that for the moment."

He stayed with Mariana until the doctor arrived. The latter's complaints about actually having to *visit* a patient *and* to have to do so late in the evening justified the old lady's comment on him. But at least he had arrived and Charles left him with the patient.

The actor went into the kitchen. He looked at the floor by the exit door, then turned the handle. It was not locked.

On the metal grille of the fire escape landing outside lay a brick, surrounded by a few larger pieces of glass.

"Mr Paris."

The doctor was standing in the doorway from the sitting-room.

"Yes."

"There's nothing wrong with her. Just a bruise on the forehead. I must say I resent being called out for something so minor."

"She is an old lady, doctor."

"If I came out on a call for every old lady who fell over, I would never get home at all."

"She didn't fall over."

The doctor shrugged. "That's not really important. The fact is that she has suffered a very minor injury and I have been called away from a dinner party."

"It's not the minor injury that should worry you, doctor."

"What on earth are you talking about, Mr Paris?"

"I am talking about the effect a shock like that might have on Miss Lythgoe's heart."

Charles sat on the side of Mariana's bed. She smiled up at him. She looked weary, but peaceful. The soft bedside light washed years off the perfectly shaped face.

"Has the doctor gone?"

Charles nodded. "He doesn't seem too worried about you. Rest, he says, that's the answer."

She grinned. "Not a lot else one can do at my age."

"No." There was a silence before he continued. "Mariana, you asked me last week to do some detective work for you."

"Yes."

"Well, I've done it."

Her greying eyes sparkled. "You mean you know who it is who's been doing all these things?"

"Yes." The word came out like a sigh.

"Who? Charles, tell me who."

"Mariana, I've looked in the kitchen and on the fire escape.

There is no glass on the kitchen floor. There is a brick and some broken glass on the fire escape."

"Yes, well, that's how he must have got in. It means—"

Charles shook his head slowly as he interrupted. "It means that the window was broken from inside the flat, Mariana."

"Oh."

"I spoke to the doctor about your health. He was very complimentary about your general condition. Your heart, in particular, he said, would do credit to a woman twenty years your junior."

"Ah." She looked up at him. Frail, vulnerable, but still in control, still with a small twinkle of humour.

Charles grinned. "Why, Mariana?"

She spread her hands in a gesture of selfishness. "What I've always suffered from, Charles—innate sense of theatre. And, I suppose, the desire to be the centre of attention."

"But to go to the lengths you did . . . Even to hit yourself on the forehead . . . I mean, why?"

"Sorry. Got carried away. Always like that on stage—really got into my parts. I never could play any character unless I believed, at least for a few moments, that I *was* that character."

"Which is what made you a great actress."

"Thank you." Once again, by her usual blend of charm and cunning, Mariana had exacted her tribute of compliment.

"And what made you so convincing to me. I believed you were really frightened because, at the moment you told me all that nonsense, you believed it. You really were frightened."

She nodded with a mixture of shame and impertinence, like a schoolgirl caught smoking.

"Have you done this sort of thing before, Mariana?"

"No. I promise. Really. When I retired ten years ago, I was determined to sink gracefully into anonymity. And I managed it. I was really good about it. I had friends, I spent time with them, and, for the first time in my life, I took a back seat. And, to my surprise, I found I didn't really mind."

"What changed things?"

She smiled sadly. "My friends died. I was increasingly alone. Yes, I must use the word—increasingly *lonely*. But what really started it was the book. Writing it, thinking about all those performances . . . and then the 'promotional tour'. I'm afraid once again I was centre stage—and I found I hadn't lost the taste for it."

"I'm a small audience, Mariana," said Charles gently.

"I know. I'm sorry it was you who got involved. Unfair. You didn't deserve it. It's just, when Mark said you were a bit of a detective . . . And then I got caught up in the drama of the situation—as I say, got carried away. I'm sorry. You were just the victim of another lonely old lady, craving attention."

Charles gave a little laugh. "And has my 'attention' been satisfactory?"

Mariana Lythgoe's famous smile irradiated her face. "Oh yes, Charles. Thank you."

He picked up her fine but freckled hand and kissed it. "I must go."

"Yes." A little silence hung between them. "But, Charles, you will come and see me again, won't you?"

"Oh yes, Mariana," said Charles Paris. "I will."

SIMON BRETT has been interested in theatre from an early age. A former president of the Oxford University Dramatic Society, he appeared in cabarets and reviews there and directed the Oxford Theatre Group's late-night show at the Edinburgh Festival Fringe in 1967. He has produced radio and comedy shows for the BBC and for London Weekend television, but he now devotes himself full time to writing plays and scripts for radio and television as well as his popular Charles Paris novels. His most recent novel was *A Shock to the System*.

RL

PHOTOS

PRINTS